Hart Street & Main

Hart Street

& Main

Book 1

Written by
Tabitha Sprunger

Featuring Illustrations by Joe Traster

atmosphere press

Chapter 1
Act of Agenesis

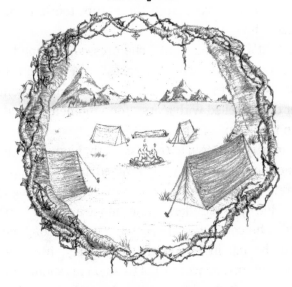

Carpenter Hills, Second World

The winds blew swiftly across the peaks of Carpenter Hills. It was a cold night in late fall, but snow had yet to break the darkening clouds that seemed to always loom overhead now. It was as if it were waiting for something... Nestled in the small valley which rested between Carpenter Hills in the east and Yodére Forest to the west was where they camped.

The tent flap folded upwards and in stepped a man wearing a long coat delicately sprinkled with frost of the bitter cold. His cheeks were blush red from the wind, encrusting a face that was once so well-shaven and flawless. Now there was a scraggly beard of a man who hadn't slept well in months. At this point in his life he had lived well past his youth but still embodied the shell of a twenty-something-year-old man. The woman, who had been resting inside the small tent, jumped at his sudden presence. She relaxed from the abrupt tension once she realized who it was.

"Oh, it's just you Clint," she pressed her hand to her brow forcing her heartrate to ease, "for a moment there... I..." she started to break off in the middle of her sentence as her eyes swelled with tears, "for a moment I could have sworn it was one of them..."

Clint rushed down to the distraught woman's side. Her long auburn hair was loosely braided and pulled up into a bun. Bits of hair stuck out every which way. Just a glimpse of her blue eyes with dark circles made a part of him wear heavy as he could vaguely remember the strong glowing woman he fell in love with. Her worry, her fear, her sleepless nights; he wore all of them on his shoulders. This was his fault. It should be his burden to bear, not hers.

He placed his arm around her back and pulled the animal skin blanket across her front. He then rubbed his hands on her cold arms, "Trinity, there is nothing to worry about. I just came from the outskirts of town. All seems to be well there. It must be the first night in nearly a month since the Château de Beaucoup has been so calm. There were very few lights lit around the market and hardly a horse to be heard out of the stables. Perhaps... God is on our side tonight?"

Neither seemed relieved by this observation. Trinity looked up into Clint's eyes. She could see his fear. She seemed doubtful about his words and remained just as worried, if not more so than before. If the Château de

Beaucoup was quiet, there was reason to believe Loucentious's men were up to something.

Helge Loucentious was the King of Humans overlooking the rule of the second territory of their world. Gresham was mostly farmland and valley. Where Clint and his men now camped. Clint was the King of Sorcerers, leader of his people and currently in disputes of land and sorcerer legal rights.

At this hour when the stars cast their gaze upon the earth, what Helge Loucentious, King of Humans, was doing had nothing to do with aiding Clint and Trinity on their escape.

All the while, Trinity had her own people to contend with. She'd taken her place as heir to the wood fairies within Yodére Forest a few years ago, at the ripe young age of eighteen. Her own parents were lost to the same senseless war they still found themselves fighting years later. Trinity was not a small fairy—here those were called pixies. She was the size of a human with similar features, but she and her people had wings capable of supporting the flight of a being their size. The wings were light but strong as leather draping their backside almost like the skin on a basset hound's ears without fur.

Trinity had told her people words of hope in these past days. She tried her best not to let anyone know that she had every intention of leaving not only Yodére Forest but the Second World altogether. Supplies had been running low within the wood fairy colony and the number of her people was even fewer. Their secret was kept tight. Not even Trinity's sister and closest friend knew of her and Clint's plans. There really had been no decision to make. It was unlike either of them to abandon ship, especially in the middle of a war.

They were both well-respected leaders with long, loyal bloodlines dating back hundreds of years. Faithful to the cause, dedicating their lives to the good of their people. But given the circumstances, if they did not leave, they themselves and their unborn child would be massacred without a doubt by the same people to whom they'd sacrificed their lives and to whom they'd devoted everything.

This child was more than loyalty, more than the oath they'd formed when they accepted their roles as leaders. This child was their realization they could not stay within the confines of the Second World. The very reason the Second World had been formed centuries ago had been tarnished at the seams. The Second World was once a sanctuary for lost souls, for those who were different, a place for beings of magic. Now it was but a memory of everything containing good. Once such a pure place now simply stained.

Clint brought his hand to Trinity's stomach, "How are the two of you hanging in there?"

It was an innocent question, but Trinity's stomach churned, and she shook her head out of her brief trance thinking about her sister and the faces of her people she was forced to leave behind. The choice to leave may have been easy, but abandoning family, friends, and an entire colony was no simple task to endure. Trinity glanced at her stomach for a moment. Choosing her words carefully, she gave Clint a truthful response, "We'd be a lot better off if we weren't here right now."

Their little secret had been stretched out as long as possible. It had been a nerve-racking six months. The morning sickness was hidden behind other unforeseen illnesses. There was little weight gain and the cold autumn made it easier to mask the growing bundle with bulky clothing.

Nothing was more difficult than keeping the baby to herself. Trinity had been ignoring her sister on and off for months. Her sister Adalina was likely furious but would know something was up regardless of being around her or not. Adalina was busy taking care of her own child, only four months old. She'd spent a great deal of time within the depths of their home sheltering her little one from harm. Trinity debated taking Adalina and the baby with her. Adalina's husband would never agree. He was a soldier through and through. Trinity found some comfort in knowing, at least, her sister and nephew were in good hands.

"I promise you, we'll be out of here soon enough. I'll just need to make sure the forest is clear and then we can go." Clint adjusted his heavy gear around his waistline.

"What happens if the forest isn't cleared?" Trinity was genuinely concerned. She knew there would be no other way out.

Clint took his hand away from Trinity's stomach and stood up inside the small triangular tent his muscular form seemed to swallow what little space there was inside. He did not say a word in regards to Trinity's question. He took both of Trinity's hands into his as he slightly bent back down to Trinity, who still rested on the hard and frozen ground nestled in the animal hides.

With her hands gently placed in his own, he spoke: "I will never let anything bad happen to you or our child. Fate has allowed us to find love, despite the strong forces that have been working against us. We shall be safe soon. It's my word."

With his words still lingering he lent in closer towards Trinity for a kiss. He made it quick and said nothing more before taking a last look at his wife. There was little time left. The tent flap brushed his bold shoulders as he departed.

Trinity felt hopeless and alone inside the tent. She heard the horse on the other side of the tent sound off, then the colossal hooves hit the frozen ground outside, its horseshoes echoed a clicking sound in the distance. The echoing kept the hope of her husband's return alive. She sat up until she no longer could hear galloping footsteps of the King Sorcerer's horse, Resbian.

Clint kicked Resbian gently on the side of her sleek black fur coat. It was a signal for her to go a bit faster towards the towering trees that were a part of Yodére Forest. Then something odd had happened for the first time with Resbian, the horse Clint had befriended almost two hundred years ago. The old mare did not follow his command. The horse of relentless obedience disobeyed his order to proceed forward along the tree line. Resbian stopped and hunched both of her front legs into the air. She let out a loud neigh as Clint held on for dear life.

Immediately alarmed, Clint pulled back on the reins. He and the horse came to an abrupt halt. Scanning his surroundings Clint could not find anything out of the ordinary. He was still facing Yodére Forest. The trees were barely swaying in the cold breeze. There was no light illuminating deep in the woods. Around him the misty

Carpenter Hills were silent, and behind him the tents made hardly any noise with just the gentle whoosh, typical flapping of the fabric.

People in the other tents surrounding Trinity were far enough away they should not have been able to hear the two of them conversing. They may have overheard the sound of a single horse departing camp, but that would not have been anything to raise alarm. It was normal for sorcerer scouts or messengers to come and go throughout the night. So just what was it that Resbian was so startled about?

"Come on, girl, there is nothing in these hills but dead people, and they can do you no harm." Even as he spoke, Clint was losing his confidence. He didn't hear any animals nor insects. Complete silence.

The old Clydesdale still seemed to be restless and refused to move, now bucking her head every which way against the tightened reins. Clint could not figure out the reason for her disturbance. It was as if she was possessed. He gently stroked Resbian's long black mane and patted down her smooth silk-black coat. Clint desperately tried again to persuade the big mare onwards and this time only lightly let go of the reins. Steadily Resbian motioned forward, her horseshoes echoing wildly through the quiet valley. "That a girl." They continued to slowly scout the edge of Yodére Forest.

Inside the dark tent, Trinity was beginning to grow restless with worry. Deep down she harbored doubts. She knew the passage to the woods on the other side of the hills was short and it should not be long before he came back to get her. If Clint did not return, she did not know what would become of her. She was currently hiding unarmed among enemy troops. The sorcerers and wood fairies hadn't been allies in all of Trinity's memory. Whatever escape she attempted without her husband, she knew she could not succeed.

She was no stranger to dangerous situations. The task of leaving the tree dwelling in Yodére Forest was no easy journey. The couple used a combination of concealing charms and some of the illusion was as simple as just hiding beneath one of Clint's long coats. Trinity was able to blend into the gathering of horses and sorcerers passing through the forest after a hunt. It was only made possible by covering her large, heavy leathery wings.

There was a slight rustling about outside the tent. Trinity breathed easy for a while. Quickly the rustling translated into shouts and the ground trembled beneath her. She wiped her tired eyes, trying to make herself more alert to the situation and she sat back upright resting on her downward palms. The shouts transformed into something resembling a stampede approaching over Carpenter Hills. Trinity leaned forward away from the back of the tent. Then she maneuvered her swelling body around the wooden post holding the tent upward.

Burning curiosity overcame the rising terror to want to peek outside to see what was going on. She froze, the tent flap came inward as she was about to grab the edge of the opening. On impulse alone Trinity stumbled backward into the tent. It was just Clint again, but back far too early to have made his trip all the way around the bordering Yodére Forest. There was no way he and Resbian were making the loud noises growing outside or causing the ground to shake.

"Clint, what on earth is going on out there? It was so quiet I had nearly fallen asleep, and then—" Trinity held her breath; she had caught a glimpse outside through the crack of tent door, "—are those torches?"

Clint quickly stood between her and the exit. "Now, darling, you must not be fearful, but we have to leave. We need to leave immediately!"

"What is going on? Were you spotted?" Trinity scanned Clint up and down. There were no physical signs of being attacked. He was frantic, and it wasn't like him to lose his calm demeanor, "What's happening, tell me!"

There was no response. Trinity felt a pang in her stomach. She was about to get sick. There wasn't time to carry on a conversation. Clint took her left hand and practically started dragging her out of the tent. "Wait!" Trinity nearly knocked him off his feet, ducking back into the direction of the tent. She dug through the mound of blankets. Then she bent down and picked up a small sack filled with an assortment of items, mostly small heirlooms.

"This is no time to gather belongings," Clint said, sweating profusely regardless of the bitter cold air, "Didn't you hear me? We must go, now!" Clint was doing all he could not to knock the sack out of Trinity's hands.

"Clint, these are all the memories of *home* I have left. Now bless it they're not much..." Trinity trailed, and her voice broke. The thought of home made her instinctively want to cry and retreat into the trees. Clint was helpless.

"Fine," replied Clint, giving in, he always gave into Trinity. He took the bag out of Trinity's hand and slung it over his shoulder. Then he grabbed a hold of Trinity's arm, and this time he really did drag her out of the tent coverings into the cold night air.

Trinity's hair went wild outside of the tent. There she stood frozen, not with cold, but with sheer disbelief. Her worst nightmare was heading her direction. Over the northeastern edge of Carpenter Hills there was an army of fairies storming towards the tents in the calm valley. Suddenly here didn't seem so peaceful. Some of the bodies carried what looked like flaming torches bobbing up and down. Others had crossbows slung over their shoulders. Most of them were riding horseback, and others were ascending into flight. None of them were too far from where Trinity and Clint stood.

The other sorcerers were stirring within their tents. There had been no men on patrol duty this evening. Clint had sent them all away from their posts, telling each of them that he would take guard tonight. It would have ensured their quiet escape. *Of all nights to have a raid?* He would be the reason for his people's defeat.

"How did they know where I was," asked Trinity. The small torchlight hypnotizing, pure disbelief across her cold pale face.

"I'm not so sure they know you're here, but if so, I don't think they would suspect it was by choice. It seems like it's just a raiding party. They could have noticed the guard was down for the night and took the opportunity to pass into our territory? The humans have been wanting the valley back under their control for quite some time." Clint was trying to assume the best of the situation.

Instead of fixating on everything that was going wrong, Clint motioned Trinity to Resbian's side. Trinity's eyes were now squinting, still determined to focus more clearly on the figures approaching the valley, low and high, streaming in by the dozens now over the hills.

"Oh dear," let out Trinity, in almost a whisper. *Was it possible her people knew she was here with the sorcerers? Would they think she was kidnapped? Had it been her sister Adalina who tipped them off?* The thoughts were maddening. The more bodies she saw come over the hills the more terrified she became. *Were there usually this many in the raiding parties?* No, it was clear as more bodies came into view this was not just a raid. Clint was trying not to worry her even more. It wasn't working.

"Come on, you first," Clint said much less patiently. He was more ordering Trinity to saddle Resbian.

"Wait," said Trinity, staring out at the nearing mob. She was focusing hard at the enlarging figures barreling towards them in the dark night. A thought pieced together in her head. Her people didn't have many horses and it was rare to see them wielding torches even in the depths of night.

Frustrated by Trinity's lack of urgency Clint blustered, "There's no time to grab anything else, we have to go now!" He patted the side of Resbian's saddle.

"Clint, those are not my people and you're not fooling me, it's no raiding party." Her eyes were welling heavily with tears.

The statement *those are not my people* broke what calm was left in Clint's body. For a second, there was no sound. He too took a moment to concentrate his eyes on the figures raging towards them, no longer specks on the horizon. No longer another mere bump in the road to their escape. Trinity was trembling from the knees down, "It can't be, it just can't. Clint, their faces, I've never seen them before in person." Fear had completely overcome

Trinity's body, and her breath was but a wisp as the rest of her words couldn't be heard.

The winged men and women ravaging towards them were not Trinity's people. The bodies approaching brandished the familiar leather-like wings, but they were not wood fairies. These fairies were full of rage, ready to kill, hungry for death. He knew just as well as his wife did, these were not beings at all. These were monsters.

"Come on, we must go, we *must* go now!"

"You see them don't you?" questioned Trinity, still mesmerized by the sheer mass of the large group of beings still multiplying as they rose up over the hills and out of the night's shadow.

"Yes, of course I see them," Clint was trying to stay calm. He had to stay calm if they were ever going to survive this night, "but it only gives us more reason to get out of here as fast as we can." Clint fought his own instincts to stay and help the others. Some of his men, oldest friends and acquaintances, were still fast asleep within the safety of their tents.

Trinity was dragging her palms through Resbian's mane, slightly bringing her peace in the moment, "They're Rodinians, aren't they? I've never seen any of them before now, we thought they had died out, maybe a handful left spread across the Northern Region."

In the far north there were caverns and mostly wasteland—not much good for crops, and the coastlines never yielded adequate fishing. The Rodinians were a happy people living amongst the wood fairies, but a thousand years prior started relations with neighboring vampires within the caverns leading to a genetic mutation they deemed superior to other beings. When the contract was penned in the 1500s, they were able to establish themselves as a separate people and were given the third territory of the north along with immunity to hunt within their boundaries. The seclusion and lack of necessities along with years of unusual flooding led to rumors Rodinians were growing scarce.

"There's no mistaking them though. The numbers, there does not seem to be an end." *Scarce? The rumor of their people dying out obviously wasn't true. Maybe it's what they wanted other beings to believe all along?* Her body wouldn't move, the thought of the Rodinians thriving was terrifying. Clint was not wasting his breath. He lifted Trinity's body onto Resbian's back.

As the first flaming arrow was sent whizzing past, Trinity was able to hoist herself up on the horse the rest of the way. Now the camp was in a full uproar of sound and movement. Word was spreading, Clint's people were lighting their own lanterns, wiping their eyes, complaining about all the racket outside. They were convinced there may have just been a brief disturbance and would be back to their beds or cots in no time. As it came with many other nights in the sorcerers' camp it was likely just someone having an argument with their tent neighbors.

How wrong they would be... how unprepared. Clint shook the image of his people's naïve thoughts. It took only a short instant for Clint to mount the large Clydesdale behind Trinity. Resbian took off on his command.

They needed to get out of the camp before either of them was spotted. At that moment complete chaos broke out. The tents were becoming engulfed in flames from newly fired arrows. Clint's men were realizing this was not a mere disturbance, but a full-blown ambush. Many tried to form a fighting stance wand or sword at hand, others were forced to duck back into their tents to retrieve a weapon.

In any other circumstances the sight would be amusing. Clint witnessed men in just their pajamas or underwear in the cold frozen with shock, dumbfounded. Most were not fortunate enough to make it back out of their tents alive. Clint had to withhold his voice to shout orders to form ranks or address a spell. He and Trinity needed to blend in and get away from the attack. It would not benefit them to draw more attention to themselves.

What was even more, was what was taking place at the eastern edge of Carpenter Hills. Another swarm of people on horseback began to appear over the horizon. This was beyond coincidence. Someone somehow must have tipped them off.

The newcomers appeared to be soldiers of Gresham. Their signature armor and fighting tactics signaled they were surely human. Clint and Trinity's heads spun back and forth with confusion. Tonight, there would be a great battle, possibly the deadliest since the war began. It would be a battle of which they hoped they would never see the result. Neither of them dared to think of the outcome.

Regardless of wins and losses, together they were bound to share the loss of loved ones—despite how it all ended. One of their peoples, if not both, would face the consequences of defeat. The idea of the humans or the bloodthirsty Rodinians ruling every territory was appalling. As much as the thought bothered Clint to admit his distaste, none of this was his problem anymore.

Resbian raced through the valley quicker than she had

ever retreated before. Beings were entering the valley at every angle by this point. Including yet another cluster of beings approaching from the shadows of Yodére Forest. There was no fear of the possibility of being spotted anymore. There was too much happening at once to think clearly. Lives were at stake. Too many spells, arrows, people flying about to tell what was going on.

Trinity buried her face into Resbian's black mane at the first sight of a man she had known her whole life back in the forest. The wood fairy was well-armed and appeared to be a strong fighter. Yet the wood fairy was easily struck dead, the image of him falling to the frozen earth stamped her memory. She had looked him directly in the eyes just before he was struck with the axe of a human soldier wearing a rather large and elaborate metal helmet. The human soldier retrieved his axe from the wood fairy's chest, as the fairy's body fell lifeless to the ground. Next, the human soldier carried the axe in one hand and started off towards a sorcerer with his back turned.

Shaken by the pure bloodlust and complete senselessness, a gasp escaped Trinity's flushed lips. It was not death she feared, it was of what she saw another soldier do, this time, clearly a Rodinian soldier. The blackened, torn wings, and barred teeth were gritted clasped on the arm of a human. As much as Trinity disliked humans and their selfish greedy ways, no one deserved what she saw next. It was as if she felt her heart tighten and her gut wrench. Another Rodinian stunned one of her old wood fairy friends in the back with an arrow to keep him from thrashing around as the female Rodinian soldier stood over his mangled body. She then began to take his blood, devouring all she could from the dead man's gushing wound.

As everyone well knew, the Rodinians lived off of other beings, but mostly deer and large vermin. This was a new level of disgust. How or what they had been living off all these years to achieve such numbers was beyond Trinity's imagination. They barreled on before she could see the Rodinian twist the fairy's neck then pluck away the fairy's wings, breaking bones with each tear.

Clint was aware of the three peoples that were closing in around them, but it was Resbian who deserved all credit for safely navigating them in and out of the crowd. She was taking shots and arrows to the breastbone, legs, and hindquarters. Some of the blasts and arrows ricocheted off her tough hide, a few Clint was able to block, but the rest penetrated Resbian's skin.

This was truly a nightmare. Clint was relentless and had survived many battles, but never with his wife, never with an unborn child. His only prayer was that this bloodshed would all blow over quickly. There was a glint of hope that perhaps in the end it would just seem like Trinity and Clint had been killed in battle. It was still possible to not go out looking like a coward. Then again, there was so much more at stake than his reputation.

They had nearly two hundred yards before they were out of the valley. The end was within their grasp, but it was not a very comforting distance to travel in the middle of warfare.

"It's going to be all right," Clint said to Trinity's backside. She was still burying her face into Resbian's mane—the surrounding images of death were too much. Clint too wished he could close his eyes and let Resbian guide them the rest of the way. Not much bothered Clint, after all he had witnessed a great deal of death and gore in his prolonged life, and he himself administering a fair share. He'd grown almost accustomed to how battles resembled each other even over the course of centuries. War was blind to time. Anger, death, and war were nearly as constant as the existence of life itself.

Clint found himself lost in the past, back in the days when he had watched the same people warring against each other. *Would this insistent hate ever end?*

"Clint!" Trinity screamed.

Wham! Like being thrust into a stone wall, Clint was thrown back into the present time. Trinity was snagged at Resbian's left side and was being pulled ruthlessly off the towering Clydesdale's moving saddle. With one hand yielding his sword and the other on Resbian's reins, he neglected to maintain a safe grasp on his wife's body. She was gone, pulled into the entangled mass around them. Resbian hadn't stopped right away, too busy trying to forge forward and dodge hits. Clint pulled on Resbian's reins and forcefully turned her back in the opposite direction.

Through the mess of wood fairies, humans, Rodinians, and sorcerers Clint tried to make out where Trinity seemed to vanish. He spotted her loose braid and darkened complexion, but only after he pinpointed her screams from the others in the cluster of pure devastation. There she was being overpowered by two winged men who had a hold of her. At this time all four sides were fighting amongst themselves, so he could not tell if it was the Rodinians who had hold of her, or her own people.

After turning around, Resbian recognized immediately

what was wrong. She had to help her master retrieve his one and only true love, no matter the cost. Without instruction to do so, Resbian stormed faster forwards towards Trinity's screams. Resbian trampled all beings in her path. The bodies were easily swatted to the side like flies.

Eventually, the loyal mare arrived back at the point where Trinity had been ripped from her saddle. With two crushing gallops, Resbian was able to take down the figures who were pulling Trinity's body one way and ripping her wings the other. Then Resbian was at a standstill.

"You're a godsend Resbian, shall we never part ways." Resbian's instincts were quicker than Clint's own eyes and ears. The horse was far more powerful than the royal sorcerer's toughest hit. Clint stroked his arm down Resbian's side as he slid off her back and joined Trinity who was now alone lying motionless on the ground. Resbian stood blocking arrows on her one side, keeping the two royals out of sight as much as she could. There were two dead Rodinians on the ground next to Trinity.

"I'm so sorry, honey. You're going to make it, you're going to be okay." Clint kept frantically talking before he made it to her side, as comfort more for himself than of hers. He couldn't even be sure if she was alive. There was blood, and he couldn't see her face. Her wings were nearly shredded and parts of them were completely pulled off and lying here and there near her body. Trinity raised her head; she was alive.

In one effortless swoop, Clint held up her entire body and then desperately searched her teary eyes. He knew nothing could make her want to kill another being. She did not deserve this pain. Trinity had always been against the war. The war which was coming and going now for nearly five centuries. She'd forgiven him for his past crimes and made her peace with his unbearable history. Now they'd been married his actions were hers and his actions wore heavy on her soul.

Perhaps it was her upbringing. The wood fairies were a peaceful people who did not fill themselves with greed. It was more their strategy to stay out of the fight and care for their own. After all, she did spend the majority of her life in hiding within Yodére Forest alongside the rest of the colony.

It was time for this war to be over, and instead of staying behind to have a chance to see it end once and for all, Trinity was leaving. Forcing her own younger sister to take her place as both a new mother and provisional queen. A part of her was still wondering if it was her sister Adalina who ordered the wood fairy soldiers into the valley or if they had been forced out of their dwellings?

Clint knew Trinity longed to see her sister one last time, just to tell her goodbye and kiss her nephew. Even to see her, to know she was alive through all of this. Adalina would have such big shoes to fill. All Trinity could do was wish her the best. Death and more death was all she'd find in this place. Leaving the Second World would be her most selfish act.

Clint and Trinity re-saddled Resbian, it was time again for them to set out on the trip to escape the valley. They were so close to freedom. There was no giving up now. Both as comfortable as they could be on Resbian's back, Clint once again lifted the reins and said, "As fast as you can run, girl, our exit is within view. As long as we don't have any more excitement."

Resbian easily obeyed her master and started to head out of the valley. Trinity hoped the baby was okay. Desperately, she tried to suppress her pain and ignore her worry for the baby's safety. As she closed her eyes, she pictured what the future could hold for her baby, not wanting to see the death Resbian and her husband had caused. She wished that when she opened them that the fighting would be over. They trailed away from the battle, but the cries could be heard for quite a distance. The echoes bounced off the surrounding hills at both ends of the valley. The sound was haunting.

They managed to avoid any contact with anyone or thing through the rest of the valley and Northern Hills. Most of the fighting seemed centralized to what remained of the sorcerer's campsite. Clint was especially alert at this point. If any of them had kept a second line of defense for the battle, they would be filling the outer limits Clint and Trinity were fast approaching. So far, it seemed like everyone was all-in tonight. *Perhaps it would really be the end of the senseless fighting? One last battle to end the war.*

Trusting Resbian to hold steady, he let go of the reins. Clint wanted to be certain there would be no chance of Trinity falling off again. He kept one hand on his sword and the other one strongly around Trinity's waist. With his hand near her abdomen he could sense the life growing inside her was still strong. A true fighter. Her fall had not harmed the baby, but he would not take any more chances of letting her slip away from him again. Born into the sorcerers' line of royals, Clint had been blessed with many medical talents, but even his powers could not heal the damage that had been done to Trinity's wings.

Over time, he would be able to mend where the wounds broke open on her back. They were serious, but if further treated they would not be life-threatening. In the back of his mind he was thinking of the whereabouts of the rest of Trinity's wings. Clint grabbed what he could salvage, but the larger pieces were left behind for others to collect as the bloodshed subsided. Fairy wings had long been prized and the envy of other beings for their magical qualities. Even wood fairies would harvest them ceremonially from their dead to repurpose. The sorcerers would have their pick after the battle to make fresh wands. *If* there were any sorcerers left alive who knew the trade.

Resbian rode forward out of the valley, gliding over the ups, downs, peaks, and crests of Carpenter Hills. Just up ahead there was a maze of gravestones, elaborate and somewhat eccentric markers, and randomized mausoleums here and there. Clint guided Resbian a little of the way using the heel of his boot to gently prod her bleeding sides just to make sure she led them to the right mausoleum. Resbian had taken this journey with Clint many times over the course of the centuries. It was only more recently Clint began to pass back through and never with Resbian in tow.

When they arrived behind a peculiar stone mausoleum marked 1519, Clint dug his boot just a tad more firmly into Resbian's side, signaling her to calmly come to a stop.

"What is it, Clint?" asked Trinity. Immediately alarmed, she lifted her head. By now her face was smudged with blood and tears. "Something's wrong, isn't it? We are never going to make it out of here."

"Always assuming the worst of things," mumbled Clint

under his breath, wondering to himself the same gloomy fate. With the luck they were having tonight, the worst seemed possible.

"I'd say we're beyond assumptions at this point," Trinity retorted, "Well then, what is it, why did we stop, did you see someone? Is the entrance blocked?" By now, Trinity was near frantic, listing off their disparities of the evening.

"Yes, I did see something," Clint was short with Trinity, trying to strain his ear to listen.

"What was it, who was it?" Trinity tried desperately to stay calm, but it was all too much. When she was torn from Resbian's back she left behind every bit of calm there was left. The amount of blood she'd lost was making her feel even weaker and irrational. It was like being drunk on emotion.

"Would you please be quiet just for a moment," Clint's adrenaline and impatience were surging through him, "I'm not certain what I saw."

Trinity finally went quiet, though there were a hundred bad situations running through her head. She'd rather be thinking of them, rather than the terrible bursts of pain that kept shooting through her back. Like knives, they were.

Clint dismounted Resbian's back and Trinity began to shakily follow him off the saddle, but Clint instructed her to stay seated and to keep low.

"Where are you going? Don't leave me here. Why can't we just go? I'm ready to leave, do you think we've been followed?" Her questions ran together as she found herself trying to support her upper body gradually drooping on Resbian's back.

"I'm not going anywhere," he said as he stretched his head forward, "Now, please be quiet."

Trinity did as she was told, yet again. She knew there was not much she could do. After all, she was six months pregnant and wingless. There had never been another time where she felt more useless.

Taking a few steps to his right, Clint peered around the side of the stone wall. He looked upon another mausoleum not far away from where they were concealed. There they were, just as Clint had feared. Restlessly standing were three horses tied to random gravestones. They were just outside the entrance into the First World. The horses were riderless, but that only meant that whoever had been on them were now somewhere on the other side of the entrance. With others still in the First World, Clint and Trinity could not pass through just yet.

Clint audibly moaned as he more closely examined the horses. He noticed his family's seal. There was no mistaking these were his men. They were surely performing Agenesis. Agenesis was a magical fluke or anomaly. In the 1400s, the Second World had experienced its first true threat from those in the First World: a threat of overpopulation and overexposing the beings of the Second World's sanctuary.

The humans marked all five entrances with elaborate markers and enchanted gates equipped with locks and keys. During this era a team began working on something that would change the Second World forever. The team included the likes of Leonardo da Vinci and King Benevolence. King Benevolence was the ruler of the humans at the time and considered one of the most admired innovative rulers to have ever lived in either the

First or Second Worlds. The last known reign of peace. As they were creating enchantments to ward out unwanted First World beings, something incredible yet barbaric occurred.

The humans began entering and stumbling upon the entrances as the First World grew more dangerous and human beings multiplied tenfold in a short period of time. Thanks to Leonardo da Vinci and his work on searching for the soul, he accidentally discovered the answer the beings of the Second World needed to keep their world protected. In the beginning, the five known entrances didn't keep unmagical beings from safe entrance. The Second World was originally recognized as a sanctuary to all.

Leonardo da Vinci fell upon the solution by coincidence while working on anatomical healing practices for King Benevolence. It merely kept those who entered the Second World without magical blood from returning to the First World alive. After duplicating the discovery, the sorcery enchanted the entrance within the cemetery of Carpenter Hills. All those who were caught entering who did not truly belong in the Second World would damage their nerve-endings in their eyes to complete, unhealable blindness. Da Vinci quickly learned what he'd done to replicate what he'd accomplished in the entrance within the human's territory. The leaders of the remaining four territories had him replicate the incantations on their entrances as well.

Not even the worst part, if it was not enough to lose your eyesight if you did not have magical blood when you entered the Second World. If an unworthy being tried to leave the Second World and re-enter the First World after losing their eyesight, their soul would separate from the body. It only took a few years for dark sorcerers to develop the magical enchantment to fuse the bits of life to their own, collecting the years left, the years the dead person was yet to live. Rumors of both Leonardo da Vinci and his apprentice Francisco Melzi may have also been responsible for this vile pursuit.

These beings were considered not worthy to see the beauty and purity of the Second World or witness those who were considered worthy of inhabiting its land. As years went on, this practice was not uncommon in the middle of a battle. He had done so himself countless times, but it had been years. Ever since he had met Trinity, he had stopped all of that. Still the men would return to the other side with new life and the energy and strength to continue in the long battle.

With his head down, Clint returned to where Resbian and Trinity were anxiously waiting for him. Trinity looked down from the height of Resbian's back. "Can we make it through yet?"

As badly as Clint wanted to say *yes*, he couldn't. There was no way to sugarcoat this one either, "No," he said. "Unfortunately, because the Rodinians decided to attack tonight, a few of my men have passed through the First World, no doubt to perform Agenesis." The portal leading back into the First World was their last chance of a haven.

Disappointment shot across Trinity's face as she fought back stomach acid, "Is there anything we can do?"

"If we want to secure the entrance all we can do is wait," it was all Clint could reply.

Clint guided Resbian and Trinity to the side of another mausoleum trying to disguise them between two tall hedges. He remained standing and on high alert as they waited in silence. Resbian's tail swayed back and forth, catching in the dry bushes. Trinity was lying down on Resbian's warm back drifting in and out of light sleep. The blood was beginning to dry, and Clint draped his outer coat around her for warmth.

With his wand held out in one hand, Clint began a few healing incantations with his other palm over Trinity's back and shoulders. The relief the spells gave wasn't much, but maybe enough to keep Trinity from slipping in and out of consciousness. When Clint had recited every healing cure within memory, he moved downward to tend to Resbian's wounds. He pulled out all the visible arrows and performed similar healing rituals on Resbian as he had his wife. The Clydesdale's thick muscles and fur coat seemed to resist most of the incantations. As he took a moment to heal a gash he'd gotten on his own arm, Clint observed his surroundings.

The graveyard in the hills was much quieter than it had been down in the valley. It was eerie and unsettling. Occasionally, Clint would peer around the mausoleum's wall watching and waiting for the three men to appear out of the mausoleum. At this point, Clint had two choices. For one, he could try to fight the men when they came through the entrance. His chances were slim to none if he wanted to survive that choice. Clint was already injured, Trinity was defenseless, and as tough as Resbian was, she had seen better days herself. The numbers alone were odds against him, but the soldiers would be strong, full of youth, especially if they had found young children. It was taking the men an ample amount of time; Clint was certain this was their intention.

His other option was to remain hidden let the soldiers perform Agenesis, mount their horses, and return to the battle. There was still hope Trinity, Clint, and Resbian could pass through unnoticed. They waited and waited; it may have only been an hour or two, but to Trinity and Clint it felt like days. The night was getting colder and the wind blew even harder. Clint's hands felt frozen to his metal sword. His grip weakened with exhaustion and the bitterness brought along with the winter winds.

When the time did come, it was too quick. The first screams were, as feared, the cries of young children. Trinity abruptly sat up on Resbian's back, awakening from a fitful sleep. She was not mentally prepared to witness Agenesis. Clint too was startled forcing his senses to thaw. He signaled Trinity to stay calm and not make noise. She did not make a sound, other than a light breathing and even Resbian was stiller and quieter than before.

Clint edged his way to the corner of the mausoleum and then he saw where the screams were coming from. It was just as he feared it would be. Without seeing, Trinity was certain of what was going on, a part of her still didn't want to believe it.

The door to the mausoleum near the other horses swung open carelessly. Out came three sorcerer soldiers; in each of their grasps was a child. The oldest was no more than ten, the youngest, a three-year-old boy. All three of the non-magic children were grabbing in agonizing pain at their eyes. They stumbled blindly in the grasps of the strong soldiers. The old enchantments stripped the eyesight from them upon entering the Second World. Their struggles were easily overpowered. The least amount of strain exerted from the seasoned men.

Less than a few years ago, Clint would have found himself doing the same thing and would have felt no remorse for his actions. Now, as he watched his own men take part in Agenesis, the sight was too much for him to bear. He did all he could to fight the knot in his stomach. His men disgusted him, taking the lives of innocent human children. *What had he ever gained?*

Clint watched the actions of the men as if it were déjà vu. Every step of the Agenesis process that proceeded was so familiar he could go through it inside his mind. To begin, his men had found young human children living in the world just through the other side of the large stone mausoleum. Then they lured them into Webb Cemetery, located on the opposite side in the First World. Given the long time they were gone, they had difficulty finding children whose parents were foolish enough to let them out at such an hour.

The small town on the other side was very remote and it was difficult to take children without much suspicion. His people had been accustomed to traveling a fair distance before hunting children. Three was an impressive number during these times and at this passage. Of course, by now it was almost morning. These kids could have been getting ready for school. Some of the other entrances into the First World were easier prey. A few were even in the heart of cities.

Children were not the only option for Agenesis. Youth only increased your chances of finding someone in the First World who had a great deal of years left to live. Sometimes, young adults in good health could provide their fair share of life. Then there were those who were brought through on a bet or out of spite, even for sport. A person further along in the lines of forty or fifty. Of course, because of Clint's work over this year those locations were no longer available to pass through.

There was so much shame, disgust. Now, Clint was feeling too much of both. It all seemed so wrong now, Trinity helped him see that, his unborn child helped him realize his wrongs.

Next the men would make sure the children came all the way through the mausoleum. Then one at a time the men would release one of the children, telling them word for word how to get back through the mausoleum. They would say that when the children arrived back to the other side, they would have their eyesight back and would no longer be suffering.

The soldier with the only girl child went first. The other two soldiers backed away a few yards. The soldier gave the young girl instructions. She was hesitant and shaking as she walked. The oldest boy was the quietest of the three. He was talking to her calmly, trying to reassure her everything would be okay and to listen to the man's voice.

The soldier pulled out his wand and recited the ancient text memorized by the many times he had incited it. The girl kept walking, forcing her unsteady feet to trust the man's directions through the darkness. It did not take long to get through the stone building and walk back up the steps. There was one last deafening scream, a burst of light, and then the blinding beautiful gold-metallic flash. The strike hit the soldier who had guided her through the tomb in the center of his chest.

Chapter 2
A Whole New World

The remaining two children gazed up at the soldier. They couldn't see, but he had a ravenous smile across his smug face. The soldier let out a menacing bout of laughter easily scaring the children. The first soldier then backed away and let the second soldier who held the ten-year-old boy in his arms go next. The boy was trying to shake the three-year-old off his leg. He was really still just a child himself, but for his little brother he tried to stay strong and not seem scared. There was no denying his fear and hearing the neighbor girl Sophia's scream was not making him feel any better. *What choice did he have but to listen to the man? What would be of his little brother Bo?*

His little brother had been driving him crazy all morning and his mom and dad insisted he let him follow him down the long drive to the bus stop. *This was the one time he wished he was on his way to school. Not here, not in this place smelling of burnt hot dogs. Not with these strange men and in such pain.* Before he walked, the older boy leaned down and blindly found his little brother's blanket. He pulled it up to the little boy's face and told him to take good care of it, "Stay strong. little man, this will all be over soon."

The little boy did not have time to respond, he only pulled his blanket up to his burning eyes. His brother's voice faded. He was being dragged away. When he crossed back to the other side. He refused to scream; he could not let his little brother worry. Then it was all over. There was a second burst of light and the same beautiful gold luster escaped his body hitting the second soldier in the chest.

Clint's body ached to watch the brave young boy pass willingly through to the other side. The three-year-old stood bold with his little fists balled up around his blanket, staying strong and brave just like his big brother told him to. Clint watched as the boy wiped his aching eyes. His youth was reflected in his innocence.

The boy was so young that he could not fully comprehend the third soldier's directions to walk as he was being told. Instead, the young boy stopped he said, "I's tired," and sat on the ground with his blanket, "you promised you were going to get me a cookie." The soldiers laughed at first, but they were growing impatient. If the boy was going to take any longer, they would have to drag and throw him through the other side.

This was all far too much weight on his soul. Clint's conscience was already bursting at the brim. Trinity was too far away from Clint to see what was going on at the entrance, but she saw when Clint bolted off towards the mausoleum with his sword clutched tightly in his hand. She reached out towards him, but with no measure of gain. The odds no longer mattered, Clint ran around the side of the mausoleum and to where his three men were positioned. The soldier who had held the boy was now kicking him, trying to force him back through the mausoleum's entrance.

"Stop this madness, stop it all at once. That is a direct order!" All three of the men found Clint's words funny. They broke out in hysterical laughter. They'd been drinking too. The harsh smell of fire whisky wafted from their gasps.

"Oh, come here to have the boy for yourself did you sire?" The men laughed again and went back to kicking the boy. The boy could not hold back tears now. He was on the ground and still gripping his blanket in the fetal position.

Clint lifted his sword to the man's throat, "Touch that boy again and you shall taste the end of my sword!"

The soldiers could not believe the words they were hearing come out of the king's mouth. The long blade pressed harder up against the soldier's neck.

"Sire, what's gotten into you?" Clint knew this man well and was shaken by the familiarity in his tone. He appointed General Monrow himself, "We're just messing around. You know how it gets when we're losing. We must do this. It's just First World skum muts," sweat and spit spewed from the ungroomed man's hairy face. General Monrow knew the king possessed one of the few weapons that could not only injure but kill those who'd performed Agenesis. During the battle the soldiers discovered some of the Rodinians appeared to have found weapons of their own capable of the same.

Clint was not in the mood for small talk. He wanted to be out of this world before the sun came up. He slit the general's throat. The other two soldiers stood and stared back at their well-known leader. They had never witnessed or heard of Clint killing his own men, especially over something so casual to them as Agenesis.

It was as if he had gone mad or was cursed. They saw their king lower his sword to his side, his chest rising and falling with pulsing rage. Their friend and commanding officer lay dead on the ground. The lack of sleep fueled Clint's need to get out of this world as soon as possible. The two soldiers were not sure what to do. At first, they didn't move as they stared back into their leader's vindicated eyes.

Then Clint made the decision for them, he brought his sword up into the air and pointed directly at the other two soldiers. "Leave now, live the life you have stolen with greater purpose than your friend who lies before you. Tell no one of what you have witnessed if you wish to keep your own lives."

The soldiers still seemed confused, something like this was completely unheard of. *Had they gotten ahold of some enchanted whisky? What was going on with their leader? Had he gone completely mental?* Whatever was running through their heads, they obliged, knowing their ruler to be a man of his word. The men scrambled off the ground and then they mounted their horses without another word and disappeared out of the cemetery, into the valley, and back in the direction of the battle.

His actions would not be something his men would

soon be able to forget, and he knew it was unlikely they would truly keep their promise of secrecy. Once the word was out, he would no longer be remembered as an honored and respected leader as he had done so for hundreds of years. Killing one of his own, defenseless, would not be easily forgotten. Since the passing of his father Charles, Clint had lived and breathed the succession of his ruthless reign with no exceptions.

None of that mattered though. He would no longer be *their* King. There was no heir left who would wish to rule and he would *never* permit his future child to follow in his footsteps. It would be endless bloodshed to decide who would lead now, if there was anyone left to lead. After all, the soldiers did say they were losing. Would they surrender?

Trinity could not stay idle by Resbian. She had walked over to the soldier's dead body turned sideways and oddly bent over a gravestone. His face was familiar to her, but he had been an enemy, so his name went unknown, and her remorse for him was less than for the men Resbian had trampled down in the valley, the ones like the sorcerer guard, whom she knew by Clint's stories.

She stepped forward passing Clint with a cold shoulder. He had almost forgotten, but she hadn't. The little boy was still on the ground but was cowering up against a tall gravestone, probably completely unaware of what it was. It turned out another's fear was his sanctuary. At first, the boy pulled away from her small hands. Her voice was calming to him. He called her, "Mommy?" before she told him her real name. The boy repeated her name with difficultly, "Trineeny," was what it sounded more like.

Regardless, he allowed her to scoop him up in her welcoming arms. She calmed the boy by stroking his long blond curls. The boy was quick to warm up to her kind heart. He wrapped his stubby arms around her neck.

"We cannot leave him here, not like this," her words hung in the crisp air. Clint hadn't really put much thought into what they were going to do with the boy after he saved his life. If the boy tried to get back through the entrance, he would die a very instant but painful death. The magical enchantments that allowed the soldiers to harvest the soul of the children from the First World would kill him. His years would be wasted. There was no way he could take him with them but leaving him here in the cemetery meant certain death.

"Trinity, I told you to stay with Resbian. What if those men were to come back and bring others with them?" Clint was furious, mostly with himself. *How could he kill so freely? Had he not changed?* He'd grown up with General Monrow fought alongside him, believed the man to be his equal. *Was he still just a senseless murderer? Did he deserve to live through this battle?*

"And I told you to stop trying to order me around as if I were one of your soldiers," Trinity was quick to respond.

He sighed, "You should not be lifting him." Clint walked to her and tried to take the boy from her arms. He resisted at first, feeling Clint's grip, so familiar to those who had caused him so much pain. With Trinity's soothing words he finally let go of her neck. When he recognized Clint didn't want to hurt him, he immediately latched onto him.

This man was warm, just like Daddy, and he felt so cold. His fluffy bear slippers he wore down to the bus stop with his brother were lost several blocks before the place where they put dead people. One of the men he thought was nice to him, even carried him so his feet wouldn't get too cold.

"What am I supposed to do with him? We obviously cannot take him with us," argued Clint.

"There must be something we can do," reasoned Trinity, "isn't there a spell or hex we can use?" She was determined to protect this boy's life.

Clint stood with the weeping boy, thinking about what he could do. There really wasn't much he was able to conjure to help with his wand and killing more people to save this boy's life wasn't practical. Trinity was thinking hard as well, but both knew they were biding their time. More soldiers were likely to head this way. If the others had talked word would spread quickly, even during a battle. His people's mere curiosity would draw them to the cemetery, whether they believed the men or not. *If there was anyone left alive to listen to them.*

Resbian had followed Trinity over to the mausoleum and was now brushing her snout against Trinity's shoulder.

"I know what to do," declared Clint out of the blue, keeping fine details to himself, "but I will have to go alone."

"What is it you're going to do?" asked Trinity, unable to imagine where Clint would be allowed to take the child to be safe at a time like this.

"The boy and I will travel towards the Château de Beaucoup, and I will make sure that we are seen. They will not fire upon us if I have a child. His life would surely be spared by the townspeople."

"That's absurd," the idea of just walking back towards the fight and surrendering the boy was insanity. He'd never make it back to her alive. "What of *your* life? They'll surely recognize you and spare no expense of your life regardless of the child." Trinity demanded; she took Clint's arm recognizing she hadn't convinced him. "What of *our* life? Our child's life. I need you and our baby will need you more than ever."

Clint did not answer. After killing General Monrow he didn't feel like he was worthy of life anymore. He acknowledged he was choosing silence more often than he preferred. All he did was give Trinity more instruction. He would be valuing and risking the element of surprise. *Perhaps if he covered his face and concealed his wand, he'd stand a chance?*

"You will take Resbian and go through the entrance. I will follow you shortly. It was never my wish to flee separately, but if it's the only way we'll both be able to depart from this world then so be it."

At first, Trinity was speechless. Neither of them knew if the Château de Beaucoup had been taken. It didn't seem to be the target of tonight's battle. She looked fondly at the young boy with frozen tears streaking his rosy cheeks. They would have to chance it. There was no way she could willingly leave the boy to die, even if it meant losing Clint. Still, she did not know this boy, no one would witness if they left him here, no one would be able to follow them to the other side, and nothing would be stopping them from their freedom.

"But Clint, you have risked not returning to me on so many occasions tonight, what if... what if this time you don't return?" Trinity's body was shaking.

"I swear I will see you again, we will part ways one last time. It'll just be a short while and then never again. You know where we'll meet. At least with you going ahead of me, I know you'll be safe."

The boy was restless in his arms, so Clint heaved him higher on his waist. He fought his mind and the strong part of him who was willing to set the boy down along the path and never look back. There was no surrendering to his blame. There was an aching for this to all be over. He wanted the dead soldier to disappear, the blood on his sword to melt away, and for this night not to exist. Here he was holding a child he hadn't raised, flooded with mistakes he made many years ago, and a single choice.

He couldn't kiss her goodbye. It would be too permanent, so certain he wouldn't make it through. "Go to the farm. We will be together soon. I love you, now go, I will not move until I see you pass through." Reluctantly, she pulled herself back onto Resbian's saddle. "Take care of her with your life, Resbian." He knew the loyal horse would. Then she was gone.

"I love you..." it was more of a whisper, but Trinity passed through the mausoleum passage, knowing it was the only way they were making it out. She was so ready to get away from this place but longed to be back in the woods. Clint pushed the door to the mausoleum closed behind her, leaving her in temporary darkness.

His arms were already numb and there was the continued burning desire to set the boy down and follow his wife safely to the other side, never to see the boy or know of his fate. Instead Clint turned away from the cemetery. He looked out at the destruction. Flames lit parts of Yodére Forest and smoke billowed in the night sky, blending with the darkening clouds and flashing against the glow of the almost full moon.

Screams could still be heard hours after the invasion, but not as loud as before. These screams were different— more the fading moans of those who lay dying within the valley. It was time.

Clint was fortunate to find a place farther outside of town and so quickly. He walked just shy of two miles from the cemetery before finding himself standing before a white-painted gate. The house seemed aged, but Clint couldn't remember ever passing the home in his many years. He must've always taken a different passage. The Château de Beaucoup was still a few miles away. The small home might have been the first bit of luck he'd experienced tonight. There was a fire lit inside the home and through the windows there was life inside, no doubt kept awake by the fighting. They may have come up from the cellar not too long before he arrived at the gate, likely forced out by the cold.

This was where he would try to leave the young boy, more than just a boy corrected Clint inside his head. The boy in long pajamas had a name, Brody Adamson. Not just Bo, as Clint heard the older boy call him. Brody could hardly pronounce his own name and was three and a half years old. He had a blanket he called *bankey*, a big brother named Thomas. He had red feet, a red nose, and chapped cheeks from the cold.

Every life he'd ever taken flooded before him. It was too much of a burden and now was not the time for repentance. Instead, he held every ounce of their life's worth in his stiff arms.

The cottage he found before the boundaries of the

Château de Beaucoup and the edge of the woods was surrounded by a short fence painted white. There were things strewn about in the front yard, a trellis to the back of what appeared to be an untamed garden, left bare for the coming winter.

By this point, Brody had his head laying on Clint's shoulder. He even had part of his thin inner coat draped protectively across Brody like a sheet. The tears on his cheeks were gone and dried away. After Clint convinced him this was all a bad dream and he would be warm and awake soon, Brody calmed down. It seemed to comfort him enough that he briefly became the chatty ball of energy he was before crossing into the Second World. He had talked on and on to Clint for several minutes and now was exhausted, clutching to his *bankey* and holding firmly onto Clint's arm.

A wholesome calm was surrounding the perimeter of the house. There was a glimmer of resistance at the gate before he seemed to stumble through an invisible wall. Then all Clint could hear was the clinking of the gate as it closed itself behind him. Clint walked up the stone path to the door. The lamp outside was not lit. For a second, Clint contemplated whether to knock on the door or to knock it down. Clint really was not in the position to arm himself. His sword was too awkward to hold with the sleeping child in his arms and his wand was out of reach on the other side of his waistband.

There was no need to do either. The door opened just a crack. Clint lowered his hand away from the door knocker. The man at the door was not very old, and just by shapes moving inside there was a young woman trying to hush two small children and the cry of a newborn baby, she clung tightly to her chest.

The man examined the unarmed Clint up and down, curious how the soldier had made his way to their home and that the gate had let him pass. "We cannot take any wounded at this time. We don't have the space or the means. Tell Kalli I'll be happy to help in the stables if there's time, but no more beings until the spring."

The door began to close in Clint's face. He was confused at the man's response. *Kalli Loucentious? These were workers for the human royal family? How had their home not already burned?*

Clint blocked the door with his thick boot. They were wasting his time and there was no telling where the next closest occupied place would be. Carefully, he forced his way into the small home. His body was quickly warmed by the fire. The man tried to shove him back out peacefully.

"What is the meaning of this? We said we couldn't take anymore!" The door pushed up against Clint's foot.

Trevor stood frozen as the firelight revealed the nightly visitor's face. It was common for the human Queen Kalli Loucentious to send wounded or orphaned children to their dwelling without notice, but since the arrival of their fourth child in late summer, it was clear they would need time before they could help any further.

However, this was no mere man of Gresham. He had never seen Clint, King of Sorcerers, in person, but he'd been around for so many years, taken so many lives, filled so many people with hatred, he knew unmistakably it was him standing just inside his doorway, steps away from his wife, his entire family. A glimpse at the crest branded into his armor and royal sword at his side confirmed it.

Trevor and his family were defenseless. While they

shared the same surname as Clint Teagardin, being distant relatives after centuries of elongated life and a messy strand of bloodlines wouldn't be enough to save them. *What was he doing with a wounded child? Could this be a trick? Was this how the gate had allowed him to pass? Was it the little bit of ancient bloodline they shared?* The white gate around their house was built and stood enchanted for at least a quarter of a century. It had protected his father and his family as well as Trevor's. It served them well. *Could such an enchantment wear off over time or had this seasoned sorcerer found a way to break the old protection?*

Trevor had worked and dealt tirelessly his whole life to protect his family and what good resided in the name of a Teagardin. He made deals, trades, promises all for it to end here. He wouldn't stand for it.

"Elizabeth, go. Take the children and get out of here!" The words were sharp and quick.

Except no one moved. One of Trevor's children, his son Alexander, the oldest at eight, was inching closer to the door.

"Daddy, his eyes?" Alexander was scared, but his relentless curiosity overcame fear. His gaze fixated on the boy in Clint's arms. The little boy's eyes flickered open as he raised his small head off Clint's shoulders.

Clint was quick to dissipate any alarm Brody would have waking back up, "Where am I?" Brody's eyes opened, but he was still left in darkness. His eyes were scarred, swollen, and raw. He was alarmed at the new sounds and unfamiliar voices, "Thomas, Tommy is that you? This isn't funny. I can't see anything. What happened? What did you do? I'm telling Mommy on you."

"Hush now, you're still sleeping, remember: this is all

just a dream," Clint stood the boy up in front of him on the wooden floorboards. He was relieved to have the feeling in his arms again and placed his palms on Brody's shoulders.

"It's not Tommy, your brother is gone. This will be your new family." Clint was trying to seem compassionate and to the point.

The Teagardin family didn't speak; they couldn't. They just watched in awe as someone they had feared their entire lives talked to the young blind boy as if he was his own, Clint looked up into their questioning eyes as he said to the boy, "This is your home now."

The children of the house were quicker to accept the young stranger. Theodore, Trevor's second son, just a few years older than the boy, stepped out of the shadows.

"My name is Theodore, but everyone just calls me Theo." Trevor quickly put an end to his son's conversation trying to encourage him towards the back of the house. It was too late though. Theodore was already holding the boy's hand the other one still clinging to his *bankey*.

Trevor deflated; his efforts would be helpless at this point. The young boy willingly held Theodore's hand. He liked Theodore, he already reminded him of his brother, very talkative. He bet he had lots of friends too, just like Tommy.

Elizabeth, Trevor's wife, whispered the word, "Agenesis," as if it were poison leaving her lips.

"We want nothing to do with your evil plans, Clint, no matter how much life it could give us. As much as our family savors time, we value more than years under this roof."

Elizabeth was bitter at his mere existence. She was looking at each one of her children. This was her safe haven. *Why was he here?* The likes of a sorcerer, especially a king, had no place here. Clint could have killed all of them right here and now if he wanted to.

Trevor looked at his wife cautiously. He wished that her feisty temper would remain at bay, the last thing he wanted was to upset Clint, but he couldn't resist. "Excuse my wife, Agenesis is not something we think too kindly of here. What is your plan sire, to harbor the boy here until it is a good time to send him crawling back through the mausoleum to his death? What worth is this boy to you, another sixty years to your miserable pathetic life? We will have no part in your people's ways."

His words were offensive, and Clint was rather surprised that someone of Trevor's stature was so knowledgeable about Agenesis. "I can assure you; these are not my intentions. In fact, I can guarantee, you will not be seeing me again. I just ask that you take care of the child."

Trevor was not convinced. Clint quickly drew his sword. Trevor was not one to cower; without hesitation, he stood unarmed directly between Clint and his family. His children recoiled closer to their mother. Theodore held the boy's hand tighter looking directly at his father.

There was no strike. Clint never had the intention. Instead, he took a knee on the wooden floorboards and tilted his head to the ground. He held out his hefty sword as an offering. The blood from one of his own men now dried at the tip of the blade.

To be presented the sword from a royal was a great honor. To Trevor's knowledge, it had not been done in centuries and perhaps not in all of history for a sorcerer to willingly pass down a sword to a human? This weapon was crafted to kill any being, including those who had performed Agenesis. It usually signified the message of defeat or the passing down of an heir. Trevor had done neither of these.

"I don't understand," Trevor almost gasped. He hadn't taken a full breath of air since he'd opened the front door only moments ago.

"Take it! Take it, use it, sell it, there's a good chance it would fetch quite the price to the right person. Use the money to care for the boy and the rest of your family, buy a bigger home, it's yours to do as you wish. It has fulfilled my time. Use it for something good."

That was all Clint said before transferring what was once his father's sword into Trevor's hands. Trevor accepted the offering, trying not to seem strained from holding the large sword. Clint glanced at little Brody, one last time. *Be brave.* He stood and left the small home at the edge of the woods. He'd been careless for time. There was a new urgency lit within him, he needed to return to Trinity.

He could all but pray she had made it to the farm without anyone following her. Deep inside himself he felt she was safe, but her wounds would still need tending to. And as for her lack of wings—it was not how they intended for her to lose them.

There was only one last thing to do before leaving the Second World. The path back to the cemetery was a lot quicker than when he was carrying Brody. He was fortunate enough to not run into anymore of his men or others along the way. Likely all sides of the battle were busy re-grouping, assessing the damage, and measuring the severity of such a senseless battle. It was surely almost sunrise at this point, but the night hung on a while longer. A calming darkness to surround his last departure. *This was the right choice.*

At the cemetery there were a few bodies scattered about including the one he was responsible for at the mausoleum entrance. Clint searched around, it seemed safe enough. It was finally quiet, almost too quiet, but it brought peace of mind. Anyone out at this point in battle would be dead or dying.

Along the path of the cemetery were a few rows of dried milkweed. The towering green weed grew to the height of his chest. The leaves were turned brown from an early frost and the large, curved seed pods curled at the ends. Not seeing his friend, Clint started calling out for him in a whisper, "Cliffton, Cliffton Burroughs. Cliffton, I know you're around here someplace, Cliffton come out. Hurry up you little old shrew, Cliffton."

There at a grave marker hardly visible from wear and dirt, was a small trail of fluffy milkweed seeds. Clint started to lean over to get a closer look and was smacked between the eyes with a small stick. He recoiled, "What was that for?"

A green-winged figure about eight inches tall stood on a mossy rock baring the little twig angrily in his small hands before casting it to the ground, "Hours! *Hours*, I've waited and watched. I'm about frozen straight through. Have me out of my pod at the eve of hibernation season. Don't even get me started with that wifey of yours. I cannot believe you let Trinity through without you. You're damn near out of luck Clint." The small angry figure pulled his tiny coat tighter around his shivering body.

"That's what I have you for, Cliffton. I take it you saw

the boy then?" Clint wasn't surprised Cliffton knew all of this. He was always the observant and sneaking one.

"The boy! Yes, I saw the little boy and your men. Bold move even for you, sire. What I don't understand is why you didn't just leave him or better yet take his years. What was one more? You could've used the extra time on the other side. You never know what you'll run into in the First World. I hear the humans there are all crazy."

Not surprised by the milkweed pixie's honesty, Clint told him, "If I would have taken his life or left the little boy to die it would have been one more too many for me. Maybe I'm getting soft as a father."

"Sure, sure. I myself wouldn't know." shook Cliffton, "now can we get on with this before someone else shows up? Our work will be spoiled if any being was even to witness." Cliffton nervously looked all around before diving behind the dull grave marker. He resurfaced from the dying dewy grass with a large, brass-colored skeleton key. At this point, the key was one object more alive in legends than it was truth. The pathways had been open between worlds now for nearly five centuries, when the likes of Leonardo da Vinci crossed through.

Cliffton and Clint had spent the good part of the last year secretly tracking down, sealing off, and single-handedly destroying what they could of the five known entryways into the Second World. This old, mausoleum was the last of the five passages left open as a route between the Second and First Worlds.

It was one of the few to have an existing key or one that could be salvaged. Clint trusted Cliffton to lock and seal the entryway just before destroying it. The old bronze skeleton key was rather heavy for Cliffton and nearly two-thirds his height. He pulled it to the foot of the door at the edge of the mausoleum's stone steps descending downward. This was as far as Cliffton would go.

"So... this is goodbye then, sire?" Cliffton was no longer criticizing Clint. He seemed almost broken or saddened to be saying farewell. It wasn't uncommon for milkweed pixies to befriend humans, or in this case sorcerer, but they nearly always outlived them. Gaining the acknowledgement of *sire* was another honor.

"Yes, and for good this time, I'm afraid." Clint's voice trailed, "Take care of that," he pointed to the large bronze key. Then as he almost forgot about what they were doing here, Clint reached deep into his drawstring satchel riding bag. The same bag that was also holding what was left of Trinity's wings and the bag Trinity had taken with her filled with her jewelry box of prized belongings, "and be sure to use this." Delicately Clint unwrapped a piece of fabric woven from sycamore bark and mermaid hair.

Tucked safely within the fabric, Clint revealed its contents. He held out a small glass vial with a cork stopper. A miracle it hadn't shattered in battle even with protection. In his other hand, Clint drew his wand with the glass out away from his body. He pressed the tip of his wand to the vial. The specks of sand inside danced and swirled around forming small bursts of light within the clear vial.

Like stepping away from a land mine, Clint carefully placed the vial on the frozen ground and backed up. "Be sure to keep a good distance with this one. I gave it an extra echo blast, just to be sure it'll take out the entire entrance. This opening is a tad bigger than the others we've encountered. Not to mention, it goes much deeper in the earth than the previous four."

Cliffton rubbed his hands together, trying to warm them. He was still clinging to the skeleton key with his small frozen fingers as he crouched at the edge of the mausoleum. His tired senses were weak, making him easily mesmerized by the little light bursts within the small glass.

"I'll be sure to stay clear." Cliffton shook away the brief trance, "I'm not sure my whiskers have grown back properly from getting too close sealing the last entrance. They seem to be all growing back gray. I may even use a pod to propel it a little further in."

"Do whatever you must," confirmed Clint, slightly smiling at the memory of destroying the last entrance with his dear friend. The little guy did look awful silly with no eyebrows for weeks. He was thankful they'd grown back, it made things easier to carry on a serious conversation, "Now that everything is in order, I really must be going."

"Aye, sire, it is time." Cliffton was distracted looking at the 1519 on the side of the mausoleum. *What would Master da Vinci think of their pursuits? Would he be proud or disgusted?*

There was an awkward moment exchanged, uncertain whether to hug or shake hands. They'd worked closely for the larger part of the year. Once known enemies the odd duo had come together for a much greater purpose. Now they were more than friends, but not quite what you'd call family. Clint had cast all his family off over time, or they cast him off. As for Cliffton, it was unlikely for any milkweed pixies to know their own kin. The two settled with a head nod. Before Clint ducked away into the mausoleum, he turned back to Cliffton, "Just one more request, it shouldn't be too much trouble."

"Yes, sire, anything?" Cliffton truly meant it, but knew better when Clint said it, 'wasn't much,' that it was probably a great deal of work.

"Will you be sure to check in on the boy, just every now and again? I left him with a young couple in a gated-cottage bordering the forest and beyond the royal stables to the west."

Cliffton paused, he was looking forward to a calm, peaceful, quiet life after Clint retreated. He wished to live the life of a hermit, not a watch guard. "You couldn't just let me retire in peace could you, sire? Nonetheless, I suppose after the spring thaw I can check on him every now and again. The house at the edge of the woods, was it?" He reiterated with one tiny eyebrow raised.

Not to seem too invested, it was a poor grain of hope to harbor. Their own disappearances would cause a great deal of unrest, followed by only more fighting and death. It wasn't likely the family would survive, especially not with a young blind boy in these parts. If the young family had any wits, they'd keep the boy quiet.

Even with the entrances sealed, Cliffton wouldn't put it past a desperate sorcerer to make a try at harvesting his years. Brody looked very young and healthy to Clint. He'd be hard for some to resist.

However many doubts and unruly thoughts Cliffton considered, he did make note to head in the direction of the cottage after hibernation season. If it meant giving Clint peace of mind, it was the least he could do.

With no other business to attend to, Clint retreated, and for the first time in his life, he ran away from a fight. Clint took the steps down into the musky tomb with deep breaths of damp air filling his lungs as he walked through the path of darkness, he had guided so many blindly through. Without light he knew when to take the first step back up on the other side and through the entrance into the First World.

The air was not as fresh at this side, but today it felt liberating as it filled his lungs. He briskly shut the wooden door as he left, then waited for it to happen.

At the other side, still in the Second World, the small milkweed pixie Cliffton had scaled the doorway with great difficulty. The key carefully fastened to his side. It weighed him down too greatly to fly. Shimmying around the door handle, he balanced himself before awkwardly lifting the key up into the hole. Hanging onto the loop at the end, Cliffton jumped up and down on the knob until the key turned enough for an audible clink. Sweating profusely, Cliffton pulled hard on the key. The key wobbled out abruptly, sending the key clunking to the hard ground below. Cliffton landed with a *kerplunk* just beside it.

The door at the opposite end made a reciprocating clink. The entry was sealed, but only by enchanted lock and key. Both sides were locked. A fragment of weight lifted away from Clint's shoulders. He gained it all back at the sight of the two children dead on the ground just outside the mausoleum in Webb Cemetery. His body made a sharp startle as a sickening pain followed to his stomach with a lurch. They were lying serenely beside one another; no doubt Trinity moved the two bodies so they could be together at peace. There was nothing more he could do for them now.

As he walked out away from Webb Cemetery, he watched the snow begin to fall, a large flake landed on a concrete headstone just as he was coming to the road. The marker read, "Hope." Hope stayed with him as he went to meet his family, his reason for ending all of this.

Trinity had to unbury her face from Resbian's mane, when Clint finally arrived. She was lying next to Resbian among some old straw in the barn on the property of their new home. Trinity refused to leave Resbian and enter the house about a quarter-mile along the way, until she was certain Clint was safe. The embrace was comfort and answered prayers. It was safety and it was home. The pain of the abuse of her wings melted away. Every possible bad scenario erased from her mind.

Shortly after, Clint made a warm place for Resbian and found enough for her to eat and drink nearby before insisting on carrying Trinity the rest of the way to the farmhouse. The farmhouse was old, but not old in the way things were viewed in the Second World. Here old just meant not just made or purchased. In the Second World it was more common to invest in something to last for generations and was prized as such.

Things were too easily cast aside and disposed of in the First World. No one wanted to spend the time to find joy in the work of making something last. This home had character and was at least fifty years old. Clint and Trinity cherished the woodwork and strong craftsmanship. Not to mention, Trinity easily fell in love with the trees and open space. It just needed some new paint and a fix or two here and there. The plumbing was already proving to be more than good enough, and fetching water was easy.

These were little things no one in the Second World

would notice, especially during a war. Shelter was everything. The other luxuries were what made beings in the Second World dislike those who inhabited the First. Wasteful. Inside the home, Clint built a nice large fire and made food for his pregnant wife. They collapsed into a deep sleep for the first time in months on the wood floor in front of the dusty fireplace with hope forming. They had made it.

Chapter 3
Hope

Alfaro, First World
17 Years Later

The sun had barely reached the edge of the fall fields on the horizon. The tall corn stocks of early August crept shadows into the grassy field the Hope family referred to as "the ballpark." The large field was named this mostly for its size and the history of town kids meeting there for games of ball. These games were typically with the family that'd lived there before the Hopes back in the seventies. Now the name stuck, but no more children played ball, and the area was just an overgrown patch of grass. It was more of a burden to try to keep the Grabers' dairy cows from grazing in or the tall dewy grass would clog the clunky riding mower, especially after there was a heavy rain.

At the end of the field was an old yellow house beside the dirt road, a two-car garage, and a white-washed barn at the edge of the fields, well overdue for a new coat of paint. This was where Skye began her morning chores. Skye was tall for a girl her age, but not as tall as those who played basketball in her class at school. She had strong arms and thicker hair she liked to pull back, but only at home. She let it fall below her shoulders while at school. A bit young for being a high school senior, Skye wouldn't turn eighteen until the summer after graduation.

Continuing along, she made sure the chickens were well fed just after she visited the Grabers' cows along the fence to the pastures. She had taken a shortcut through the cornfield and was now gathering a couple of eggs. The cloth-lined wire basket was beginning to fill, just enough for breakfast. The barn was always her last stop in the morning and first stop back in the afternoon when school was over.

The Hopes owned all the farmland, the pasture where the cows grazed, the cornfield that they often rotated with hay, soybeans, and even wheat. The barn was also theirs, but ironically enough, as much as Diane and Vince Hope loved animals and the idea of farming, neither of them had the experience, time, or knack to run a family farm.

It was the spring after they had come to town, they made arrangements with the Graber family down the way. The Grabers had family all across the small town of Alfaro, mostly farmers like themselves. Fine people if there ever were any who raised mostly boys and kept to themselves just for good measure. The past seventeen years the Grabers had farmed the land and raised the cattle. The Hopes didn't dabble in the small profit the cows turned over for the dairy products at Graber Dairy Farm, but the fields often produced enough to share in those profits in exchange for the use of the land. It was always a fair agreement.

Originally, Matthew Graber wanted to purchase the farmhouse and the land but was not financially sound at the time due to an unusually wet planting season. He let the land and house go out from under him at an auction-estate sale. If it would've been up to Matthew, he would have bulldozed the old house and barn and expanded into pigs. Nonetheless, he was grateful for the rich land and the extra room for his cows to graze.

The chickens, on the other hand, were left for Skye to take care of, as well as their rooster. Skye had nicknamed the old rooster Lucy mostly because she had been only seven years old. Of course, at the time, she was convinced their old rooster was a *she*. Sometime later her parents persuaded her to change the name Lucy to Lucky, but every now and again Skye would holler at the old brute with an accent like Ricky Ricardo, "Lucy, now why'd you have to go'a spillin' all the food," or, "Lucy, what's the matta' with ya." No one was usually around to hear her poor attempt at an accent, and it was a joke she kept to herself.

Her last stop of the morning was at the horse stall in the barn. As she opened the doors the smell of fresh-cut hay and dry manure filled the air. It was an odor most people disliked, but Skye was comforted by it. Here in the barn she had so many fond memories. A place to truly be herself. There was an assortment of old farm machinery, more like ghosts, which were never used. There were broken brooms and metal rakes. The horse stall was two ordinary stalls combined. The black and white patched horse was a nearly full-grown Clydesdale and the Hope family's only horse.

This horse was special to Skye. He was born unexpectedly in April the same year Skye turned five-years-old. The birth was quite a wonder for the old mare. It later turned out she had gotten over the Grabers' fence and became fond of their white stallion, Hickory. The Grabers weren't too happy to find the broken fence and were pretty set on taking the foal when it was born. Skye's father Vince Hope paid to repair the fence and gave a fair price for the foal, even though he was certain Hickory had a lot to do with the whole ordeal.

Resbian fell ill soon after birthing the foal. Within a few months, Resbian died in the barn still nursing her foal. Skye's mom took Resbian's passing hard, but not as hard as her dad. He spent a lot more time working at the hospital afterwards and hardly paid much mind to the other animals. Losing Resbian was like losing a family member. Vince even insisted she be buried under the oak tree by the barn. It took borrowing a backhoe from the mill and nearly a ten-foot hole.

The foal was named Buckwheat by Skye's mother Diane because he ate more than any animal she had ever known. He still nearly ate them out of house and home, thought Skye, filling the food trough to the brim. She grabbed the coarse brush off the wall and started brushing Buckwheat's tail, his long black mane, and the white feather covering on all four massive hooves. Buckwheat had black and white patches along his body, resembling a large cow. Next, she scooped the manure out of the horse stall and untied his reins. On her way out, she left open the stall gate and barn door to allow Buckwheat to come and go as he pleased throughout the day, just as she always did when the weather was permissible.

Heading back up to the house, the sun was nearly over the barn roof. She had taken too long on her chores and would now have to skip breakfast. Dad was sleeping off a twelve-hour shift from the hospital the night before and Mom always left at four in the morning to get to the Brightways Daycare in town before parents started dropping off their children for the day.

Skye found space on the small kitchen table, towering with old newspapers, and set down the basket of eggs. She grabbed her school bag and bolted for the bus stop.

The bus was... well, the bus. It was nothing short of the long-stuffed doughnut, they liked to call it. Being a senior in high school with just a driver's license and no car was embarrassing. The bus was full of smelly freshman and even smellier potheads.

"Skye," a girl with narrow cheekbones as well as slick blond and purple hair called up from her seat, pulling one headphone out of her ear. Skye scanned down the aisle until she found her best friend. Tiffany was seated towards the back of the bus just behind the wheel seat and positioned directly in the emergency exit.

If school buses had first class, this was the spot to be sitting. After being stuck on the bus for three years, you got to know where to sit and more importantly where not to. The front was never a good option if you wanted to hide something. The back was always claimed by the potheads, and was awful bumpy on gravel roads, train tracks, and potholes. The wheel seat was the absolute worst. It was only big enough for one person, but it was inevitable, that the *one* kid you didn't know, or stunk, or was a little overweight would sit right next to you. The rest of the trip you would be eating your knees and school bag, counting down the minutes 'til you could breathe again. Sometimes you just prayed the ride would end and sometimes it was spent planning your escape route.

This left the emergency exit seat. The window went down one extra notch on hot days, the seat had a little more wiggle room, and best of all, Skye's friend Tiffany was among the other loser seniors stuck on the bus and just happened to be one of the first to be picked up every morning.

Tiffany lived in Cherry Hill Mobile Home Park with her mom, stepdad, and little brother. Like Skye, Tiffany had her driver's license, just no money for a car, and her mom's Oldsmobile could hardly make it out of the driveway, let alone the couple miles it would take it to get to and from the high school every day.

Skye slid into the brown pleather seat next to Tiffany, putting her knees up against the seat in front of her and slinging her bag full of books in her lap. Tiffany had her phone out, listening to music and texting her boyfriend, Davidson Jacobs. Skye didn't care much for Davidson. He was smug, played basketball, baseball, and football, and worst of all when it came down to it, he was very book savvy. Not only was he smart, he would often tie with Skye or score just above her in grade-point average in their classes. Skye found this hard to believe, considering all the stupid stuff she'd witnessed Davidson do over the years. She tolerated him for Tiffany's sake.

Tiffany and Skye exchanged few words in the morning. The bus was always calm and quiet this early in the day. Hardly anyone said much. A few heads were clinging to the windows fast asleep, their breath creating a gross layer of fog on the grimy windows. Some book bags were used as pillows, a few phone lights were glowing in and out of the seats. Their heads rocked back and forth melodically as the bus continued down Hart Street's dirt path through the small town of Alfaro.

The bustling of students making their way off the bus awoke Skye from a light sleep. She quickly collected her things and pushed her long black hair back behind her ears. The bus had stopped in front of Black Pine High School, a one-story brick building welcoming seven hundred students back to school, after an all-too-short summer break.

A part of Skye liked going to school. She always wanted to know more about everything there was to know about the world. Another part of her couldn't tolerate being around so many other stupid people all day.

Tiffany walked with Skye to their new locker for the year. A taller-than-average muscular senior wearing gym shorts and a black and yellow letterman's jacket was already waiting. Davidson leaned against their open locker. *Great*, she gave him their locker combination... again this year.

Davidson was a few months older than most of the seniors and had been driving his pickup truck nearly two years. He drove early for football workouts in the morning and spent most of his summer at the high school. Skye tried to ignore his presence to no avail.

"Hey, Valpot," Davidson ruffled Skye's hair, like he was greeting a puppy dog, "I missed you this summer."

Skye recoiled unconvinced by Davidson's sarcasm and tried fixing her once straight hair. She hated the nickname that she was certain he himself started a few years ago. Valpot, which Davidson pronounced val-pōe was a combination of *valedictorian* and *pothead*. As of now, Skye ironically was neither one. She and Davidson had been neck-and-neck as top of their class since grade school and it just so happened her friend Nick Burkley was a synonymous pothead at Black Pine, but she hadn't done anything. She didn't even drink like the rest of the juniors and seniors.

Davidson quickly paid no mind to Skye, which she was thankful for, but only briefly. He instantly started kissing all over Tiffany. Tiffany's mother had banned Davidson from their trailer early into the summer vacation, and between sneaking around and football practices twice a day, they hadn't gotten to see much of each other over the last few months.

Disgusting.

Skye hurriedly threw her things she thought she wouldn't need for the morning classes into the locker and left without so much as a see-you-later to Tiffany. Some things just didn't change. A whole new school year had begun and so far, nothing was any better than the three years before.

She had already looked through their class schedules. There were no overlapping classes with Tiffany. It was rare for them to be in a same period together, even lunch. Skye had been in honors classes for a few years. As for

Tiffany, who was smart, she just preferred taking lower-level courses and made sure to steer clear of anything requiring any actual work. There was something Tiffany preferred about the small workload of general classes. It saved time for 'extracurricular' activities as Tiffany put it. Basically, hanging out with Davidson and whatever guys claimed to be his friends at the time.

Most of the day, Skye kept to herself. She found entertainment in doodling at the edges of her notes in Calculus, after borrowing a pencil from an overly nice boy named Luke Stevens. Carelessly she had left her supply bag in their locker during the rush to get away from the public display of affection this morning. French class was okay but was already giving her a headache. She was taking an extra semester, mostly because of the teacher, and then there was a near-napping experience somewhere during Honors English.

This left Skye fumbling to lunch period. Lunch period the first few weeks of school could be tricky water to navigate. There was hardly time to eat; the lines were long and slow. If you didn't sit with the right group, you could easily spend the rest of the year in isolation or spending time trying to act like you were interested in the group you were stuck sitting with.

Passing by a few tables with only a half-full tray, there was the inevitable popular table, a group of girls Skye got along with but couldn't really relate to their conversations, the jocks, and the kids who no one really cared for including themselves. Skye found herself near the cafeteria window at the end of the table where the soon-to-be dropouts sat. She gave a head nod down to Nick Burkley but really was trying to keep to herself. Isolation didn't sound so terrible. It was difficult to be around some students, especially those who hadn't matured.

Her food was already getting cold and Skye picked at the burnt edges of the chewy chicken nuggets. As she stirred her spoon in the heaping glob of ketchup, Skye began to look around the cafeteria. Some of the football players were throwing pencils up at the ceiling tiles, a few tables down a young couple was making out, many students were trying to sneak their cell phones under the tables, and some—much to her surprise—were reading books.

As Skye scanned the lunchroom, she took notice of an upper-classman she didn't recognize. Not upperclassman, Skye corrected herself, fellow senior? She was an upperclassman now too, there was just no physical change or feeling like being one. It was a small school and there were never many new kids. When there was someone new to the school, you usually knew about it before the student had time to introduce themselves.

The senior classman had broad shoulders, dirty blond short curls. His black and yellow jacket was slightly oversized with name-brand jeans. Skye followed down to his shoes. The shoes were odd, nothing like the name brands most of the jocks wore. They were old, browned leather, the laces tied up higher than any gym shoe she'd seen in the mall. Not to mention the shoes didn't match the rest of his outfit one bit. The senior classman with curls kept walking but turned in Skye's direction. His eyes caught hers for a brief second. Skye quickly looked down at her chicken nuggets and slightly freezer burnt green beans. Suddenly, she wished she had her own book to pretend to be reading.

Skye jumped when she felt a hand on her shoulder. Nick Burkley and his group were getting up from the clunky cafeteria benches to put away their lunch trays.

"How was your summer?" Nick's voice was somber like an aged rock singer but smooth.

Skye was dazed and hadn't really spoken much today, words seemed to be hard to find. "It was good, kind of boring really, still no car, so the bus was as lame as ever."

Nick nodded like he could relate. Skye already knew Nick had been driving around the back roads illegally for years, but no one paid much mind. He had his own moped he like to drive around too. He and his friends had been caught mudding in the Grabers' fields a couple times.

A girl Skye recognized to be Nick's girlfriend Bailey had gotten up with her tray of uneaten food, grabbed Nick's arm at the elbow, and linked it with hers. Nick smirked and left Skye with another smile, and a "See you around." When he turned, she noticed he had cut off a good part of his black hair. It was almost spikey now. As they left, Skye scanned the cafeteria for the new kid out of curiosity, but he was gone. He seemed so much older than she felt.

The remainder of the day was just as eventful as the morning. By the time World History rolled around, Skye was starving and exhausted. Her head bobbed somewhere in between the Mesopotamia and Babylon staring down at a faded map inside the sticky, torn pages of her history textbook.

The bus was far worse going home in the afternoon. Skye's so-called best friend Tiffany was sneaking a ride home from her boyfriend Davidson before football practice. There was no good way to reserve a spot. Skye was sandwiched on an aisle seat with Dusty Thorton. He was about a hundred pounds too big for a sophomore and covered in acne. He would squeeze pimples anytime and anywhere. Skye cringed at the idea and bunkered down for the humid, loud bus ride back home.

Right about now, Skye missed the comfort and seclusion of summer more than anything. By five o'clock, Skye bolted off the bus, ready for fresh air. The bus was filled with muggy body odor and wet feet smell.

The sun was already lowering in the sky, revealing the autumn-chill in the air that was not there just this morning. A few leaves were even making their way to brown and filling the gravel driveway leading back up to the house. Her pet cat Maiji was there at the end of the path to brush up against Skye's feet as she fetched the mail from the Hope family's extra-large metal mailbox. There was never much mail, and Skye rarely received anything. There was the weekly grocery ad from Blaker's Food Mart, bills her parents couldn't figure out how to pay electronically, and some stuff from credit card companies. All of it was just junk bound for the burn pile out back.

The black and white cat Skye found in the barn about a year back was annoyingly persistent. She figured Maiji most likely came from a stray litter from the barn or the Grabers' fields, but they never found any others. It was just Maiji. Her parents let her keep him on the condition that he stay outside and just ate scraps. These restrictions lasted all of two weeks. Maiji would come and go as he pleased and ate at least two bowls of high-end cat food along with whatever else he wanted to around the barn or house.

Skye's dad Vince liked the cat because he kept him

company napping on the couch at all hours of the day, and her mom Diane tolerated him for his presence in the wee hours of the morning. The person he seemed to bother most, ironically, was Skye. He followed her all over whether she wanted him to or not.

At home, Skye's mom wouldn't be off from work for almost another hour and dad left at least an hour ago to be back at the hospital until the next morning. Skye was so hungry she had a smorgasbord of pickles and potato chips while simultaneously drinking from the milk carton and kicking her shoes off. The snack coma on the coach proved to be rather intense afterwards.

The after-school nap was not very restful, and it put her behind on her evening chores. The chores were like the chores in the morning, but she didn't need to collect any more eggs. It was almost dark now and Skye was exhausted. Whoever's idea it was to start back to school on a Monday was just cruel.

When Skye arrived at the outside of the barn, the door was still wide-open like she had left it this morning for Buckwheat to get out and graze. Skye realized she couldn't hear anything, but the humming of a few insects. Usually, Buckwheat was eagerly waiting at the food trough or could be found straining his neck to reach a crabapple off the apple tree through the wooden fence. Nothing.

Skye's immediate thought was he may have gotten out of the fence and over to the Grabers' farm, like his mother had done years ago. There was little daylight left so Skye began briskly walking the perimeter of their land, peeking behind the empty grain silo and continued along the old five-foot wooden fence.

Her school shoes dodged piles of manure and puddles

from the light rain they received in the early afternoon hours. So far there were no breaks in the fence. The pesky cat Maiji joined Skye in her search. He was not really being helpful, nearly tripping her with every step she took through the uneven field. He was no doubt impatiently implying he wasn't getting enough attention or that he somehow needed more food.

There was still the possibility that even with Buckwheat's massive size, instead of breaking the fence he may have jumped the five feet needed to clear it. Skye let out a long groan. It was looking more like she'd be taking a trip over to the Grabers' farm. With no one else at home it'd be a decent trip walking back in the dark and an even longer start to the week.

She was getting ready to text her mom to let her know she'd be gone a while when she saw the black and white mound in the grass. It was Buckwheat. As Skye turned the second bend in the fence towards the woods, Skye bolted forwards. The sight ahead was unsettling. She ran forward, as she tripped over her own feet. It was difficult to breathe. Buckwheat was down on the ground facing the woods. At first, Skye thought he was injured from an animal attack or sick. *Could a fox or coyote even take down a Clydesdale?* She couldn't see any blood from where she stood so she forced herself to walk closer.

It was rare for Buckwheat to ever lean down or rest entirely. A Clydesdale of his size was nowhere near old age. He should have another twenty years to his life. Skye was reasoning with herself. When she arrived at his side, he was just resting and grazing on a segment of high grass, almost how her cat Maiji was now laying and frolicking in a cluster of dandelions.

Skye remained standing in awe and still dumbfounded at what was going on. She felt silly for exaggerating her concerns. Then she looked closer and there was the large old white oak splitting at the center and lacking a few of its limbs. Buckwheat was laying just a few steps from where her parents' horse and his mother, Resbian, was buried. *Could he sense where her remains were?* Even still, they had ridden past this part of the woods and oak tree many times and never once had Buckwheat acted like this. Slowly Skye stroked Buckwheat's black mane. Maiji was still rolling around carefree in the muddy grass. Soon the nuisance followed Skye and gently sat on top of Buckwheat's topside batting at a fly on the horse's back.

Up close, nothing looked injured. Buckwheat didn't startle and from the naked eye there was still no visible sign of bite marks or bleeding along his fur. Maybe this was like one of those things when animals lay on a grave as if they could sense they were dying. *Or was that just dogs?* Skye lent down and checked the bottom sides of Buckwheat's hooves for anything wedged within his hooves and the colossal-fitted horseshoes. Nothing.

A sharp pain in Skye's stomach followed the dreadful thought. Skye took a step back when she realized it. Too busy trying to figure out what Buckwheat was doing she hadn't even noticed he had been saddled. *How bizarre?* Her mother and father never rode horseback anymore and there were few Buckwheat would even let close enough to be allowed to put on the large saddle.

There was an alarming determination now in Skye to get back up to the barn and into the house. A sensation of being watched arose inside of her. It was with great apprehension she forced herself to take one full look around, and into the woods. There was no sign, but she felt someone's presence nearby.

Carefully Skye coaxed Buckwheat back to his heavy feet. Maiji remained swaying on Buckwheat's rear. Buckwheat seemed strong and held his weight with all four legs just fine. Skye couldn't bring herself to ride Buckwheat on her return to the barn, so instead she guided him back walking along his side and just lightly took hold of the reins.

A few times she paused to check behind her, but Buckwheat never grew restless and Skye saw no one approach or attack as she briskly made her way to the old barn. This offered little peace of mind.

At the barn, Skye removed the saddle. It was only when she lifted the saddle did she start to think of all the hiding places someone could find in the barn. Behind the wooden wall or perhaps amongst the equipment, around a corner, even beneath a pile of hay. Skye maneuvered as though something could jump out at her at any moment. Carefully she ducked around the horse's wooden stall with an uneasy glance upward to the rafters. There was still nothing.

The saddle was put on correctly and nothing else in the barn seemed out of place or missing. Some of the old farm equipment had to be worth something, even if just for scrap metal.

"You know you really should sweep out the stalls more often?" a voice called from behind her.

Skye lurched teetering off the small stool she used to properly reach Buckwheat's topside and groom his long black mane. She corrected herself before falling on the hardwood floor covered in hay inside the barn. "Ahh!"

"Mom, don't do that!" Skye's heart was racing.

At the doorway of the barn Skye's mother Diane stood with her arms crossed kicking at pieces of dead grass and straw on the floor. Diane was still wearing her work clothes typical for Brightways Daycare, which consisted of a blue button-down top and black slacks.

The last thing on Skye's mind was sweeping out the barn. She really wanted to spend as little time in the barn as possible. After all, it was getting late.

"Come on up to the house, I'm about to put some dinner on," her mom straightened a shovel hanging by the door. There was something tugging at Skye not to mention what happened to Buckwheat.

"I'll be up in a little while, just putting away some riding things," lie number one. Skye wasn't sure she was even convincing herself.

Diane could sense Skye was acting a little strange. *Maybe it was the new school year or Skye could just be recovering from the startling fall?*

"Well don't spend too much time out here, I don't want you neglecting your schooling." Diane looked at Skye to make sure she wasn't hurt.

Skye found the last comment a little insulting especially coming from her mother. It was true even the first day back there was a lot of homework in her AP and honors courses, but Skye had never fallen behind or ignored any of her schoolwork. For her mom to assume as much was a tad hurtful.

Diane scanned the barn with her tired eyes but didn't walk much farther than the first few steps and then she was gone, walking back through the ballpark and into the yellow farmhouse. Diane was trying to catch up from the long day. She'd already forgotten to stop by the store for more bread.

For a moment, Skye reflected clinging close to Buckwheat even if she did well in school, got a good scholarship, and went off to college—what would happen to the animals? Mom and dad never minded them anymore. It was foolish to think it was one of them riding Buckwheat. Still, if not either of them, who had?

The thought of graduating and leaving the little town of Alfaro and Hart Street left Skye feeling warm and full. But losing the animals likely to the neighbors was not satisfying in the slightest.

Briefly, the mystery surrounding Buckwheat's rider was forgotten to the chores and the swirling thoughts of losing the animals. *Someone could easily be nearby.* Her conversations and interactions with the animals were never quick and Skye found a sense of security with Buckwheat close by, but she still made a point to keep the sharp metal rake leaning against the barn wall nearby too.

Tonight, Skye was sure to lock the barn. It was a tough old latch and it hadn't been locked for years, but it might be the safest route for the time being. There didn't seem to be any intention of theft or harm, but Skye didn't want to take the risk of losing Buckwheat. If it wouldn't raise suspicion with her parents, she would've taken the chance and slept in the barn tonight even if it put herself at risk. Curiosity was getting the better of reason.

It was pitch black while Skye walked through the ballpark from the barn up to the house. Inside was quiet, she was late for dinner. She ate in solitude, not too unlike today's lunch. Her mother was already in the shower and getting ready for bed.

In the morning, Skye awoke at her desk in her second-story bedroom. She glanced out her window where she could see a dimming light creep above the topside of the barn. Her stiff neck turned begrudgingly to her clock. As she willed her aching arms off her heap of school papers. Skye had overslept. The morning was a mad dash of stuffing things in her book bag and running all around the house like she was crazy.

The usual morning chores would have to wait until she got home from school. Skye threw a new set of clothes on and tied her hair up, which she *never* did in public. By the time she was decent, her bus was down at the edge of the gravel driveway viciously honking the horn. Maiji about tripped her a million times, begging for something to eat. "Sorry, boy, nothing today," she said.

While walking down the bus aisle groggy students were giving Skye the evil-eye, not forgiving the obnoxious honking waking them up just moments ago. Next to Tiffany on the emergency exit seat on the bus her own stomach was rumbling. The cold mac 'n' cheese from last night's dinner was not holding her over.

Tiffany was fast asleep on the bus, probably passed out from a late night of no homework.

Day two of school was almost as boring as the first. French was an utter and complete disaster. The teacher Mr. Laux was in one of his moods and expected the students to do work, much unlike the first day of school. Yesterday they spent the better part of the hour talking about his travels and concerts he attended over the summer months. She could hardly remember even how to ask to go use the bathroom from last year and was sent out shame-faced. She was forced to write "May I use the bathroom?" in French on the chalkboard. *Like anyone else in the class honestly remembered how to say it?*

The lunch menu consisted of chicken over rice and peas. But it turned out the 'chicken' was just leftover chicken nuggets from the day before and the rice was one sticky white maggot appearing lump. Lunch was quickly turning into study hall as she shifted uncomfortably on the gray cafeteria table. Skye was busy trying to finish her ridiculous first-day English assignment. After stuffing a spoonful of sticky rice in her mouth, she heard a lunch tray clank down to the seat beside her.

Preoccupied with rapidly scribbling on her paper, the sound didn't seem very important and she really didn't pay much mind. Her eyes shifted to the clock on the wall covered with a black metal cage to protect it when the cafeteria was used as an extra basketball practice court. There was only about five minutes remaining of the lunch period to finish the assignment. The thick English book and notepad were already awkward enough lugging around to lunch.

The lunch bell dinged with an irritating dull hum like her alarm clock. Skye looked down at her blue-lined spiral notebook, she barely finished her assignment and hardly touched any of her food. When Skye stood to take her lunch tray, she saw him. The person who sat down just a few minutes ago was the strange boy, she saw yesterday around the same time in the cafeteria. *Why didn't she look up before now?* He was looking right at her this whole time, stuffing her food in her mouth, and writing her assignment like a frantic idiot. *Should she be worried about how she looked or why he was sitting by her? What a weirdo?*

"Your shirt," the handsome boy said in his sing-song kind of voice, adjusting his sleeves.

"What?" Skye's face must have looked as dumb as she felt as her ears burned a deep shade of pink. Haphazardly, she wiped her face, just to be sure there weren't any stray pieces of rice stuck to it.

The boy was speaking English, but it had a trace of an accent behind it. Her French teacher Mr. Laux had a similar accent, but this sound wasn't quite the same. What was that, surely not French? Italian, maybe? Skye still didn't respond or move. Instead she made the decision to stand like a statue with her tray out and bulky book balanced under one arm. Nervously she glanced from his piercing green eyes to his shoulders, then back to his hands. Skye noticed his rounded fingernails.

"Your shirt, it's inside out," the senior boy smiled. She brought her eyes back to his face. *Why did he have to be smiling?*

Today he was wearing the same black and yellow letterman's jacket with nothing on it and the same jeans and strange shoes as yesterday too.

Skye realized she wasn't talking as the boy pointed to her shirt tag sticking straight up. *Really?* Skye was horror-struck by something as simple as wearing her shirt inside out. *How was it she made it to lunchtime without anyone telling her this, and of all people?* He must've thought she was such a slob. The least Tiffany could've done was look up long enough from kissing Davidson this morning to tell her. It would have still been embarrassing, but this was a whole new level of humiliation.

She mouthed a shy and quiet, "Thanks," as her face flushed a red almost as dark as her ketchup left behind on her tray. Skye turned without saying anything else. Uncomfortable and upset with herself, she nearly dropped her English assignment in the trash and threw her tray at a very disgruntled hairnet-wearing lunch lady.

This was now beyond a terrible day. She'd be lucky to make it through the rest of her afternoon classes. Ten minutes after the start of fourth period, Skye walked into World History. The most exciting thing to happen in the first few minutes was a tardy slip the teacher wrote her. All eyes perked up. The 'good kid' was in trouble, what big news.

After leaving the lunchroom, Skye couldn't resist turning her shirt back the right way and had to still gather her things for afternoon classes. She knew she'd have no problem catching up in World History. It took all she had not to roll her eyes at the teacher for even taking the time to write the tardy slip. There was no chance she would get a second or even third to result in detention. Now *there* would be some news. Skye Hope serving detention.

PE class wasn't very smooth either. Unlike the first day of just lecturing, she needed her gym equipment for class today to receive credit. Her gym shoes were left at home during the morning rush. When she approached the short woman with rather muscular calves, the lady stared Skye up and down. Then she looked back at her brown clipboard clutched in her pudgy fingertips. The gym teacher nodded her head at an old faded blue milk crate overflowing with dirty shoes on the locker room floor.

Ms. Cromsky had her borrow a pair of shoes from a collection of left-behind shoes in the lost-and-found. The milk crate and most of the shoes looked like they'd been in the locker room just as long as Ms. Cromsky had been teaching at Black Pine High School. Skye pulled out a set of shoes at least a size too small that smelled like old pizza and were covered in pink sparkling glitter. That wasn't even the best part. Just after finding the pair of shoes, a loud ear-piercing whistle rattled at the end of Ms. Cromsky's chapped lips. She then giddily announced they'd be running 'the mile' today. Then, she began leading the class of girls out of the locker room.

Halfway outside to the track there was a sign of relief. Tiffany headed out of the backside of the school carrying a yellow hall pass. She jogged over to Ms. Cromsky and gave her the slip. Skye couldn't help but smirk and shake her head.

"What are you doing here?" Skye tried to sound surprised. Inside she was thrilled to have someone to talk to today.

"My counselor thought I could use a study hall, so I dropped a computer course and traded my PE class for the afternoon. He wouldn't let me drop PE, but it looks like it worked out all right. I forgot you had Ms. Crommmsssky in the afternoon," Tiffany drug-out the *m* in Cromsky to make her sound like a boring old woman. In truth, she really was, and so was the PE class. The only good thing about it was getting to go outside occasionally. It was nice getting away from the dreary fluorescent lights within the school.

At about the same time, Mr. Jaxson, Black Pine's athletic coordinator and boys' PE teacher, was adjusting his visor on his balding head. He held a clipboard like Ms. Cromsky's and led the boys' PE class out of the boys' locker room. Sure enough, as Skye could have predicted, there was Davidson Jacobs, Tiffany's boyfriend, hitting his hand on the top side of the exit door. He strolled behind Mr. Jaxson pretending to make a touchdown in the grass, then walked like he was holding a clipboard of his own and flicked one of the less athletic boys in the class behind the ear. *Tiffany's counselor's idea... right. Meet Mr. Gullible.*

Skye was no longer listening to Tiffany, who already poked fun at her borrowed sneakers. Now she was rambling on about just how hard her Algebra II class was, the second time around, and watching Davidson in line. Two boys behind him pouring awkwardly out of the boys' locker room and talking to someone Skye recognized as the student sport's announcer at the football and basketball games. There was the guy from the lunchroom. The only person who had the decency to tell her about her little wardrobe malfunction.

Tiffany wasn't one to miss much, at least when it came to boys, "Have you gotten to meet him yet?" Skye didn't realize she'd been staring so long. She turned her body as she walked just before she ran into the metal fence post. "He's all the cheerleaders were talking about in choir class. He's the new foreign exchange student from Italy. I think they said he's staying with Mr. Laux and his family. Isn't he your French teacher?"

A lot of mystery surrounded the handsome boy, and Tiffany seemed capable of popping the bubble that fascinated Skye about him in all of two sentences. Still, Skye could feel her ears getting redder as she realized how she must look. Her unwashed hair was a big ball of frizz in her loose ponytail, the shoes she was wearing looked like a twelve-year-old left them at the park, and her clothes weren't really running material. Optimistically, her shirt was now right-side out.

He was wearing just a white t-shirt, gym shorts, and his same strange fancy (probably) Italian shoes.

"So... have you met him yet?" Tiffany prodded more insistently, "They say he's rather smart, probably right up your alley. He's a senior too."

Skye wasn't sure how to answer, "Yes, I mean no, I mean he sat with me at lunch today."

Tiffany dramatically let out a gasp before grabbing a hold of Skye's arm rather tightly. It was as if there was nothing better in the world than sitting with the new kid.

"What was he like? Did he smell good?"

What kind of question was that? Leave it to Tiffany to ask how a person smelled. There was a pause. The class was almost to the track by now, "I don't know, I didn't really notice."

Tiffany rolled her eyes and finished pulling her hair back with the hairband she had around her wrist, "Oh Skye, you wouldn't, would you?"

"What's that supposed to mean?" Skye was a bit offended more than usual by Tiffany's comments. Any other day, she would have just brushed it off.

"Nothing..." Tiffany wisped, now gawking at the line of boys trailing out of the school and heading towards the running track.

The class had made it out to the running track surrounding the football field bordered by metal bleachers. Ms. Cromsky lined up the class of about twenty-five girls and held out a faded black stopwatch. She kindly reminded them they needed to finish the four laps around the football field before the end of class to get credit for today's lesson.

"Ready, set, go." There was no shot or boom, Ms.

Cromsky just dropped her arm unenthusiastically to signal the girls to start running. Ms. Cromsky took a seat, flopping on a metal bench beside Mr. Jaxson who was holding a stopwatch and spitting sunflower seeds into the freshly cut grass. He was hollering all-too-excitedly to the boys telling them to hustle it up, along with other sprinkled insults.

A few of the girls darted away without much effort. The others took off slowly. Tiffany and Skye ran alongside each other even though Skye was much faster. "I don't want to smudge my foundation," Tiffany would protest. Besides, the slow pace today suited Skye. Her feet were already getting blisters and probably some sort of foot-fungus in the glitter pizza shoes. The boys went whizzing past, lapping most of the girls in her gym class with ease.

Very unlike Skye, she was feeling particularly self-conscious now and didn't want to leave PE sweaty and smelly. Of course, her deodorant was at home too, and she kept lifting her arm nonchalantly trying to check if she already smelt.

The boys' PE class finished running the mile a fair smidge of time before the girls. In the grass beside the track they began a game of touch football. Skye and Tiffany were walking their last lap, and Skye couldn't help but laugh at the jocks, most from this year's varsity football team, showing the foreign exchange student how to throw a football. It did not appear to be going very well. He was clumsily holding the football in one hand and trying to grip the white laces of the old ball. His masculinity seemed to deceive him with his lack of hand-eye coordination. *Perhaps his talents were more for kicking a ball or weights?*

Dusty Thorton was the only boy left on the track. He was walking the inside of the track almost in the grass. His pace could've only been faster if he tried walking backwards. He waved to Skye as they lapped him the third time. Skye wasn't paying attention to Dusty Thorton. Skye was still craning her neck as they moved watching the game of touch football to pass the time. The football left the foreign exchange student's grasp, and then something odd happened.

The air around Skye quickly turned salty, and she was suddenly up very high in the air. She could no longer see Tiffany or the track through the thick hazy fog. It was starting to get dark all around her. There was a blinding flash of light moving, flickering before her very eyes. A swooshing noise was crashing all around her swaying as if stuck in a tunnel she couldn't escape. Her back was throbbing in pain and then there was a free sensation like falling surging powerfully through her veins. Skye was weightless—no, not weightless... flying.

Skye blinked, her eyes were very dry, and she was suddenly in rather desperate need of a drink. Someone was standing over her and talking. She could see the lips moving of the woman but couldn't make out the right words. There was great strain as she tried to focus her dehydrated eyes on her surroundings better. She climbed distressed out of the haze. There was a poster from the 1980s describing symptoms of high and low blood sugar, as well as a large picture of a poorly illustrated child with various skin rashes. Skye's hand instinctively went to her pounding head.

"What happened?" Skye said it twice, she couldn't hear herself the first time or feel her mouth moving to make the words, "What happened? Where am I?"

As if the school nurse read her mind, she said, "You got hit by a football, deary; you went down pretty hard on the edge of the track." The nurse handed her a disposable cup half full of water. Slowly she supported her grasp as Skye took the water cup.

That explained why there were pieces of mud and grass all over her palms and knees. Skye noticed Tiffany was standing in the room, no doubt hanging around as long as possible to get out of going back to class. The nurse spoke to the other person in the room and wrote a hall pass, "You can go back to class now," the nurse talked loud and slow to the boy as if *he* had the head injury, "TH-ANKS FORR YOOUUR HELPP!"

Skye withheld the urge to vomit her chicken and rice all over the school clinic when she realized he'd been standing right next to her on the opposite side of the bed. The nurse was talking to Mr. Laux's foreign exchange student. *He had a slight accent, but he was most certainly not deaf.*

Skye waited until he left to ask, "What was he doing here?"

Tiffany had no problem answering, "He insisted on carrying you to the nurse. I guess he felt bad about hitting you with that football." Tiffany took out her ponytail and tried with great difficulty not to touch anything in the clinic as if it would give her the plague. "Don't you remember?"

"I don't know. I was flying, and my back and head hurt, and then I was here." At first, only silence followed Skye's response. It was instinctive to check her hearing again and so she took her fingers up to her ears and pushed on her eardrums. There was no difference in sound.

Tiffany turned to the nurse with her eyebrows raised, "I think she hit her head harder than I thought."

"Miss Henderson, I would say you ought to be heading back to class now too." The school nurse, Mrs. Dimwhittle, was a little smarter than Tiffany's counselor.

Tiffany didn't argue, "I just hope we get credit for the mile today; I'm not running it again tomorrow." Leave it to Tiffany to think about having to do more work and not worry about her friend who probably had a concussion. Tiffany threw away the empty plastic water cup for Skye, "Feel better... lucky."

Skye didn't think her throbbing head was 'lucky.' The words embarrassing and mortifying, high school yearbook maybe. Most certainly not lucky. But if it was anything to do with getting out of class, Tiffany was all about it. Tiffany left the office with her yellow pass convincing the nurse to write it a few minutes extra to have time to change out of her gym clothes. Skye knew the nurse was too naïve and it was likely Tiffany would use the extra minutes to make out with Davidson before heading to her next class.

With Tiffany and the exchange student gone, Skye took the opportunity to be vulnerable. She laid back tenderly on the squeaking brown pleather bed, aching everywhere and breathing heavily. The nurse was on the other side of the room hanging up the phone.

"I tried to get ahold of your parents, but there wasn't an answer on your mother's cellphone. I also tried the hospital's number without much success. They said your father's in the middle of a surgery with the doctor and won't be able to leave for at least another three hours."

On the uncomfortable surface Skye kept blinking her eyes open and closed. She was hopeful today could still just be over and done with. The only problem was she was stuck in this terrible limbo. Skye could've told Nurse Dimwhittle to call the Brightways Daycare and that her mother always had her cellphone on silent during working hours, but what difference would it make?

"I'm fine, really." Settling for the day that wouldn't end, she tried to sit up again and slow her breathing as the brown pleather continued to squeak beneath her with every slight movement.

The nurse wasn't very convinced, "You may have a concussion. If you feel lightheaded at all or blackout, be sure to have your parents take you to the doctor."

Obviously, like a lot of others in this school, the nurse didn't know her parents very well. Even though she may've been spoiled as the only child at times, her dad would probably say something along the lines of, "Suck it up, buttercup," before sending her to the hospital. Her dad was often in the intensive care unit and saw anything and everything. A scratch or bump on the head was nothing to bat an eye at.

"Are you going to be all right walking to your last class?" The nurse tried to sound compassionate, but it seemed more like she was just ready to leave for the day.

There wasn't much confidence in Skye's voice, "I think so."

The nurse seemed satisfied and pulled an ice pack from the mini-refrigerator. Skye took the ice pack along with the yellow hall pass with a few extra minutes to change out of the awful shoes still on her aching feet. On the bright side, Skye managed to miss all of fifth period and now would be moving onto Chemistry class. As she brought the ice pack to the back of her head, a few girls were coming into the nurse's office complaining of stomach cramps.

In a dizzy rush, Skye quickly changed out of her borrowed shoes. Then she tried to air out her clothes back in the girls' locker room with the help of the old roaring air dryer in the small bathroom cubicle. Her whole body was stiff. *What had she fallen on, a pile of bricks?* The smell of salt was resurfacing, and a halo of bright light seemed to swell her eyes to a burning sensation. *Was it sweat she kept smelling?* Skye discreetly sniffed her armpits. Although they weren't great, it wasn't what she kept getting a whiff of. She'd never been to the ocean, but she thought for sure, she was there even if it was for a moment. Water and crashing waves and... and flying?

Maybe she should've laid down in the nurse's office a few minutes longer?

Chemistry class seemed impossible to process today. They were taking a pre-test on the upcoming semester. Skye bubbled in what she could remember quickly and put her head down the remainder of class. Her teacher didn't seem to notice either way. Students were cheating left and right, and the teacher was behind a computer trying to hide her own phone.

The bus ride home was agonizing. Tiffany was sneaking home with Davidson again, and it was louder and rockier than ever.

Off the bus, Skye could already tell all the farm animals were restless because they had not been fed in the morning. The chickens were clucking angrily at each other and with some comfort, Skye could hear Buckwheat pacing in the barn. Even Maiji was losing his cuddly welcome and was feistily biting at Skye's calf.

Exhausted, starving, and aching Skye grabbed a dusty baseball bat from the garage in case she would need protection from anything and headed towards the barn.

Chapter 4
Ike and Olli

Gresham, Second World

The hills put off a steam this time in the day. A hovering mist stretching clear to the heavens. The main square buzzed with life as people finished their errands and work for the day. Through the towering gate and center to the main square rose the Château de Beaucoup's stone walls. The massive walls blocked the light of the setting sun, leaving a long dark shadow cast through the center of town atop the constant motion of people.

The town of Gresham had been calm now for almost two decades. Sure, there were small pockets of destruction or senselessness here and there, but these disputes were always resolved through order of the council. The army of

Gresham human soldiers were well-trained but never had to be involved. The woods were at peace and the dwellings of the wood fairies undisturbed. The Rodinians had been chased back to their lands nearly two decades ago. At that same time, territories were clearly drawn and marked by the ancient stone pillars. A new treaty was established as a moral extension of the ancient contract. Every current leader signed the treaty, and no longer could the peoples involve themselves with each other.

It was a peace their world had not known for centuries.

The five entrances to the First World had been sealed. There was new human leadership rising within the Château de Beaucoup, across the lands of the Rodinians, Yodére Forest, and new ruler ship amongst the sorcerers brought a sense of hope, change for the better, or so everyone wanted to believe.

Olli Loucentious was skeptical for the future of the Second World. He had his father's sense and mother's persuasive skills, allowing him access to information others did not. There were worrisome activities happening around the five territories enough to scare him, and things he knew were running short of control. Enough to act upon rumors of a possible heir to multiple thrones that could threaten everything.

His butler Henry was updating him on most of the recent activities. A great deal of the information was of a man causing corruption through areas of a land known as Preadence and as far as the edge of Carpenter Hills outside of Gresham. Whoever the man was, he seemed to be avoiding direct areas around the Château de Beaucoup.

Olli and his close confidants couldn't gather much about who was to blame for the attacks. As far as they knew, his name was Fideleroi. Assuming Fideleroi was even a man, he was likely a sorcerer running short on years and not only causing fires and explosions but also making it around parts of the Second World trying to re-open the entrances into the First World.

If Fideleroi had other intentions besides performing Agenesis—such as finding the rumored child of Clint Teagardin and Trinity Amadori—there were much more pressing matters at stake. If the child did exist, they would be coming of age soon and would have the ability to rule at least two regions of the Second World. If someone like Fideleroi knew this confidential information, he would have the ability to change the course of the future of this world or may want to kill the kid to ensure the current exchange of powers kept on course.

The attempts to mend entrances seemed to follow the blazing occurrences set as diversions. After the third attack, particularly within Yodére Forest, suspicion was mounting, and most leaders of the territories took precaution by heavily guarding the entrances within their territories. Unlike the others, the entrance within Gresham's cemetery was left unprotected, much to both Olli's distaste and benefit.

Trying to disturb the closed entrances was a direct violation of the treaty. However, the treaty was only a set of guidelines to end the war and bloodshed. It was not magically bound like the contract. He was by far not the first to try to re-open the entrances but seemed to be the only one to succeed in current times. *Were his own endeavors in the First World more of a crime than what Fideleroi was trying to accomplish?* Olli tried to reason that having the upper hand on the most current happenings in the First World could only benefit his kingdom if someone else did succeed in repairing an entrance. To top it all off, the mermaids were in an uproar over territory disputes and the price of grain had inflated tenfold.

Slumping like a marionette, Olli sank into the armchair inside the Château de Beaucoup's study and knocked off his shoes. He was physically and mentally spent, and the long second week in the First World had beyond worn on him. He wasn't truly sure what he was trying to accomplish anymore. If the council were to find out about his activities he'd be overthrown and shunned by thousands of his own people. It was risky, he'd even admit, but there was far greater danger if he chose to do nothing.

"Young Olli," said Butler Henry in his reassuring tone, "Were you able to speak with the girl yet? Do you have any idea of what she knows?" Henry shuffled about the room with towering ceilings. His tall build was in good shape for a man of his age. Must've been from all the walking and climbing stairs Henry did day to day wandering about the Château de Beaucoup, Olli often thought. The black hair with peppered gray wasn't fooling anyone with the strength he still had in his bones. There were veins sticking out of his callused hands. He had lived a very long and weary life.

Defeated, Olli turned, "No, not yet. It's been rather busy. It's harder to blend in than I originally thought, and it seems most of the advice you've given me, Henry, is well... outdated. I've really been struggling with the technologies. Even these clothes," Olli gestured to his leather jacket as he flung it over the chair, "they are uncomfortable and gaudy to me."

Henry was growing impatient; there was too much at stake, but he hid his anxiety as well as he could manage in front of the young prince. There was more to be told about their mission that young Olli wasn't prepared to handle yet, "All in all, they'll pay no mind. Does she seem to know anything?"

"It's hard to tell. From what I've observed there's been nothing, not a single trace of evidence, and neither parent seems to observe our ways. Is it possible we have the wrong target?" Olli was serious, the girl they'd been tailing just appeared to look like every other First World teenager.

The old man exhaled, not realizing he was holding in his breath, "No... no... I'm almost certain we've tracked them. If only I could go through to the other side with you, we would know for certain..."

"That's not happening, old friend." Olli was using his *this is my moral responsibility* voice Henry hated but admired, it reminded him of his own son, "I'm afraid we've wasted enough time. Fideleroi has crossed the line too far." Others had tried over the years to get through the openings (including Olli), why was Fideleroi any different? It was unlikely he would be successful.

"Time, risk, it's all a part of the job," Henry was pouring a hot footbath from the metal pitcher that hung above the billowing fireplace. He added a little drop of lavender and something extra from his pocket while Olli wasn't looking, "The dwellings have had some light attacks, but they don't want to sound any alarm. As far as I'm aware, Reynaldo and Marconi are the only ones who know." Henry rattled through the current leaders of the wood fairies.

"And what about Adalina?" Olli picked and pulled at the tips of what little remained of his fingernails, peeling pieces of his nails off as they conversed.

"For now, she knows only what she needs to, but it won't be long before she does find out." Henry's head throbbed, "Those wood fairies aren't ones for secrets, all close together like they are, and with their loose tongues..."

This seemed to settle Olli for now, "We haven't had a breach in the treaty of this magnitude in years. A few messing around, but the entrances were always left locked tight."

"We may have to gather the council." Henry was battling his own shortcomings. Olli cringed as he placed his feet into the hot bath Henry had placed at the base of the chair. The thought of the council made another wrinkle in his brow. He was almost of age now; he really didn't need or want their advice.

"I know they are a bunch of old misers, but it may be the only way you'll get the numbers." Henry weighed the odds in his head, "There are still a few good men left supporting the council."

There was truth in Henry's words, but Olli was hoping not to need the numbers. The more people who were involved in this... this mischief-maker Fideleroi... the more deaths there would surely be. Maybe just for once he would like someone to take just him seriously. His youth was his greatest asset and his greatest weakness, "Then I'd have to share with them what I know, everything we've been up to, everything we've gained, and I'm not interested." They both knew they'd have to admit their own violation of the treaty. A minor detail he hoped the council would overlook if the time came. If they had truly found the child of Clint Teagardin and Trinity Amadori, so much could change—so much misfortune could be avoided.

"I understand," was all Henry could muster since he really didn't want the council in this business either. Their conversation came to a halt just before the double doors to the library burst open. Olli hastily covered the hideous jacket behind his back. A tall, lean, blond curly-haired figure, a mirror resemblance of himself was cockily strutting in. His mouth opened in a long yawn and arms flanked into a stretch as he flung an apple up in the air and caught it. Henry pretended to straighten a shelf of books off to the side.

Ike was quick-witted and just as smart as a fox. He was fast to realize the pathetic charade. A part of him chose not to say anything about the awkward silence following his grand entrance. This was nothing he wasn't accustomed to around the Château de Beaucoup, especially when it came to his goody-two-shoes twin brother and the butler.

In one swift motion, Ike flopped into the armchair adjacent to Olli's. Immediately he demanded Henry to pour him a footbath, "This time be sure to it, it's not too hot. The last time you made it, I could have sworn I suffered third-degree burns on the bottoms of my feet just from the steam. You're lucky our father put it in his will that you remain on staff, or I'd have made certain you were gone years ago. You old swaggert." Ike relished in demeaning the mere existence of the old butler. He took a large and loud bite out of his green apple.

As usual, Henry pretended to not hear the prince's rude remarks. Especially the part where he insulted him by calling him a swaggert. He poured the remaining water from the pitcher as Ike tossed his boots caked in mud and grass across the clean study's rug. Henry neglected the lavender in Ike's bath.

"How was the polo match?" Olli tried to immerse himself into Ike's leisure lifestyle. He could hardly relate to him anymore. Growing apart from the boy he had been near inseparable from as a young child. Sharing every speck of loss alongside each other. After the death of their father they were never the same, as if losing their father was too much. Then knowing Olli was going to be king far sooner than either would've ever imagined was a breaking point. Now even the idea of playing a game to pass the time baffled Olli.

"Ah, we killed them, as usual. No thanks to Murphy or Triton." Crunch. Crunch.

There was rarely a shot of them losing. Ike always insisted on riding his horse he'd inherited from their mother. It was a special breed of a Clydesdale and thoroughbred. His name was Rapscallion, and he was big, strong, and fast. Most of all through and through he was a brute. He favored Ike early on even though he was originally left for Olli. Rapscallion only would take to Ike riding him much to Olli's own annoyance.

Every polo match Ike would mount the ridiculously large animal and parade around. The horse stood a fair two feet above the other polo ponies. He even insisted the town blacksmith Cameron Dole forge a mallet long enough to accommodate the height difference.

Regardless of wins and losses, polo was just something else that came easy to Ike. There was nothing in his life too strenuous. Ike was in the middle of letting out another exaggerated yawn. There wasn't much left of the apple now except for the core, "What are you looking all guilty about in here, my favorite brother?"

As usual with Ike he made a point to try to frazzle Olli. In turn Olli, wasn't sure how to respond. Ike was aware of just about as much as he was, he just didn't seem to care much with his do-little attitude. To top it all off, he had the council convinced his own outlook on Fideleroi's attacks was the only solution.

Unfortunately, Ike and the council shared the concept of, "It's on someone else's territory; let them worry about it. Why do we have to always be in everyone else's business?" The approach had been working for several years and saved Gresham valuable resources, time, and money. Why would they question his side? This would also explain the negligence of guarding their territory's entrance to the First World. A lucky coincidence currently paying favor in Olli's pursuits of the possible royal child.

With the mind of a true ruler and ample anxiety, Olli could never resist or risk the question of just when *would* it be their territory? How long would it be before it *was* their problem? Aside from Rodinia, the remaining three territories at some point over the many centuries shared protecting the Château de Beaucoup's region. If the other regions needed help, now was the time to pitch in. For the time being, Olli would have to stick it out with the rest. He convinced a part of himself it was someone else's problem. The 'someone else' would just have to be him.

If the attacks were isolated and the infringement of the treaty remained outside of Gresham, Olli knew there was nothing the council would be interested in being a part of. The risk of involvement was greater than the incidents. All of which were outside of their assigned territory.

There was a tinge of pain in Olli's eyes. The lack of sleep was making him more anxious than usual and paranoid about everything. When Ike did pipe up again, he had to rub the sleep away from his heavy eyes in order to concentrate on what his brother was saying. The footbath was beginning to cool so he lifted his pruned feet out of the water. Henry immediately came over to pat them dry with a cotton rag.

"Off playing dress-up?" Ike was making a jab at the bright-colored jacket slipping down from the back of Olli's chair as he slouched forward for his feet to be dried, "You know court jesters went out of style decades ago?" Olli flinched again; he'd forgotten he was trying to hide the hideous thing.

The bright yellow on the jacket was difficult to hide. It was made mostly of a fake leather not found anywhere in Gresham or the surrounding territories. Here you'd only find real tanned leather in black or brown. The colors were too bold and not common dyes used around the Château de Beaucoup and surely not afforded the luxury to the tanner in the main square.

There was a second time Olli opened his mouth to talk to Ike but was unsure of what response to give to his brother. It was not uncommon for Ike to know everything about Olli even without the two seeing each other for days. When they were younger, they could have entire conversations with just the use of their eyes. It used to and still did drive Henry crazy.

He was often left prying the speechless conversation out of Olli at a later time. The unusual trick also made it easier for the two young boys to create schemes and practical jokes throughout the Château de Beaucoup without ever leaving a trail. Those were pranks Olli could only cherish through their memory and had abandoned years ago. Some out of the respect he'd gained in Henry's companionship.

It was pulling at Olli to confide in his brother. The work he was doing was more valuable than Ike's gallivanting around the Château de Beaucoup or so he kept telling himself. There was an even deeper almost instinctive form of protection that begged Olli not to share everything with Ike. Olli didn't wish the sleeplessness or guilt on anyone else. Henry was sharing his worry and unease in other ways. The old man was just better at carrying secrets and burden. *Perhaps Henry would have made a better heir. Too bad his father left that out of his will, not that the contract—or townspeople—would allow such a thing.*

Ike's own feet were soaking in the little footbath, he was pulling off a hangnail on his big toe, as sudsy water dripped all over the clean carpet, "How you ever convinced that little milkweed pest to hand the key over I'll never know."

No, you won't, thought Olli to himself. As much as he yearned to confide in Ike, he didn't trust the key in his hands. He'd probably travel to the First World just to joy ride and look up the last known celebrities. Carelessly squandering away what little true wealth remained? Not too unlike he did in the Second.

There had been a great deal of speculation that the key to the fifth entrance was never destroyed, but instead left in the care of the milkweed pixies. The key had been hiding in the confines of a rather be known Cliffton Burroughs.

With a fair amount of bribery and a hair away from a wild-goose-chase Olli had managed the trade.

"Did the little nuisance manage to get that out for you?" His brother pointed at the hideous jacket. Olli wondered if Ike even knew what the jacket was used for in the First World. A part of Olli was still trying to understand the custom.

He knew Ike was prodding. Olli hadn't told him he was spending time in the First World or about Mr. Laux. He was just as curious as Olli about the other side. There were rumors the other side of the cemetery entrance had been obliterated along with the other four, in which case the key would be rendered useless. The jacket could be proof the sole entrance to survive Clint Teagardin's destruction was in their territory of Gresham. Maybe he could pass the jacket off as a gift. Strange things turned up for the twins all the time, including a box of glasses with red and blue film. They were collected from the First World decades ago.

It was tempting to let out everything. The exhaustion was too much. The secrets of a double life were overwhelming. Just as he was about to spill everything about his travels, the large doors came swinging open again.

Ike instantly flung his wet feet out of the tub. Bubbles and water were sent splashing all over the carpet. Olli immediately stood barefoot, and Henry concealed the letterman's jacket beneath the nearby lunch cart's draped cloth. Dumbfounded, Ike's apple core dropped to the luxurious rug with a dull thud beneath the chair.

Through the doors hobbled a stout woman nearing her fifties. Her wavy short brown hair bobbed along with her walking. She was pushing in a table on wheels along with a book, a stack of napkins, a set of china, and a case of silverware. The plump woman who came through the entrance let out a rumbling chuckle. "Well, if that isn't the most excited, I've ever seen the two of you about your lessons... After all these years, I've never doubted I'd get through to you."

Ms. Hockenberry looked thrilled to see both brothers present for class, even if her tone was full of joyful sarcasm. The shell-shocked expressions on their faces weren't turning her away. Henry could hardly register a concealed chortle behind his clasped hand. They had both genuinely forgotten they had a lesson just now. It was more than common for them to both dip out or suddenly they would turn up 'missing' during the tutoring lessons. Ike looked nothing shy of a trapped mouse inside the study. Olli was relieved to have held his tongue but about sank to the floor. He didn't have any shred of energy left to humor Ms. Hockenberry. Today's lesson featured The History of the Château de Beaucoup and table manners.

Bless Ms. Hockenberry. Her enthusiasm didn't seem to be bothered during the lesson despite Olli's half-asleep eyes and Ike working on his third attempt to sneak out of the study. As much as the twins wanted to be anywhere else, they respected the time they had with Ms. Hockenberry.

Aside from Henry, Ms. Hockenberry practically raised both the boys as her own children. Today she was refreshing how to properly set a table. It was all she could to ignore Ike when he commented, "Isn't this why we have Henry?" Henry restrained throwing a teacup across the room at the back of Ike's head. Ms. Hockenberry was not in the least bit offended, "Believe it or not, you'll soon be expected to move out of the Château de Beaucoup and marry. Your inheritance will be stretched thin if you think you can afford to take Henry or myself with you."

Ike crossed his arms, ignoring the subordinate's remark. Ms. Hockenberry was completely unaware of his connections or just how much money he had stored outside of the council and chateau's walls. Olli on the other hand, could not believe they'd be of age in less than a year, making the Château de Beaucoup rightfully his by only a matter of minutes. Not that he could imagine evicting his brother. The Château de Beaucoup was big enough to raise ten families.

Meanwhile Olli truly was trying to seem interested in the lesson. He was just as thrilled as Ike to hear they would eventually get to eat. If the two were able to recite the history of the Benevolence Ruins prior to the current Château de Beaucoup's construction and then properly set out dinner plates, they would all be able to eat early this evening. Olli found himself starving. The food they served in the First World was rather dismal. He'd take oatmeal for every meal instead of what they served in the Black Pine High School's cafeteria. It was tasteless and left him hungry every day.

Retelling the history of the Ruins of Benevolence was rather easy, almost everyone knew the old stories even given the long centuries. As for the latter, it was a lot more difficult to remember the order of silverware than either boy could've ever imagined. Ms. Hockenberry and Henry were enjoying watching Ike and Olli struggle. Silverware was being placed all over the table. As often as they used the fine spoons and forks, neither Ike nor Olli seemed to be able to remember where they were positioned. In Olli's heart, he really was trying to get it right. His mind seemed to have other plans. There were so many more important things he should be doing than setting a table.

When they mastered a decent plate-setting on about the fourteenth try it was near the end of the hour. They all sat down then for a quick dinner. Ike dispersed almost immediately after finishing his dinner. He stuffed his roasted quail and rice pudding into his mouth wiping his cheek and flung the cloth napkin on his scraped-clean dinner plate. Ms. Hockenberry scolded his poor table manners as he exited, giving Olli the opportunity to sneak a sample of the spare food into his own cloth napkin and inside a pocket within his vest. Olli wasn't far behind Ike's departure, but did take a moment to thank Ms. Hockenberry for the lesson as well as her time and then asked to be excused. As much as Olli loved and appreciated her efforts, she really did still treat Ike and Olli like children.

During the lesson, Ms. Hockenberry even chastised Olli about not putting his napkin in his lap and Ike for talking with his mouth open. The whole situation was rather silly, regardless of manners. Within the next few months, Olli would be crowned King of all Gresham and ruler of all its peoples. These lessons would really be child's play. There was far more the council should have been doing to prepare him for his role.

Unfortunately for Olli's sake, there was still a great deal of the council looking for a way to name an older more experienced successor. Sometimes, a part of Olli wished there was some sort of loophole too. However, he'd read over the old ordinances set within the contract as many times as they had. The contract was different than the treaty that'd been signed seventeen years ago. The laws within the contract were magically bound and sealed. The treaty his own parents signed, along with the other four rulers was more of a promise to keep the peace within the Second World.

To change or abolish the contract, it would take all five true rulers of each kingdom to come together and sign with their blood. All five would have to agree for anything to change. The thought alone was laughable. It was rare for even two rulers to be near each other, let alone all five. Getting them to agree on anything these days was next to impossible. Being able to trace the true heirs back hundreds of years was also a lot harder than it sounded. Some of the bloodlines were close to the First World soap operas except with unspoken incest and an abundance of deceit. At the present time, they were much better at leaving each other alone and staying within their territories. Making it even more urgent for Olli to succeed in his First World mission.

The Château de Beaucoup of course was being led by the council for now, until the next in line to reign came of age. Their heir known well for years as Olli Loucentious. After him Ike presided by less than an hour of birth. Yodére Forest was being ruled by Adalina, but a bit of controversy was surrounding the authenticity of her leadership. A merman named Jamison Atlas led the mermaids in Pirates Cove. Kayala was the disputed Queen of Rodinia. Lastly, there was a veteran sorcerer who served in nearly every war prior to the time of peace in the Second World, Sargent Danelaw who was standing in as temporary and presumed ruler of the sorcerers but possessed no true bloodline as rightful heir to the throne.

As far as the council was aware, the sorcerer next in line to rule would be coming of age this year along with Olli. The sorcerers had been keeping it a tight secret as to who this person was. They said it was for the safety and well-being of the young sorcerer. What they didn't like to mention was it was likely they were protecting the sorcerer from their own people. Of course, no one would know with utmost certainty unless the person was of age and the succession of crowns took place performing the sacred oath. The oath must take place on a full moon and the crowns were a crucial factor in revealing a true heir. The successor would place a drop of their blood on the magical-binding contract. The final commitment to their people. The five crowns illuminate a shimmer when placed on a true heir and the contract did the same by touch of royal blood.

There simply was no other way: unless he died or was killed anytime soon, he was next in line and would become Olli, King of Gresham. The title sounded made up when he repeated it in his head and when he wrote it, and the words didn't look like they belonged together at all. There was always such an outpouring honor for his and Ike's father Helge, King of Gresham, even after people found out how he died.

Regardless of how people felt about his father, he was gone and without a mother or father to reign the town of Gresham was viewing the Château de Beaucoup as a place wasting the taxpayer's money and no one left to fill the empty pit of leadership. The council did their best, but the people had their own afflictions even with the old leaders. They were too divided and hardly productive. The widely known corruption within the council put a bad taste in everyone's mouth.

For now, it was how things had to operate. It's how things had been within Olli's living memory. Without the council's help, the people of Gresham would be blind sheep.

Leaving Henry and Ms. Hockenberry to clean up after the lesson, Olli raced away, stumbling as he slipped his shoes back over his feet and headed out to take care of business. Olli moved quickly out of the Château de Beaucoup's doors, across the moat, pulling his hood up over his face through the thinning streets of Gresham's main square, and let his tired legs carry him past the courtyard and beyond the horse stables. Olli tried to slip around the large barn known as the royal stables. He'd caught a glance at Ike's backside dodging behind the large wooden structure. Ike had already met up with his not-exclusive girlfriend, Victoria. He didn't want to know what they were up to in the royal stables. A girlfriend was just another luxury Ike could immerse his life with, and Olli could only dream.

While Henry and Ms. Hockenberry still treated Ike as he was next in line; most of Gresham—including the council—left Ike alone. Olli was in good health and so close to succession that there was no emphasis on his twin brother. Olli wondered what would happen if he suddenly fell ill or went missing. Would they care as much about him then or would he just be the lackadaisical brother without cause or care or worry? Then would he be free?

Chapter 5
The Five Entrances

Olli walked well out of the Château de Beaucoup's grounds toward Yodére Forest. The stables were a respectable distance behind him. In the few weeks he'd spent traveling between the two worlds he had gained a greater appreciation for the simple things. The glow of a fire, pastime of a book instead of a screen, and human connection. He was grateful to find the entrance led to more a farming community than a city. The books he'd read about the First World made it seem like a filthy place full of too much artificial light and human waste. The books turned out to be accurate about the environment but out of date in other areas.

Even the color seemed more realistic and truer here in the Second World. It was still warm for fall. The relief of what the First World humans called 'the weekend' was welcoming with the changing of the leaves. The trees had turned a bright shade of red, yellow, and orange. There were specks of purple here and there with the fading of the green.

As he walked, Olli carefully shuffled, trying not to crumble the biscuits and strawberry tarts he'd taken from Ms. Hockenberry's cart. His pants pockets were also jangling. There was the large skeleton key clinging against the coin currency used amongst Gresham as well as the strange fake metal coins he was using to buy lunch within the First World.

At the edge of the dirt path, the clanking came to a pause as Olli approached a short white fence. Over the worn edges of wood showing through the chipped paint, the backyard was full of life. There were birds swooping in from the forest and finding a refuge amongst the dozens of handcrafted birdhouses and feeders. There were bird feeders against the fence, hanging from the low apple trees, positioned along posts poking out of the yard, and a few resting against the small house located within the confines of the white fence.

Their songs were calming and brought Olli back to a place before he had so much responsibility. Before Olli's father died, he brought Ike and him here to play with the estranged Teagardins and their many children. Those times of carelessly playing amongst the chaos were long over.

However, the home still brought great comfort. There was only one Teagardin remaining in the residence at the cottage at the edge of the woods. The other children left to live in town a few years back. Elizabeth and Trevor moved to be closer to the Château de Beaucoup for Trevor's job consulting with the council on agricultural pursuits within Gresham's territory.

Trevor Teagardin's wife Elizabeth stayed in the townhome with their youngest child Julianna. Julianna was close to Olli's age. Their other children were grown and lived on their own now, working trade jobs within town.

Alexander apprenticed with the town blacksmith and now had his own shop, mostly making clocks or doing repairs on household items, and a growing family of his own. Theodore worked in the royal stables taking care of the animals for the Château de Beaucoup. He worked with a much younger Ike and Olli a few times during riding lessons growing up. It was common for him to jump in for a polo match here and there. Theodore was one of the few riders within Gresham evenly matched with Ike's riding ability. He might have also been the only other person alive who could handle Ike's horse Rapscallion.

Then there was Adam. When the family moved into town, Adam volunteered to stay back and care for the old cottage. Everyone who knew Adam knew he preferred the life of a recluse. Many years ago, there had been a great deal of gossip spread about Adam. Some bits and pieces were easy to believe while other parts were highly exaggerated. Olli didn't care much for old-woman-talk and Adam wasn't one to let a bad word bother him. Every now and again, he'd even spread a rumor or two of his own while at the market, just to have some fun.

Olli left the past behind him. It was the future he needed to worry about now. For a moment, he hesitated in front of the latched gate, surrounded by stacked rocks.

There was a minute before there was a subtle clink, then he pushed the gate forward unlatched. The ritual of entrance at the protected cottage took some getting used to, but from recent visits it was starting to grow on him. There was still a worry there'd be a day where he wouldn't be able to pass through.

Inside the gate Olli brushed by Adam's garden. The corn was taller than he was; along with the mammoth sunflowers full of honeybees, there were the lower crops of squash and young vining pumpkins, still green. There were signs the tomato vines were drying out the last few tomatoes a bright red on the browning vines. A small patch of milkweed was nestled at the edge of the garden, the pods full, beside the tall weeds was a purple-splashed butterfly bush with patches of blooming flowers.

At the front steps there were two red mums. It was obvious Adam had adapted to some of Trevor's healing abilities and Elizabeth's green thumb. Even without the bustling movement of a family, the yard was full of life and fertility. Olli went to turn the doorknob. It was unlocked. Of course, Adam would already know he was near. Inside it was quiet, the table already set for three.

There was the aroma of a freshly brewed coffee flooding the home. Adam was maneuvering down the creaking wooden stairs from the cottage's second floor. He carried a crate overfilled with old scrolls. Adam made it down effortlessly with a thump of his barefoot on the last step, each pace accounted for. The crate plopped onto the small open space on the table. He acknowledged Olli with an excited but nervous anticipatory nod. Adam had been working and sifting through Trevor's old papers since the rest of the family moved into town. Most of the morning, he spent going through yellowed ledgers filled with receipts and maps trying to find ones of use.

Unable to meet with Olli earlier in the week, he wanted desperately to hear about his days in the First World. It was unlike Adam to get excited about much, but he wanted to know everything there was to know. Adam refused to reveal his vulnerability and his curious mind. He remained calm and collected trying to distract his thoughts.

Around the small first floor of the home everything seemed to be overflowing. The large metal sink had many dishes, mostly cups, spewing out of both sides. The table was full of odds and ends, just cleared for space to sit. There were more piles along the walls. Olli suppressed the urge to tidy stuff up—he knew better. This was how Adam functioned. This was what worked for Adam.

Lately, Adam's face was a scruffy mass of dark fluff. His hair was shoulder length and dark brown to match the hair on his face. Today it was tied back in a loose ponytail. As he began flipping through the crate, there was a moment Adam didn't move, but never looked up or startled. Olli hadn't noticed any change, "About time you showed up," Adam called towards the door, but that was all he said.

Sure enough, a subtle fluttering flashed the space between the wooden floorboards and the table, leaving a dusting of fluffy white seeds trailing to the floor.

It was only when Olli saw the small curly shoes land at the edge of the kitchen table and the tiny coat settle from the short flight that he realized the little figure followed in behind himself. Any slower and the miniature hat sitting atop his small head would've been caught in the door.

"You could have held the door open for me a tad more,

or is that above your status?" Cliffton adjusted his cap the size of a thimble on his small head directing his remarks rudely at Olli.

The six-inch winged figure stood atop the table beside the wooden crate. Olli ignored the milkweed pixie's snarky comment. He loved taking jabs at Olli, fully aware of how much he resented having royal blood. Cliffton removed a small tin cup from under his cap, blew into it to dust the cup off and helped himself to some of the coffee. It was still very hot and the steam made his bushy little eyebrows curl upwards. The cup was more like a ladle scooping up the coffee from a much larger mug. As he had on many other occasions, Adam had set the shorter mug aside just for the milkweed pixie.

Olli unrolled the biscuits and tarts from his pocket, placing them on the table for all of them to share. He knew it would've meant more to make something himself or to stop through the market, but he didn't have time. Plus, Olli thought it was rude not to bring anything to their little meetings. In the back of his mind, Ms. Hockenberry was both nodding in approval in the kind gesture and scolding his presentation of sweet delights. Not that Adam or Cliffton cared where the food came from or what it looked like.

Adam didn't sit down. He was unraveling one of the larger scrolls and sprawling it across the odds and ends on the table pacing about the room nervously. Olli wondered how many cups or pots of coffee Adam drank today. When it was as flat as he could manage, he placed his own coffee mug on the corner of the scroll to hold the curling edge flat, not minding the coffee ring stain it was leaving behind and placed another edge underneath the wooden crate.

Absent-mindedly Adam started nibbling on a strawberry tart, and he realized it was the first thing he'd eaten all day. He quickly scarfed down three of the small tarts, brushing the crumbs away from his rough fingers. Olli looked out of the corner of his eye, always surprised at Adam's accuracy. *How'd he known the tarts were on the table? Could he smell them as Olli pulled them out of his pocket?*

The three were quick to get straight to business. Cliffton was eager to call Olli out, not paying much attention to the scroll, but at Olli's pants. "You best be finding a better hiding place. I can clearly see the outline in your pocket from here."

The second blow in less than a few minutes. *Cliffton was on a roll today.* Olli was aware his pocket was by far the best place to hide the irreplaceable skeleton key. In the wrong hands, it'd prove disastrous.

"If you can't find a better place or use, I'll gladly have it back," Cliffton gestured towards Olli placing out his tiny little hand.

Of course, Cliffton was half-joking. He trusted the young prince with his life and greatest possession. As for Olli, deep inside a part of him wanted to hand the key over more than anything. Ever since he coaxed it away from Cliffton he'd wanted to give it right back, taking all that was promised to Cliffton along with it. There wasn't a full night of sleep since then. On top of the lack of sleep he was so paranoid of losing it, he'd worn a faded spot outside of his pants pocket from brushing his palm against it hoping others didn't notice it. He made a mental note to figure something else out in order to better conceal the precious cargo.

Across the table, Adam was hardly paying any mind to Olli and Cliffton's ongoing rant. He had no place for it. Instead he was targeting his focus on a large map of all five territories including the Ruins of Benevolence's Castle. He was busy reading the map, not with his eyes, but with his callused hands. Softly he slid his cracked palms across the parchment, feeling for the ink marks and for blemishes in the old paper. Not all the maps included the ruins these days. The land was never traveled and not occupied as far as they knew. This map was old enough to still picture in ink the castle in one piece, a few marks for rocky land were where the Château de Beaucoup now stood. Adams hands weren't concerned with the ancient history, fortresses he'd never see. They were focused around the areas near Pirates Cove and Lighthouse Point.

"Here's where the most recent activity on the entrances have been spotted. It seems Fideleroi and his people retreated away from the entrance in Yodére Forest. The entrance was too heavily destroyed and the Amadori family has been sure to keep it well-guarded."

Cliffton scuffled closer to the ink markings on the large map. He sat on the edge of the saucer admiring the symbols. There were old fragments of memories flooding back to him of similar talks about these same entrances. Here he was again. There was pride in the work he and his old friend Clint Teagardin accomplished. Shame remained for work unfinished and a sense of urgency to make sure the sacrifice and dedication of sealing these entrances stayed protected.

Nibbling on a piece of strawberry tart and in between a sip of coffee Cliffton stared at the spot Adam was pointing to on the map and asked, "The lighthouse? Isn't the entrance more towards the cove?" The little black-penned structure was only partially visible under Adam's finger.

"Yes," responded Adam, just as concerned. "The lighthouse has been inoperable since you and Clint took out the entrance. I'm not sure why someone would want it up and operating again. It'd be a waste of materials, time, and energy." There were now pieces of tart crumbs along the map and forming clusters within Adam's untamed chin hair.

"It used to be for trade ships from Benevolence Castle and the fisheries within Pirates Cove, but that's been centuries." Olli was confused, "There's little trade between territories now with the treaty..." even Olli's voice trailed confidence.

Adam corrected, "Little trade within territories that we're aware of, but Olli you and I both know we never stopped trade with the wood fairies in their dwellings within Yodére Forest and much of the fuel within Gresham to this day comes from Jamison Atlas's mermaid colony within the same cove. There's no reason to think others haven't made similar arrangements."

Great, something else he needed to worry about. Olli thought to himself. Naïve to even consider the other territories sticking to an old word.

Cliffton widened his squinty eyes, "Just what would they be trading large enough to need the lighthouse to wield it in?"

Neither Adam nor Olli had a response. They weren't sure they wanted to know the answer to the question, so he continued, "Do we know if any of the entrance itself was restored?"

Cliffton was genuinely concerned, "When we closed the entrance, we depleted the exterior structure, but neither of us had the key. There could be small chance of passage through the entrance within the cove."

All Olli knew was the mermaids had tried for years to restore the strength of the entrance to pass but as far as he knew had never succeeded. It was possible some of the mermaids were trapped on the other side of the entrance as it was destroyed. There had been great hatred towards both the sorcerers and milkweed pixies ever since then.

Besides the chance of family members being left behind, there didn't seem to be a great desire for the mermaids to pass to the First World. The increase in the human population around coastlines over the last few hundred years drove many of the First World mermaids out to dangerous seas. Most dwelled within the Second World. There was too much pollution in the First World waters and hunting any creature there for sport was too common. The mermaids were smart enough to know by having a functioning entrance would only attract trouble, particularly from the sorcerers.

"Where did the entrance near Lighthouse Point lead to in the First World?" Olli wasn't sure if any of them knew the answer. If the mermaids were able to pass through it, there was a more than fair chance it was near the water or underneath.

Cliffton ran his small fingers through his ruffled hair, "If memory serves me correctly the entrance was off the coast of Scot..." Cliffton paused glancing at the edge of the table then finished, "... Scotland."

Distracted, Olli turned to where Cliffton was irritably shuffling his feet to the edge of the table, "In all my years,

I've never seen anything like it."

"What's that?" retorted Adam, sensing something, but unable to pinpoint the cause of Cliffton's increased irritation. He didn't know anything about Scotland and thought the place Cliffton was talking about on the other side of the cove's entrance might be causing the sense of alarm.

Olli fixed his eyes at the black, white, and yellow creature crawling up the edge of the table. A monarch caterpillar was creeping towards Cliffton, brushing its antennae against the curled tip of his left shoe like a puppy. "This little striped-worm booger has been following me around for days." Cliffton bent over and picked up the caterpillar stroking his back as if it really were a pet. Then he reached in his small jacket's pocket for a piece of torn-up milkweed leaf.

"You must be getting soft," Adam chortled, realizing what was going on. He imagined what he knew of caterpillars as a boy. A day catching them in a bug box with his older brother Tommy, but they weren't yellow striped. The caterpillars they caught years ago were fuzzy with pokey brown and black bands. *What were they called?* Woolly bear seemed right. Adam didn't know if those were around in the Second World.

"I found him nibbling on my ears a few nights back, so I fed him a few of these chunks of leaves. I haven't been able to shake him since. Cliffton nestled the little guy in the bend of his arm.

Adam returned to the map and said, "It's going to take several days to make it to Lighthouse Point if the weather holds out. It'll be nothing but luck if we are able to maintain our cover in other territories for just as long."

Cliffton piped in, enunciating, "Especially through Preadence there's been a lot of talk of stirr—ings through the valleys and the edge of Tromperie Desert."

Olli was the first to speak, "I'll go, but... it's going to have to wait a while." No one protested.

"How long?" asked Cliffton.

Olli knew the milkweed pixie was worried he'd miss the journey completely. If Cliffton waited too long to hibernate, he wouldn't survive the winter. There wasn't much reason to wait too much longer.

"We're talking weeks maybe a few months," Olli was truly at a loss. *Could they afford to wait so long?*

Adam echoed Olli, still examining the maps, with a sharp sigh, "Did I hear you correctly? Months?!"

There was more confirmation in his tone this time, "I'll have to check what days are free of school in the First World. The days are long, and they go five days each week. I want to say there's a break in November for a few days and the weekend. That would give me enough time to make the journey. Just in case, I'll keep things packed and notify Theodore in the stables to have my horse ready."

"If we must wait to go to the cove, we may have to look at alternative pathways other than the trade routes." Adam scratched his beard knocking the tart crumbs down to the table. "If you didn't notice, your face is easily recognizable. There are basically two of you."

Even the blind guy could tell how closely Ike and Olli resembled each other. "You may be right, Adam, we might have to try other ways. Even if we don't run into Fideleroi, there's still a good chance we could cross paths with a black-market trade group."

"Going later into the season may lower our risks of

seeing poachers," added Adam.

Olli hadn't considered poachers either. Perhaps he shouldn't have volunteered so quickly.

He went on, "Until then, I'll try to make progress in the First World. With any luck I can either abandon the mission or have an answer by then. It may also give me a chance to ask around about anything in the news for Scotland. I had been looking for news in England, just in case they pursued the entrance in Yodére Forest."

"There may even be other areas to review," Adam had his hands almost flat to the table, "We are left with the entrance in the caves as well as the Ruins of Benevolence Castle. The cave has been collapsed since Clint's time, and no one has been able to pass through the system of caves or through the passage near Rodinia."

"As far as we can tell," chimed in Cliffton.

Adam announced, "Then the entrance in the well at the ruins has been gone since Leonardo da Vinci's time. It was destroyed when the castle was taken. The cave's entrance to Milan, Italy, and the deep well within the ruins of Benevolence Castle to a place now called the Middle East should have no chance of reopening."

"I'd say your best off trying Lighthouse Point, as you said. I'm not sure you're going to want to go alone." Cliffton scratched his small head of hair, "I'll try to scout ahead and see how much activity is going on in the area. I've got a little time before hibernation season."

Without a great deal of evidence, there wasn't a lot of time to consider an actual threat being at Lighthouse Point. Olli had to question, "Who else could come along without the council's approval? We can't risk bringing any other beings into this mess. Besides, we don't even know if there's anything there to need protection against."

There was no sense in putting too much at risk, Adam was looking towards Cliffton, "You can check things out quietly, then turn back before we'd need to be concerned. Staying within a safe distance of Tromperie Desert and far from the eastern trade routes along the coast of Preadence. This may be the chance we need to get more support. If there was proof Fideleroi was trying to gain entrance, we'd have all we needed for the troops to dispatch."

Adam was smart and by far the most level-headed of the three. Olli trusted his judgment as much as he trusted Henry's. It wasn't a great plan, but it gave them a direction to turn their energy and focus. If they were wrong, nothing was at stake but a few wasted days. Still, the weeks they'd have to wait would cost... If they were right, weeks could mean losing the upper hand or people's lives.

A sudden tremor rippled throughout the small home. Droplets of coffee slashed up spotting the edges of the map and scorching Cliffton's face as it dripped from his small scraggly beard. The little caterpillar clung around Cliffton's arm, curling just beneath his elbow.

There was a reverberating boom, followed by another ripple. Olli reached for his dagger in the inside of his vest as he ducked. Cliffton gripped the side of the chattering saucer, rapidly tucking his wings back into his green teardrop-shaped pod like a turtle. Once inside he leant over the little caterpillar-like a shield. As for Adam, he flinched and wrinkled his face at the falling soot, but he held his stance.

A second, more powerful boom erupted with a stronger blast. Adam nearly lost his footing on the wooden floor. This time the loud echoing boom seemed to keep going. He covered his sensitive ears. They were under attack.

Chapter 6
Third Sight

Alfaro, First World

There was relief in the first breath of the morning. Saturday. It was like hanging onto summer just a little bit longer. Around these parts of Alfaro, they called the unusual warmth their 'second summer.' Skye slept in until sunrise and took her time on the morning chores. She even stayed in her pajamas as long as she possibly could, pulling on her tall rubber rain boots over a pair of sweatpants and throwing a hoodie on as she headed out to the barn in the early morning fog.

There was a steady rain the night before, leaving behind the musky sweet smell of hay with a hint of soggy worms. Her mind was free of stress as she stomped through a few of the fresh puddles as she walked. Stuck inside the night before, she finished her homework and could easily enjoy the next two days. The bump on her head was almost fully healed from Tuesday and the rest of the week was optimistically uneventful.

Pouring grain into Buckwheat's food trough, Skye kept getting a whiff of the salty smell again. Wafting through the damp morning air. She instinctively smelled her hands and her long hair pulled back in a messy bun. Then used the garden hose attached to the spicket outside of the barn to spray down Buckwheat and his horse stall. When she was finished cleaning there was still the strong odor of salt and fish.

Skye tried getting away from the barn and gathered the eggs and visited Lucy like any other day passing the Grabers' fields, watching the tips of Queen Anne's lace and milkweed plants full of seeding pods bobble in the light breeze. Skye kept getting the strange feeling of being watched but shook off the feeling as she tried to move on from the neverending week back at school.

The salt scent seemed to increase as she continued her chores. The basket of eggs in her hand was nearly full and weighted her right side with its bulkiness. The Grabers' cows were huddled along the fence. Skye paused to let them lick her hand while she watched a woolly bear caterpillar glide along the slanted wooden post. The little guy was striped brown and black but had almost no brown in his stripes. Her dad once told her that meant there would be a long hard winter. The thought of her younger, happier dad telling her this when she was about six years old made her happy, the thought of a long winter did not.

The nice memory popped when there was a screeching

sound from up above. She glanced up to find a white and gray seagull gliding overhead. When Skye turned her head back towards the cows, she wasn't alone. The boy from school, the foreign exchange student, was standing along the Grabers' wooden fence. Except now the cows were gone and the wood was a rusted twisted metal. What was his name again?

When Skye blinked, she jolted. She wasn't on the ground anymore. Her feet were covered in loose straw on the second floor of the barn at the edge of the open hayloft. The boy's broad shoulders and muscular face faded as he turned to say something. Was he trying to shout something to her? There seemed to be a forceful blast and a flash of bright light. Her arms were outstretched, she tried to grasp her bearings but was too thrown off and confused at how she made it to the top of the hayloft. Had the boy even been there?

It was too late, Skye stumbled as she stared down dizzily at her muddy rain boots. The jolt sent her arms forward uncontrollably flinging the basket full of eggs airborne. She tried to catch herself, but there was no possible way to remain grounded on the hayloft. Down she went.

Back in Gresham, Adam was rolling with laughter. Olli wasn't sure if he heard him right. His hands were over his head ducked underneath the kitchen table like they were in the middle of an earthquake. Before the door lurched-open Adam let the edges of the two map parchments fold back into a loose roll.

Olli froze trying to straighten his hair as he stood. The

small home had finally stopped shaking, but he was having difficulty hearing out of both ears or finding his balance after all the blasts. His hands clasped over his belly. The tall, lean, brown and blonde highlighted braids bobbled as she jumped forward to hug Adam, "Oh, did you hear that last one? Wow, what a punch that one packed! I'll have to see if Leona has any more of the turquoise powder. I think that's what did just the trick... a little expensive, but I bet I could talk her down if I order in bulk." Julianna, Adam's younger sister, began to ramble, not talking to anyone in particular.

Julianna released her arms from her brother's neck and pulled at the uneven chin hair, "When are you going to get rid of this? It looks like you should be living in the hills."

Adam ignored the comment, "I see you've been practicing your orb blasts. Does Dad know you've been visiting Leona Harlow again, squandering his hard-earned money away? Bet he'd be interested in knowing you want to do business with that woman."

"No, and he's not going to find out about it is he?" Julianna flipped one of her braids back over her shoulder, examining the cottage.

He let her be, he'd never really tell their dad about Julianna's illegal exploits just as long as she kept quiet about what *he* was up to. After all, the new ruler of Gresham was crawling out from under his coffee table.

Olli stood up as straight as he could and then brushed off the dust from his pants shaken loose by the blasts. He then flicked away a stringing cobweb he'd gotten stuck in his hair from the underside of the kitchen table.

"You should've seen your face," said Julianna, trying to

cover her mouth from giggling. Clearly, she was enjoying scaring the living daylights out of her future king. Julianna picked up the edge of the half-rolled map. "Going somewhere?"

"That is none of your business, Julianna," Adam was quick to respond.

She didn't ask any more questions but took a mental note of what crate Adam pulled from the attic of Dad's things.

"Leona kept warning me storms are coming while she was giving me another lesson on dice reading. Would you like me to try one on you?" Julianna lifted the overturned coffee cup, Cliffton slowly popped out of his pod and stood trying not to seem too shaken as he checked over the little caterpillar. He was dripping with warm coffee. He overturned his hat, dumping a few drops into the cup.

"Perhaps you, Cliffton, could use some advice on your future." Julianna was now reaching into her jacket's deep pockets.

"Young Julianna, I think I'd better pass." Cliffton coughed hacking on the dry dust shuffling about the room, "We milkweed pixies don't need advice on our futures. We have our own natural instincts to rely on to predict what lies ahead. Besides, I've been around too long to believe in that hocus..."

Adam was scolding Julianna with his blank eyes, "You really shouldn't be meddling in people's futures, Juli."

Juli. She hated when he called her that, "Don't worry, Adam, I'm sure your future will be just as boring as ever."

"How about you, then?" Julianna had a small drawstring bag, almost a sea-green, she pulled out of her pocket. Inside dangled and clanked five wooden dice.

"Care to see if anything has changed?" Cliffton and Adam both turned to Olli, disgusted yet intrigued.

He immediately felt guilty for having gone to Leona and Julianna in the first place, but there were certain things Olli needed answers for back before he crossed into the First World. In all fairness, he didn't know Julianna was going to be there and he was a fool to believe she'd keep his visit to Leona's shop within the main square a secret.

Olli shook her off; it was enough to think about the answers from his first dice-reading. He'd gotten a triple set of fives for death coming nearer and a pair of snake eyes for love. Julianna hadn't let it go since. He was pretty sure she was more interested in teasing him about the love part than she was concerned for imminent death. Olli blushed just thinking about it.

Yet, even he knew not to roll the dice twice. It was bad luck. You're given what's been rolled just as a tarot card reading. Even Leona was taken by the roll. It was rare for someone to get one or the other told to them in a reading, let alone both extremes at one time.

The old fortune-teller had worried over him ever since and could now be spotted reciting protective enchantments behind his back. Even though she meant well, Olli tried to avoid her in the market. One day Olli barely dodged a heavy necklace of garlic Leona tried to hastily bundle around his collar.

He was mostly embarrassed. What did he expect from Leona Harlow's hocus? As much hocus as it was, the people of Gresham had a great deal of faith and coin invested into it. Now to be sensible, Leona had plenty of readings that came to be real and a decent share to never play out. Or so her customers would claim. Most of them seemed more frustrated their future wasn't as bright or luxurious as they were hoping. Some of them were just too proud to admit what came of the dice reading or vision telling.

"What did you want today?" Adam's voice distracted Olli from the memory of knocking on Leona Harlow's door. Adam was tired of Julianna showing off and was losing his patience. Olli made eye contact with Julianna, trying not to think of the two snake eyes.

Adam wasn't trying to be rude, he just wanted to cut to the chase. Besides he was certain Julianna's orb blast took out a cluster of sunflowers and a few roof shingles. He'd be busy with harvest and crawling on a roof to beat the cold soggy winter quickly approaching.

"What makes you think I want something? Maybe I *brought* you something today?" Julianna was quick to notice the little caterpillar crawling on the edge of the table. She placed her dainty hand to it and it swiftly crawled into her palm.

"It's not my birthday, and I know you aren't just feeling generous." Adam was blunt, trying to straighten items in the house bashed around by the blasts. Entire stacks had toppled over on their sides.

"I wanted to share with you a few things," Julianna stepped over a pile of books, "I may or may not have overheard Dad talking in the stables."

Briefly, Adam's interest piqued, "The stables?" Adam stayed busy rebuilding the towers with messy precision, "Theo already told me everything he's heard come and go there."

"Well, The-o-dore, doesn't always get all the

information, if you understand what I'm trying to say," Adam was really intrigued now, even if he was trying not to fall for Julianna's theatrics.

Julianna gently let the caterpillar crawl out of her hand. She watched him crawl eagerly and effortlessly back towards Cliffton. "You should really consider naming the poor thing if he's going to hang around. I'm thinking he looks like a Juniper."

"Juniper," scoffed Cliffton, "No sense in naming him, he'll chrysalis within a few weeks or so and then I'll be rid of him. But if you insist, I think he's more of a Gordan."

"Gordan?" Julianna said aloud, "What kind of a name is Gordan? I do like Gordy though."

Cliffton rolled his eyes. Gordy bobbed his antennae up and down as if in approval. "Gordan it is then."

"Now that the important things are settled. Julianna would you care to tell us what you came here for other than to put holes in my roof? There's no one here I wouldn't share the information with. No one will incriminate Trevor." Adam craned his head downwards taking a sip of his half-spilt coffee, "The council needs him too much."

Olli knew this comment was directed at him, even if Adam didn't face him when he was speaking. Trevor Teagardin was well-liked by the council and knew the most about trade and agriculture pursuits in all of Gresham. He'd also gained a great deal of knowledge about sections in the depths of Yodére Forest.

There was still some hesitation within Julianna, but she chose to continue. The nearly dry Cliffton was at the edge of the table, enjoying the light breeze wafting through the open window in the cottage. Olli tried not to be invested in the news. More likely, it was gossip.

"Very well then," Julianna finally continued, "I may have overheard Dad carrying on about trades with fairies from Yodére Forest. It sounds like there will be another shortage of morel mushroom... what was it they said... two more fields blasted to smithereens? It could be another full harvest season or more before they come back. At the earliest spring thaw."

"Morel mushrooms? You expect me to believe you came out of your way to tell us about a mushroom shortage? That's old news Julianna." Adam was already rolling back out the map of Gresham to study the outlet near Lighthouse Point, seeking safe passage through the Tromperie Desert.

"I was getting to the good part. Would you just let me finish?" Julianna went on, "We all know about the illegal trading with the morel mushrooms. It's been on the low end of trade, everyone eats them but never question where they come from."

"People will be up in arms if they find out where they were growing," added Cliffton. "There's no telling what they would do if they knew they were paying that price to the wood fairies in Yodére. Not that the council minds. They get their own pretty penny paid to them through the hidden trade tax."

"Hush, Cliffton, you're stealing my glory here," Julianna was being sarcastic but quieted him down nonetheless. "As I was trying to say, parts of Yodére were up in smoke, blasts not too far off the orb blast I just concocted outside of the fence. Leona and I have been trying to mirror the blast they described. We can get the blast to absorb the smoke and ash, but we haven't figured out the silencer part."

Adam and Olli nodded like this was all supposed to make sense. Considering an orb blast capable not only of absorbing smoke, but also producing no sound. That explained why no one in the Château or council had been made aware of the explosions.

"Orb blasts have been around for centuries, what's your point, Julianna?" Adam still didn't stop scanning the map with his hands.

Julianna shook her head, exasperated by her brother's lack of concern, "The point is they're only illegal in our territory but would still be practiced elsewhere, especially by the sorcerers in Preadence. I heard after the blast cleared and those fast-paced wood fairies cleared up the mess, they found something more than cooked mushrooms in the burnt fields."

Olli could hardly restrain himself as he, unlike Adam, wasn't distracting himself. He was holding onto every word Julianna had to share eager to know more, falling hand for hand with the suspense. Olli blurted out, "An entrance?"

Julianna and Cliffton gave Olli a side glance. "No," Julianna clearly put. "It was a body."

Now Adam was all ears, he turned from the map not moving the placement of his hands hovering over where he knew the above-ground morel mushroom fields were within Yodére Forest.

"A body?" He echoed; the word hung. *Could it have been a fairy working the fields or one of Fideleroi's soldiers?*

"Yes, a dead body," Put Julianna as casually as she could restrain before adding, "Well... I mean, sort of."

"What do you mean *sort of*? How do you *sort of* find a body?" Cliffton didn't like Julianna dragging them along like this.

"It sounded like a merman body, but he didn't have a fin," Julianna continued a little more quickly this time, "He had legs instead, but his gills were still intact. The person Dad was talking with said the body of the merman was charred."

"And you don't know who Trevor was talking to about this within the stables?" Olli's brow was furrowed in concern.

"No, I couldn't see, I'm assuming someone who conducts the illegal trade network within Yodére Forest. I'm not sure, maybe a scout or a royal?"

"Why would they be sharing information with Trevor like this and not the council or myself?" Olli was outraged and completely thrown by the information.

Then there was Adam to add to his discontent, "Unless, the council *does* know. It could have easily been the wood fairies just heeding a warning of precaution when entering Yodére Forest."

Adam wasn't trying to be hurtful. Without the use of his eyes for so long he had this strange way to see through things like no one else Olli knew. Without body language or other distractions Adam could almost read between what people were saying. It was the same talent that made it nearly impossible for other people to lie to Adam.

If the council knew something like this without passing the information along to him, there could be corruption within the council or they were planning to stage a new reign, legally bound or not.

Olli tried to keep up, "Focus, Julianna. Did you happen

to hear anything else or see anything worth sharing?"

"No, that was it, the big brute of a horse—Rapscallion, I think—kicked a barrel of water over and I had to get out of there fast."

"I don't understand," declared Cliffton, "a merman in the middle of Yodére Forest? Why, that's a good hundred miles from any body of water."

"I thought the same thing when I heard, but I was asking Leona..."

"You told Leona Harlow about this!" Adam threw up his arms, "Is there anything you *don't* share with that woman? You really need to be more careful."

Julianna ignored her brother's caution, she trusted Leona with her life, "Leona told me, it was common for beings of all kinds during the reign of King Benevolence to alter their forms to become more equal with one another. It was very accepted. She was also saying how wood fairies would clip their wings to go live in the First World or for humans to practice sorcery. It was how they discovered fairy wings could create wands. Leona believes it's also how the vampires became extinct and the land of Rodinia was formed..."

Olli was only partially listening. He couldn't shake the feeling someone was working behind his back. *Was someone working to try and upstage his reign as king?* The thought of people wanting to kill him and his brother was worrisome. *Who succeeded them?* The next in line may not even live within Gresham or even be human. Olli would have to ask Henry to check the family bloodline later.

The kingdom favored his mother and father so greatly he never second-guessed their loyalty for his reign when it came time. There was too much at risk now. He had to work more quickly as well as watch his own back. He had no choice but to return into the First World tonight. It might be safer there in the months leading up to his coronation.

Chapter 7
Swings

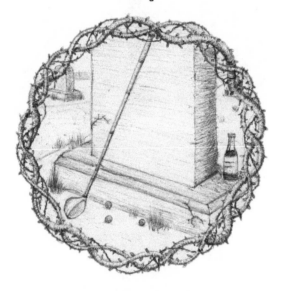

Alfaro, First World

It took all of Skye's energy to open her eyes. The brown, orange, red, and white fuzzball was pecking around her face. Lucy was out of the chicken coop. He was currently strutting around the barn bobbing his head up and down at the pieces of hay all around the ground. Skye chuckled. *What a silly rooster. Was this what a hallucination felt like?*

Lucy started pecking away at Skye's cellphone not too far from Skye's head and lying flat against the floor. Her head felt too heavy to lift, so she didn't move. The floor of the barn felt good on the side of her face. It was cool and smooth. Instead of moving she just kept watching Lucy and smiling, "Hey Lucy," she laughed once more, "Who you talking to? Is that Ricky bothering you?"

Buzz, buzz. Now the ground was vibrating. Again, Skye thought to herself, *was she high?* A part of her was enjoying flying, feeling weightless and free. She liked being surrounded by the seaside and the boy. Where was he from? Ireland? Iceland? Italy? Skye closed her eyes and tried to reimagine the exchange student by her side looking out over the water. Her body was slipping out of consciousness, she smiled, it was so peaceful.

Lucy was almost dancing as he hopped away, buzzing. As much as she tried, her brain wouldn't take her back to the dream. As both of her eyes opened again there was a tugging and pulling at her head. Her body felt like an arm or leg that fell asleep when she laid on it wrong, but the tingling feeling consumed her entire body.

"Ouch! Lucy!" *Buzz, buzz.*

The rooster moved away from the phone and was plucking at Skye's frizzy messy-bun hair. *Buzz, buzz.* Skye's thoughts were swirling sorting out everything that was blurry and trying to straighten reality from the dream. You don't feel your hair being pulled in a dream. *What was going on?*

Her body started recognizing the surroundings. The tingling feeling began to dissipate, and pain edged at every muscle and joint. Everything seemed too out of place to be in a dream. Her palms found a gooey-yellow slime and there were pieces of hay scattered all around. Everything was tilted on its side. Even the cobwebs at each wooden post seemed to slant. Buckwheat's shovels and brushes came into focus, away from double vision.

Skye was laying on her stomach with her face

sandwiched on the ground. There was the basket beside her and about a dozen eggs splattered to pieces. Instead of comfort and softness as her face previously felt there was now a burning in her back and on her left cheek.

In a few moments she could stand. How was nothing broken? The hay must've broken her fall. Did she fall or had she jumped face first? How had she gotten up to the hayloft? Skye's head was started to hurt as she continued to sort out the facts. There was so much fog. In her head and all around her. A mist of the thick smoky white was lingering just outside the barn. Another thought dawned on her: *Why was Lucy out of his coop?*

Buzz, buzz. Skye looked back down, among the eggs, and to her horror she saw her cellphone covered in yellow slime.

Already coated in yolk herself, Skye cleaned her screen with her soggy shirt. No cracks from the fall, but there were five text messages from Tiffany and two missed calls from Dad. Clearing all the slime using the corner of her sweater, she called her dad first. While she was talking on her cellphone, she shuffled Lucy back into his pen, limping around.

Dad wanted her to know ahead of time that he was called in for a double shift at the hospital and wasn't going to be home until after lunch. He added that an intern from the hospital named Izzy would be stopping by the house in about an hour to grab a couple cartons of fresh eggs.

He was talking as she scooped out the mess from barn. She worried he sounded more tired than usual. The intern would have to deal with some eggs from the fridge. Skye wasn't ready to tell Dad what was going on. A few times while he was talking, she had to shake her phone to try to hear through the goo in her speaker a little more clearly.

There was no way she was going to tell him she just jumped from the hayloft. Especially with how much extra he was working. He didn't need any additional work to come home to. She wasn't even sure what was going on, maybe she was completely losing her mind. For now, she was going to blame it on her unofficial concussion.

Halfway through her fourth goodbye to her dad, the jumpy cat Maiji joined her in the barn, licking the egg yolk from her shoes and the floor of the barn. She put her dad on speaker while she moved on to trying to finish her morning chores. The sound got a little better. Like clockwork she added more food and water to Buckwheat's stall.

At the last minute, as planned, Skye waited to ask her dad if she could go out with Tiffany the rest of the day. She'd been glancing through her texts while he was on speaker. Tiffany was bored and desperately wanted to go out and do something. He seemed hesitant, but said it was up to her mother. Dad didn't like it when Tiffany drove. Somehow, he knew Tiffany had already gotten two traffic warnings. One for speeding, the other for yielding at a stop sign. In this small town, even boring news traveled fast.

After Izzy the hospital intern stopped by for the eggs, Skye prodded her mom to let her go out. Her mom gave her permission after Skye swore she finished her homework and chores. Diane was going out to shop for groceries and only slightly guilt-tripped Skye that her mom would have to go to the store all alone. Skye rolled her eyes when her mom wasn't paying attention.

It was almost six by the time Tiffany pulled up in her mom's red sputtering Oldsmobile, "How'd you manage to get the car for tonight?"

"Mom's going out with Mark; they took the bike. I just have to fill the tank before we head back home," said Tiffany.

Mark was Tiffany's stepdad who'd been around for as long as Skye could remember, but Skye had never heard Tiffany call him her dad. It was always just Mark. "What about Allen?" Skye asked curiously.

No sooner than Skye finished asking did Tiffany adjust the rearview mirror to the backseat. Sure enough there was Tiffany's half-brother, the five-year-old boy with spikey black hair, shoes untied, looking down at his tablet and not making a peep.

"Hi, booger." Allen looked up and smiled at Skye in the mirror. Tiffany hated lugging her little brother around, but Skye didn't mind much. It usually meant they couldn't be getting into too much trouble. Besides, Allen liked Skye.

"Call me squirt. Boogers are gross," Allen said without hardly glancing up from his game.

"Okay, squirt it is then," Skye must've gotten her likeness for kids from her mother, "Where are we going tonight?"

"You'll see," then Tiffany peeled out of the gravel driveway in reverse with the bald tires skidding down the unpaved road leaving a screechy sputtering sound trailing behind. Tiffany sped along down Hart Street and the three other dirt roads they sped down through Alfaro. A trail of dust clouds and grime was left in their path.

The sun was almost out of view by the time they pulled through the stone gate. Above was an old metal sign reading in braided twisted lettering: Webb Cemetery. Skye couldn't help but cringe. Their group would hang out at Webb Cemetery on occasion. It was situated out a few miles from town and not a lot of people came or went anymore. There were only a few plots left before the cemetery filled, and a history of strange happenings kept most smart people away.

After they got out of the car, Skye noticed Old Blue was parked behind a few shrubs in the back lot of the cemetery. The old rusted-out blue pickup truck belonged to Tiffany's boyfriend Davidson. Sure enough, he was standing out with his posse, golf clubs in tow.

When Skye took another step outside of the Oldsmobile she heard, "Fore!!"

A golf ball went whizzing over Skye's head and beyond the top of the car, rolling down the side of a grassy hill. She resisted the urge to jump in the car and drive herself home.

Tiffany bolted from the car towards Davidson, furious as she spotted the golf ball zip by. He was clearly aiming for the car. "Do you realize just how grounded I would be if you broke the windshield? I'd maybe see you again when I was fifty."

The fury was extinguished like a match as soon as Davidson flung his arms over her shoulders and laid a big smooch on her lips. Allen was standing next to Skye, he hardly noticed the ball whoosh over his own head, still buried into his video game. When he did look up, he wasn't too thrilled to see his sister kissing a boy, it was just gross. Allen shook his head and scrunched his nose up like he smelled something bad at the spectacle. He didn't seem to be too excited to be in Webb Cemetery either.

Skye leaned over the backside of his shoulder, "Don't worry, squirt, I'll make sure no one here messes with you."

"Does that include ghosts? My dad says this place is haunted."

Skye gave Allen a cross look. *Of course Mark told him the cemetery was haunted.* Suddenly, Allen got very quiet and his cheeks started turning white. She shook Allen. He gasped, "What are you doing? You scared me!"

"I was holding my breath. Dad always holds his breath when we pass by the cemetery in the car."

Skye sighed deeply, "That doesn't really work, and this place is not haunted." As the wind dragged in the cool early autumn air, Skye tried to seem braver for Allen's sake. She would have never been out here if it wasn't for Tiffany.

This seemed to comfort Allen a little. Skye took off her jacket and flung it to the ground next to the back tire of the Oldsmobile. "Here, why don't you stay by the car? If you need anything, just come get me. And, squirt... no more holding your breath, okay?"

"Okay," Allen responded, scrunching up his face and swatting at a mosquito buzzing around his shoulder. Tiffany was hanging all over Davidson already. He was helping her hit her first golf ball of the night off a small white tee next to the granite headstone. *Would it be okay if she stayed at the car too playing a video game? Getting eaten by mosquitoes seemed less irritating.*

This was not what she imagined when Tiffany asked her to hang out tonight. Regardless, Skye left Allen beside the car along the dirt path and headed towards the group of boys taking turns drinking out of a bottle Skye was going to pretend was soda. They were sipping and swinging endlessly at the all-too-fresh gravestone.

It was common for Davidson to drive out to Webb Cemetery on a night when he didn't have a basketball, football, or baseball game. Usually he could be found with a group of friends, sometimes he was all alone. He lost his older brother a few years ago in a bad car accident. Some people in town still talked about it. The faded wooden cross along the back road next to the telephone pole was always a haunting reminder.

Skye could barely remember Davidson's older brother, but of what she could he looked much like Davidson. They shared the same athletic build with broad shoulders, same charming dimples, and same talents. He was also smart and played football and... "Fore!" Skye ducked to the side again... and whop.

"Hey Valpot! You make a pretty good target." Skye lost any sympathy she had growing inside her for Davidson as she rubbed at a welt forming on her right shoulder. *First a football and now golf balls?* She noticed Tiffany was taking her turn swigging from the glass bottle as she prepped a new ball and tee to swing the golf club again.

At least they weren't swinging towards any of the other graves and the only plot they ever teed-off of was Davidson's brother's. Skye looked down at his name, Riley Jacobs echoing eerily back at her.

After about a half an hour, Davidson was on his third bucket of golf balls. Allen had made his way over away from the car. His video game battery died and was now busying himself collecting the golf balls along the sloped hill leading down into the small valley.

Skye was standing around bored and anxiously convinced a police car was going to pull up at any moment. When somebody did show up, it wasn't the police, but it might as well have been. Both would've made Skye feel just as sick to her stomach and make her want to hide behind a tree.

"Hey, look who decided to join us." From the other side of an old mausoleum, the foreign exchange student suddenly appeared. He was wearing the letterless letterman's jacket, a pair of jeans, and his same brown shoes. His expression seemed just as surprised to see them standing around in the cemetery as Skye did to see him here. *Where'd he even come from?*

Olli walked closer and hesitantly stood near a gravestone, turning down a drink from Davidson. He was taken aback to see so many familiar faces in the cemetery this late at night. It was usually empty by dusk.

A part of Olli's memory recalled something Davidson was talking about during gym class a few days ago, but so much was going on that it was a lot to try to keep track of.

Why were these kids in a cemetery drinking something? What was the game they were playing? It seemed to be something in between polo and... before the word could come to Olli, Davidson intervened, "We missed you at the scrimmage game Friday."

Olli shrugged, "I had a lot of homework to do."

"Oh, just tell them you can't translate it. The teachers aren't going to care," Davidson adjusted his golf club and placed a grass-stained golf ball on the crooked tee. "If I didn't know any better, I would've thought I was talking to Valpot over here."

The remarks were hard to ignore, but she chose not to comment, she was careful not to draw attention to herself. Olli didn't ask what the nickname meant. Hopefully, he didn't think it was her real name. There was the *tink* sound reverberating from the golf ball as Davidson swung away. He watched until the ball plopped somewhere out to the bottom of the grassy hill. Then Davidson held out the golf club towards Olli, "Would you like to try?"

Olli glanced around, finding Skye. *What was she doing here?* He wasn't sure what to do or how to respond. He had to admit he wasn't familiar with the First World's burial practices, but he couldn't bring himself to feel comfortable hitting a ball off someone else's burial site. Knowing their remains were directly below his feet was already curious enough.

Skye didn't have much time to react to the new arrival. She was almost certain this was a part of Tiffany's hidden agenda. Allen was lugging a full bucket of golf balls up the grassy slope. He placed it directly in the middle of everybody. A few of the golf balls rolled out of the bucket into the cut grass. Olli looked more startled than ever at the sight of Allen in the cemetery.

"Tiffany, I have to go to the potty," Allen said.

Tiffany gritted her teeth. "Can't you just hold it?" She was furious.

"No." Allen wiped at his eyes, crossing his legs dramatically.

"Then you're going to have to find some bushes or something. I'm not leaving, we just got here."

"I'm not going to go *outside*." Allen crossed his arms. Olli looked horrified, like he'd never seen a young child throw a fit before.

Skye and Tiffany both knew what would be next if they weren't careful. Allen was already dropping to his knees preparing for a full-on meltdown.

To save them both the embarrassment, Skye thought quickly. She was sure he was just getting tired; Tiffany was crazy or just plain stupid for bringing him here in the first place.

"Tiffany, I'll take him, I think the restrooms by the park are still open. We can be back in about a half-hour if we cut through the grass and not walk along the road.

A wobbling Tiffany scooted closer to Skye trying to whisper in her ear and dragging her *rs*, "Arrre you shurrrre?"

"It's no problem," Skye almost jumped on the opportunity to get out of the cemetery, "I'm not really having a whole lot of fun if you haven't noticed."

Tiffany didn't take it personally and paid no mind to Skye's obvious irritation. "Thhannksss, Skye, I rrreally owe you one."

"Come on, squirt. Can you hold it for a few minutes?" Skye put out her hand for Allen to take as she helped him stand back up.

Allen nodded, thrilled to be getting away from the cemetery as he swatted another mosquito buzzing around his ankle. Skye tried not to seem just as excited to be leaving.

"Wait," a voice called from behind Skye and Allen. Skye had to turn around, not recognizing to whom the voice belonged. They were just beyond the dirt path out of Webb Cemetery when they heard the voice calling after them.

"Wait, Skye, someone should go with you. It's getting dark." Skye was dumbstruck when she realized where the voice was coming from.

It was the foreign exchange student Olli, who was jogging behind them. Skye could hear the boys, *oohing* and *ahhing* in the open air, as a golf ball flew over Skye's head. *He did know her real name. Why did it sound so mesmerizing when he said it?*

"How do I know I can trust you?" The words came out of Skye's mouth before she even realized what she had said.

Immediately, she tried to hide the sick feeling she was getting in her stomach all over again. So much for ghosts, she could be haunted by something much greater, embarrassment. They really didn't need anyone to tag along, even at night. This was Alfaro, and nothing exciting ever happened in Alfaro.

Olli didn't respond to Skye's question, acting as if he didn't even hear it. Regardless he continued to follow along. For Skye's silence and shyness on their short walk, Allen sure made up for it.

"You talk funny." Allen dove right in with his questions, not shy for once, "Where are you from? What kind of shoes are those? Do you have a girlfriend? I have two girlfriends. Is Skye your girlfriend?" Allen's questions were an endless reel.

Skye was beyond embarrassment at this point. However, Olli seemed to be comfortable walking with them and talking to Allen. He was playing into Allen's infinite questions and curiosities with relentless patience. His posture was so straight, even how he walked was elegant through the thick grass. His hand motions seemed to paint the air while he spoke.

There was a recurring feeling in Skye's insides tugging

or egging her to say or ask something, anything herself. The silence between them seemed long and obvious, even with Allen's ongoing banter.

"I'm sorry," said Olli suddenly as if he'd been waiting for the chance this whole time. His words seemed to fumble.

He'd beaten her to asking anything. She had to admit she was thrown off by his choice of words. Skye was enjoying his conversation with Allen and she was finding herself rather fond of Olli's voice. There were several times she had to force herself not to laugh or smile. Secretly, she was keeping mental notes of Olli's answer to Allen's silly questions. His favorite American food so far was ironically pizza. He didn't really care for golf or basketball but was rather fascinated by how much people here could watch sports on the television.

It was amusing to hear Olli annunciate words like *television* and *cellular phone.* Skye was so caught up in the conversation that Olli had to repeat what he had said directly to Skye, "I'm sorry."

"You're sorry?" *Had she heard him right,* "For what? Did I miss something?"

"The other day at the school. Davidson threw me the football in gym class. If I would've done a better job throwing it back to him. Then he may not have missed, and you wouldn't have been knocked out."

The dull ache could still be felt in the back of Skye's head.

"It's nothing really. Besides if I know Davidson well enough, he probably missed the ball on purpose because I was behind him. If anything, I'm sorry you had to carry me all the way to the nurse's office." They shared a bit of a laugh.

Allen seemed to be out of questions and was now walking a few feet ahead of them kicking a discarded aluminum pop can they passed in the taller grass of the low-lying valley.

Skye thought to herself after the pause that followed, *Should I ask something?* "How are you liking Black Pine High School?" Skye scolded herself. *What a dumb, generic question to ask.*

He didn't seem to think the question was too boring and was quick to reply, "Oh, it's all right, not like our schooling back home. The students at Black Pine act like they don't even want to learn. Like it's best to act out and be funny. I'm not sure I understand it much."

Skye had to smile again. She was rather taken aback, by the comment, having thought the same through her years at Black Pine High School. It wasn't what she expected him to say at all. Maybe she liked Olli more now, "I know what you mean. I once got an A in a class for not talking and staying in my seat while everyone else goofed around. I tried to convince my mom to homeschool me that same year."

"Are you close to your mom?" Olli asked innocently.

There was an ease of talking to Olli, Skye found unexpectedly, "No, not really." Olli looked confused, Skye hurriedly added, "Well, we get along all right, but she works. She works a lot. There's a daycare in town."

"Miss H," piped in Allen. "She can be kind of mean."

Allen had Skye's mom as a teacher his first year at the daycare. Instead of a teacher, Diane was currently the director who oversaw the financing and management of the other teachers.

"So... she takes care of kids?" Now it was Olli's turn to look disappointed.

Skye was suddenly desperate to make her life sound more exciting than it really was, "My dad works as a trauma nurse at the hospital. He's gone a lot too. When he's not working, we do things around the farm." *How was he listening so intently? He was almost too easy to talk to.*

This was coming to a surprise to even herself. She hardly shared anything about her personal life or what she really felt about home or school, not even with Tiffany. If she was being truthful with herself, Tiffany seemed to only half-listen to anything Skye shared anymore.

When the three of them got to the park, Allen ran into the small concrete building. Thankfully, the city's parks department forgot to lock the public restrooms tonight. This left Skye and the foreign exchange student awkwardly standing together outside the restrooms. They were both out of their element.

Allen stepped out of the concrete building flicking his small hands, splattering blots of water every which way. His shirt was tucked into the front of his shorts. "There's no paper towel left, and it was pretty dark in there."

"Here," Skye pulled the bottom of her hoodie towards Allen. He willingly finished wiping his hands dry on the bottom. Then he looked up.

"Oh, the park is right there," Allen begged, "Can I go play? Please, please?"

Like there was a choice in the matter? She barely had time to say anything before Allen was off running up the small slope to the old playground. Relentlessly, Skye followed, "Just for a few minutes. I don't want your sister to get worried," she shouted, but her voice tapered off. It was just a waste of breath.

Skye and Allen knew better. The others would be at the cemetery for a while. It was unlikely anyone would worry they were gone. The longer Allen spent playing, the fewer golf balls he would have to track down and the less dumb stuff Skye would have to witness or listen to.

"You can head back if you'd like." Skye turned, offering Olli the chance to have a good time hanging out with Davidson and his friends. He declined, refusing to leave the two of them alone out here. Olli trailed behind Skye and Allen up the grassy hill to the sad-looking playground.

The playground was a rather sad sight. There were a few old swings with rusted chains, a slide with all kinds of writing, and to top it off, there were parts here and there fading to an unpleasant shade of orange. Nearby there was also an old wooden train, a set of monkey bars, and a rickety bridge. Aside from the orange were random pieces of metal held together with a combination of makeshift rails and plywood boards. The icing on the cake was a merry-go-round, once eight colors but now a combination of white, yellow, and rust.

A part of Skye remembered when this park was bright and vibrant, full of families picnicking and children playing. She hadn't been here in years. *Where'd the funding go or were kids just too busy glued to electronic screens to notice?*

Allen didn't mind the faded paint or rust; he was already well ahead of them, jumping and climbing along the bridge. Skye stopped at the set of swings and sat down, lightly pushing off the tips of her feet in the dry dirt. She smirked at Olli who was clearly looking at the contraption with curiosity and disgust.

"It's called a swing." Skye wasn't sure how to approach explaining what a swing was.

"I know what it is. I'm just not convinced it's safe to sit on," Olli wiped the rust and grime from the chain on his pants. "I've never been on a swing like this one before."

Skye rolled her eyes and stood back up. "Here, sit down."

Olli was still side-eyeing Skye like she was a crazy person. Something in him trusted her, and he decided he ought to give it a try if he was going to earn her trust anytime soon. All he could think about was how he was going to get the information he needed. Now he wasn't sure if he would survive this clunky rust-covered child's play.

The nearly six-foot-tall boy scooched his bottom side to side in the swing seat. The rubber seat sunk and dipped under his weight. He held onto the chains with a death grip. Skye glanced up to check on Allen. He was still running across the playground pretending the ground was hot lava and escaping the clutches of an imaginary t-rex.

"Hold on." Skye nervously placed her palms on Olli's shoulder blades, looking at the back of the letterman's jacket. Chills shot right through her. Briefly she questioned whether Olli was right to worry. The rusty swing might not hold up with his build and weight. More chunks of brown rust rubbed off on his palms. It was too late now. *What was I thinking?* Skye tried to stop her brain from overthinking things for once and went ahead and pushed onto his backside.

"Put your feet out," sure enough up he went like a little kid. After a few pushes Skye sat back down in the swing beside Olli. He caught on fast and was propelling himself up slowly.

Allen didn't think anything was out of place about the two teenagers swinging on the playground. He simply came over and picked a swing on the opposite side of Olli and started pumping his feet back and forth. Allen looked back over at Olli who was slowing down and going a lot lower.

"Like this," Allen was up much higher now, kicking his legs together quickly like a little professional.

Out of instinct, Skye cautioned him, but she wasn't too concerned. She had seen Allen swing countless times at the daycare without any issues, "Not too high," she said out of habit.

Olli was studying him and was trying to copy Allen's leg motions slowly working his way up and getting more relaxed on the uncomfortable rubber seat. He forgot a great deal, transfixed in the moment. There was no kingdom to rule, no morphed merman dead in the forest, no council plotting against him, no fortune teller reading. He was so focused in learning how to get higher, somehow, he forgot why he was even there.

His worries melted with each fresh breath of air whisking by. *Could he just stay here in this innocent moment? Leave all his worries on the other side? Who would miss him? Henry... Cliffton... Adam... Julianna?* Suddenly Olli reasoned with Clint and Trinity. Guiltily, he concluded he too would have left the Second World if he was ever in their shoes. Especially for her. Olli watched as her hair streamed back in the wind, and he reveled in her smile.

Allen was giggling now as well. He was clearly much

higher than Olli. So much higher his seat was starting to jump up leaving his little body bouncing on the seat with each peak.

"Olli, Olli, watch this!" Allen bellowed enthusiastically. Olli snapped out of the trance and turned to the swing Allen was sitting in high above the ground.

Even though she knew what he was going to do, Skye's heart leapt. Olli nearly burst out of the swing to follow him. Allen had let go of the swing chains and leapt off as soon as he was as high as he could go. He landed effortlessly on two feet on the worn dirt spot in the grass below. Allen took a bow, still giggling. Taking deep excited breaths, he asked, "Did you see that one? I was flying, really flying. High to the sky!"

Skye had stopped her swing too because she was laughing uncontrollably. Olli looked like he was going to have a heart attack and brought himself to a complete stop dragging his shoes in the worn spot on the ground beneath him, like he had a chance to catch the airborne Allen.

Allen got up and ran back towards the slide and monkey bars. After that, Olli didn't want to swing anymore and just sat trying to keep his rear end situated tightly in the swing beside Skye.

"Do you not have swings in Italy?" Skye couldn't resist the question.

"No, no, not like these. We have rope swings with wood, but not like this one. Sometimes where I'm from they are hanging from a tree or along a pond."

Skye shrugged it off, feeling certain there were swings like these, maybe even nicer ones, in Italy.

"So... what do you do back home for fun? I'm sure compared to Italy; Alfaro is pretty boring." Tonight, was proof of just how much there was to do in town. Truly the finest entertainment Alfaro had to offer. Nothing to do but golf off an old relative's grave in a possibly haunted cemetery and hang around quiet rusty playgrounds.

Olli was looking back down at his feet. He was kicking at a loose piece of dry dirt, "Well, sometimes boring isn't so bad."

"Do you do a lot with your family?" Skye wanted to know everything she could about this peculiar stranger swinging beside her.

Family. Olli hesitated again. *How was she doing that?* The word family was still painful for Olli. The loss of his mother and then his father was too much to think about even now, years later. He hadn't met someone who had caught him this off guard, ever. Not in a way like Julianna who needed explosions to distract him. This was just an innocent and simple word.

Now wasn't the time to talk about his hardships. "Sometimes, my brother and I will do... things." Olli was catching his words trying not to give anything away. As much as Henry told him to study Italy and know all he could about it. Instead of telling this girl about his personal life he was supposed to be making up a fake life he lived in Italy. Like the rest of his studies it was placed at the end of his ever-growing list of priorities. It was a lot tougher to lie to this girl than he thought it would be.

"Must be nice having a brother. I mean, Allen's about the closest thing I have to a sibling." Skye looked fondly over at Allen who was still playing and then back to Olli.

Again, Olli wasn't sure what to say about Ike. "It's all right; sometimes it's not all it's made out to be. I'm just lucky we have a big... house... to give each other space."

Skye was trying to keep the conversation going. She couldn't help but think of her apparition from earlier today in the barn. *Would she blink and wake up somewhere else?* For a moment he wasn't saying anything, but he looked up from his feet and gazed directly into Skye's eyes. His were green. His eyes seemed to look right through her. It made her feel warm and terribly uneasy all at the same time. She was immediately self-conscious. *Was it possible he could tell what she was thinking about?*

An ear-piercing scream shook them from the brief trance. They both shot up from the swings and ran over to the monkey bars where Allen was lying on the ground holding his knee. If this was another illusion, Skye thought she could've been more creative.

Luckily, Allen just scraped it. The way he screamed Skye could have sworn he broke some bone in his body. Allen immediately grabbed a hold of Skye's neck and wiped his eyes. He was exhausted as he laid his head on Skye's shoulder. She stood up with him wrapped around her neck. "I think we should be heading back now," Skye said to Olli without looking at his eyes this time.

There was no reason to protest. Olli agreed as he tried to convince Skye to let him carry Allen. She insisted it was fine, and he wasn't all that heavy. Allen was already putting his head down on Skye's shoulder half-asleep. They walked back towards Webb Cemetery together.

When the pair got back into the cemetery, Allen was fast asleep over Skye's shoulder. Davidson's friends were still snickering, surely making stories for Skye and Olli's lost time. When Skye spotted the swaying and giggling Tiffany,

Skye was beyond fed up. It was more obvious than ever there wasn't just soda in their drinks tonight. Tiffany could barely walk. She was swinging several times at the golf tee with no ball, then she fell forwards slumping down against a tree stump, trying to keep her eyes open.

Skye could only shake her head as Olli helped get the sleeping Allen into the back seat of the Oldsmobile. She draped her jacket over him and shut the door. *Now what?* Tiffany was supposed to drive them home.

"Where's Davidson?" Skye asked, livid.

Tiffany flopped her head up. "Party pa-ooper, home, coachy coach, curffff-few."

"What a gentleman." Tiffany drew her arm up around Skye's shoulder, and they stood. The other guys kept drinking and hitting the last few golf balls. They obviously weren't as concerned about the coach's curfew. It was less likely the coach would call to check in on the defensive line than the quarterback. Skye was certain at least two of them were currently suspended for low grades anyways. *Why would they care about other rules?*

It was plenty dark now, just a few streetlights and a buzzing cemetery lamp. Time to get out of here. With nothing else to do, Olli helped Tiffany into the passenger's seat half-asleep and snoring loudly. Skye slid into the driver's seat of the Oldsmobile, uncomfortably adjusting the squeaking rubber seat and mirrors. She didn't want Olli to notice how little experience she had driving, especially this oversized boat. Her nerves were already shot. Driving a drunk underage friend home wouldn't help her out any if she was pulled over by the police.

"Do you need a ride?" Skye asked feeling obligated to make sure he got home safely, especially after he'd proven to be so helpful. Skye tried to place where Mr. Laux lived. *Did he even call Mr. Laux's house his home?*

"No, no, no, I'm fine. Someone has to make sure these guys get back home all right." Skye put off a sympathetic nod, looking over. *Could Olli drive here legally?* The way he just kind of appeared tonight, she figured he walked clear out here.

Tiffany popped her head up from what seemed like a dead sleep. She was giggling, "Mom, gas, dead."

Adding to Skye's frustration she remembered Tiffany promising her mom she'd fill up the tank in the car before going home. That was the deal. Skye considered Tiffany getting grounded. It didn't seem like such a bad idea. If Skye was her mom, she'd do more than ground her, but she was Tiffany's best friend and Skye needed rides in the old clunker just as much as Tiffany would want to still have the privilege of driving it.

Skye flipped through the center console and scanned the change at the bottom of the two cup holders. The $0.79 she found wasn't going to cover even fumes and Skye knew there was nothing in her pockets. She didn't bring her wallet; Skye didn't think she would need it.

Olli was still leaning over the driver's side door window. Skye must've looked as desperate as she felt. Without even as much as of complaint, Olli reached into his jacket pocket and pulled out a crumpled $10 bill and some change.

"Will this cover it?" he said, as if he read her mind.

Now embarrassed, Skye felt a little less uncomfortable knowing she wasn't the only one who was helpless. He had no idea how much money he had on him or what the price of gas was.

Grudgingly, Skye accepted the money as Tiffany face-planted into her seatbelt and fogged up the side window with her heavy breathing. Tiffany was probably going to bum the gas money off Davidson but forgot to mention it before he dipped out.

"I'll pay you back," Skye put out her palm accepting the money and hastily adding it to the cup holder beside her seat.

Anxious to get Tiffany home, Skye sheepishly told Olli good luck and to be safe. She said she'd see him at school as she thanked him again for all his help. Awkwardly and slowly, Skye hand-rolled up the Oldsmobile window.

Although Skye passed her driver's test for her license, she had only driven a handful of times, but never the Oldsmobile and never after dark. It was on her mom and dad's much newer car. Convinced she wouldn't make a fool of herself in front of the guys and definitely not Olli, Skye put the car in drive. If Tiffany could figure it out, then she must be able to as well.

She fumbled around for the lights and then pulled abnormally slow out of the cemetery toward Frank's Gas Station.

There were a few cars on the road, no deer, and thankfully no cops. The gas station was easy-going, and the money Olli gave Skye was enough to at least get the tank to a quarter of the way full. It was enough that Tiffany's mom wouldn't have a complete fit. Skye used the ten but kept the change. There was a normal quarter she kept in the center cup holder along with a few pennies, but there was a strange gold-covered coin that must've been Italian. She slid the peculiar coin in her pocket and kept that one for herself.

Chapter 8
Distraction

Gresham, Second World

Rain spit at the glass window with metal lattice of the third floor of the Château de Beaucoup bedroom. The large bedroom had a towering four-poster bed, a lounging area, and small book nook. "Do you think he'll go through with it?" Ike's girlfriend, Victoria asked in a bit of a mischievous wisp.

"Go through with it? Go through with it? Have you not been paying attention at all?" Ike was fuming.

His bedroom was a complete disaster. Food trays were left half-eaten atop of bookcases. He'd ordered Henry to stop cleaning months ago. The bed was unmade. There were books and papers on and under every surface. The window seat even had the pillows thrown off and the paintings that used to hang elegantly on the wall were turned backwards some broken on the ground surrounded in a pool of shattered glass as they leaned against the stone walls.

"Sorry... you are a little... distracting." Victoria picked up one of the pillows and sat down next to Ike on the chaise lounge. She put the pillow on her lap as she sat behind him flicking her long-flowing hair across her pointed shoulders.

He sighed, calming down and sounding rather half amused with himself, but still irritated nonetheless. "Replogle has already confirmed it. He's saying he made it through to the other side all too easily." Ike had been using the old milkweed pixie Replogle to spy on his twin brother. As Olli hastily accessed the First World entrance in their territory, he was unaware he was not alone in his pursuits.

The entrance was believed to have been destroyed on the First World side, but not in the Second, as the other four entrances had been. It was thought the mausoleum at the access point was saved out of respect for Senior Leonardo da Vinci. Most beings didn't think the key still existed, let alone the entrance. *How very wrong they all were.*

Thanks to Ike, the council members were among these naïve humans. The fools had not even been guarding it. The other entrances were under heavy surveillance for no reason.

"I couldn't help but notice Olli's been bringing back things helter-skelter through the entrance ever since. If he's not careful the council will know the entrance is active before the next full moon. Can you imagine what those old idiots would do with the key?"

Ike rubbed unconsciously at his temple where a blue vein was beginning to throb with boiling frustration. The streaky blond-haired girl named Victoria scoffed, "I knew your brother was narrow-minded, but I didn't think he was stupid. It's as if he doesn't even understand what kind of power he has. He spends his days in the First World chasing after some girl."

"Some girl... that girl is more than what she seems. Not only does she potentially have the power to overthrow Adalina as rightful heir as the true successor of the wood fairies, but it'd also mean she'd be the next in line for the sorcerers. Let's face it, you'd become obsolete. Even you'd have to admit it's more than just 'some' potential threat," corrected Ike, "If it's even who he thinks. You and I both know you could be at risk if it is her. If she's not, though, she may just be a useful diversion."

Victoria softened again, wrapping her arms skillfully around Ike's shoulder. She plucked a green grape from an old dinner plate. She paused to check her reflection in the metal tray, but quickly looked away. Then she squashed a gnat as she sat down on the edge of the lounge chair.

Ike continued, "I just can't even imagine the great Clint Teagardin staying so close to the entrance. He surely would've traveled hundreds or thousands of miles even if he was more careful ensuring the destruction of the entrance. How had he not destroyed the other side? How did this side go untouched? Unless... unless... he intended to return all along?"

"Well, he was dimwitted enough to leave the key and the responsibility of destroying the last entrance in the pestilential hands of Cliffton Burroughs in the first place," reasoned Victoria, agreeing with Ike's growing speculations.

"This is true," Ike pressed his cold fingers to his burning eyelids. He hadn't slept through a night in years. There were always too many changes, always more work to be done. He was trying to be two people in two places for far too long. The time was nearing when he could become his true self and only true self, not an airheaded, carefree adolescent he was pretending to be.

"Where was I with the distraction," Victoria started to run her own fingers through Ike's curly hair, "I'd say we need to get our hands on that skeleton key." Her eyebrows raised noticing some tension was being let out of Ike's shoulders with the movement of her hands.

He was still doubtful, "My brother may not be the brightest bean in the jar, but I don't really believe he's just going to leave it lying around."

"It'll be easier than just waiting," she scoffed placing another green grape into her mouth.

She had a point. Victoria always had a point. As she removed her arms from his shoulders, Ike sat up.

"It's getting late," she said bluntly, "If I'm going to get out of here without that snooping butler of yours noticing, I best be heading out."

"Psh, that old necromancer? What would he do? Scold me some more?" Ike took Victoria's hand in his palm, "Won't you stay tonight?" Ike was trying not to sound too desperate for company.

For a moment, Victoria seemed to consider the request. She looked into Ike's sleepless eyes. Sometimes she felt she might be his only weakness. "No, not tonight. I need to be getting back. There's work to do and the council seems to be cracking down more and more on entrants after dusk."

"I thought you weren't using the gate anymore?" Ike questioned.

"I haven't been in the evenings lately, but the strange man in the moat seems to be catching onto me going down Main Street and not coming back."

"No one in their right mind would listen to the weasel in the moat. He lost most of his marbles years ago."

"If I remember correctly, you used to listen to him," Victoria liked to throw it in his face.

"I was a child at the time and his stories were... how you would say... *entertaining*." Ike couldn't help but think warm-heartedly of the old man with baggy eyes, long hair, and white beard. He was skin and bones. Often, he could be found collecting litter of an array of all sorts of things being thrown or lost within the surely toxic water of the moat. The man had evaded paying taxes for decades by technically living or trespassing on the Château de Beaucoup's property.

"Okay, then now what are you if you're not a child?"

Ike hardened his face and looked away to the rain. "Are you insinuating I'm crazy?"

Victoria said, "No, I'm telling you. You are crazy."

Ike threw his jacket at Victoria; they were both smiling. "You'll need that. It's raining."

Chapter 9
Talks the Least Says the Most

Alfaro, First World

Go Panthers!" exclaimed the crowd of Black Pine High School fans rumbling the metal bleachers. There were trumpets and tubas blaring in the background. Tiffany and the other cheerleaders were down on the running track surrounding the lit football field. The cheerleaders were primping their hair and stretching for their next cheer of the night.

The school's first football game of the season was underway and was now well into the opening quarter. *What am I doing here?*

It was rare for Skye to ever attend a school sporting event. Now all she could do was regret coming. For the last half an hour she went from sitting watching the game and pretending to be interested to walking mindlessly around. *Where was he?*

Skye continued to walk, checking the scoreboard the seventieth time and thinking about every possible scenario of why he wasn't there yet. *Could their times be different? Did he really think he was asking me to a soccer game? Wasn't that what they called football in Italy or was that a myth?* There were several whistles blown. Skye turned back to the football field, not sure which team had possession of the ball.

She kept walking, 7-0 in the first quarter. Thanks to Davidson and his touchdown in the first five minutes of the game, the Black Pine Panthers were looking optimistically well in the homecoming game against Hawthorne Heights. Skye tracked down Davidson who now had the ball again and was bracing for a tackle from the opposing team.

The whistles and cowbells started to fade out. She headed toward the concession stands, hoping a hot chocolate and a bag of candies would make up for some of the naiveté she'd been feeling. Behind the bleachers heading back from the concession stands—that's when she nearly ran into him.

"Nick, what are you doing here?" Skye almost wore her hot chocolate; the drink had already burned the tip of her tongue. She tried to make it seem like she hadn't just stuffed ten colorful candies into her mouth even though her voice was audibly muffled.

He was nearly as surprised as she was. Nick might have been embarrassed being seen at the game as well, if he had been the type to get embarrassed. He was always right where he intended to be. Nick dropped the nub of a cigarette butt to the gravel ground, smashing what was left of it underneath his gray-torn high tops. Skye noticed the bulky camera around Nick's neck.

"Well, you see, Bailey is in the color guard. I told her I'd stay until the half-time show, and then I'm out. How about you?" Nick shifted his eyes to the group of parents and cluster of freshmen walking behind them. "Doesn't seem much like your crowd."

Skye was still struck off guard. "I'm— I'm not so sure why I'm here. Tiffany's cheering again this year, but I'm not very confident I can tough it out until the half-time show. I've been bored out of my mind. What's with the camera?"

"Bailey's also on yearbook. She's supposed to be taking pictures of the game, but between you and me, I'm a better shot." Nick popped the lens cover off the end of the camera, snapping a few pictures. His first of the night.

Nick smiled, tucking his lighter back into his jacket pocket. He was nodding like he completely understood.

Before she knew it, they were walking together behind the towering bleachers along the chain-link fence. *This was a lot better than watching the game.*

It had been such a rough start to the year, Skye could only think of what was on her mind. She and Nick had been friends since they were little kids. The past couple of years made it hard to stay in touch, but in the moment, there was comfort. "Do you know what you want to do after graduation?" *Why did she always ask such stupid questions?*

"Ehh, I haven't really thought about it. I may get a job at the factory with my dad. He says there they're always hiring." Nick was being his usual smooth-talking self, but there had to be some part of him worried for what lay beyond high school, "And what about you? Miss Valedictorian is it or 'most-likely-to-succeed'?" Nick was teasing, but there was a near physical pain in Skye's side at the mention of the unofficial titles. Nick snapped a few more pictures of Skye's not-so-enthusiastic face as she put her hand up to block the lens.

"Stop that, they haven't even voted for senior awards yet." Skye punched his shoulder jokingly, "You shouldn't be wasting space on your memory card."

Nick didn't listen to Skye, taking another picture as she flung her hood to her jacket over her head, "No, but I'm sure you'll get it." Nick side-smirked for the second time since they bumped into each other tonight, and he also didn't stop snapping pictures. "The yearbook could use a few more authentic photos, not just posers playing a part of a game."

"It's just football." Skye replied seriously, "I don't think I want an award. It's jinxed or something. Most of the people who get voted 'most likely to succeed' end up broke, working a job they hate, or pregnant before they even make it anywhere."

"There's nothing wrong with any of those things... but I mean, that's not going to be you," Nick said. He seemed to be so certain, Skye's confidence was already down this year, especially with everything going on in her head. Even if it wasn't true, it was still good to hear Nick say it.

"I don't even know what I want to be. Everyone else seems to think they know, though."

"If it makes you feel any better, I'll vote something else. What would it be if you had the choice for an award?" Nick was being thoughtful.

Skye tried to think for a second and then she considered the likelihood of Nick taking the time to fill out a ballot. Honestly, she didn't want any award. When she didn't say, Nick had his own suggestion. "How about... 'talks the least, says the most'?"

At first, the suggestion seemed like an insult, but Nick wasn't trying to poke fun. He was being serious. The rare occasion of Nick being sincere was almost flattering to witness. It was worth considering and noted somewhere in the back of her mind that she couldn't possibly be too disappointed if she got that one. She shook it off.

"Give me that," Skye pulled the clunky camera off of Nick's neck. If he took anymore pictures of her she was going to have to smash it. She clicked the shutter button a few times trying to take pictures of the football field and then snuck in a couple shots of Nick who nearly tackled her to get the camera back. Skye was certain he was the last person he wanted to see grace the pages of Black Pine's yearbook. No one needed to remember Nick Burkley, but maybe she did.

After walking around the outside track of the football field at least twice, Skye's hot chocolate and candies were long gone. As they turned the last lap, Skye looked up at the bleachers. It was half-time, and people poured from the bleachers. The two football teams were running off the field with all the whooping and hollering trailing behind them. The blurs of yellow, green, and black brushed by. There was excitement in the air as the Panthers were now up 18–7.

The band and color guard were getting ready for the half-time show and the cheerleaders were reciting their newest cheer and forming a small pyramid while no one paid much attention. Near the entrance, a shirtless boy came barreling towards her with a black smudged letter A on his chest. He elbowed his way through the thick crowd.

Nick couldn't help but side-eye Skye as he snapped a squinty-eyed blur of the shirtless boy, purposely using the flash. It took her a minute, and then she remembered why she even came to the game tonight. The boy struggling to put his white shirt back on, half-blinded and running in their direction, was none other the foreign exchange student.

A part of Skye wanted to pretend she hadn't seen Olli and to keep walking past with Nick. Anger swelled inside her. Who makes a date and then has someone wait an hour and half before doing anything? Of course, Nick was so much better at hurdling by the awkward situation.

"Well, I better be off. I'll be needing a seat for this half-time show." He tapped the camera, "I may actually have to try to get a good shot of the color guard. I'll leave you two to it then." Olli was wrapping his black and yellow letterman's jacket back over his shoulders. Black paint and sweat was seeping through the white cotton of his t-shirt.

Nick turned around the corner of the bleachers. Skye swore she saw him leave the fence and exit. He pulled his lighter out as he walked. It didn't seem as if Nick intended to return back to the game or to the football stands to watch his girlfriend perform in the color guard.

Olli was a blubbering mess once Nick was out of sight. "I'm sorry, I ran into Davidson, and they were saying I had to paint my chest to get into the game. You see, I didn't have enough cash to get in, and he said I could use his student pass if I did it."

He was talking so fast it was difficult to make out a single word he was saying. It was pathetic, but it was more than likely the truth. It was completely believable for Davidson and his group to use someone to get something they wanted or for a joke.

As Olli poured out his apologies, Skye wasn't sure how he didn't somehow end up in the Black Pine Panther mascot costume. The situation could've been avoided entirely if it wasn't for her. He likely didn't have any cash left because of the money he loaned her and Tiffany for the Oldsmobile last week. Guiltily, Skye remembered she hadn't paid him back, and she didn't have the cash on her to offer him. She'd borrowed Tiffany's student pass to get into the game tonight and spent the cash she had on snacks for herself.

Skye lifted her hand up to Olli's face. She could feel the light stubble on his upper lip as she placed her fingers gently over Olli's mouth trying to get him to be quiet. You really can say sorry too many times. She quickly pulled her palm back as she realized how impulsive she was being.

The half-time show was starting as the crowd of people were shuffling back and forth from the concessions to the bleachers. The awful sound of trumpets and out-of-tune drummers had begun. Skye's eyes shifted uncomfortably to the students giving the odd pair the look, especially after she'd spent half the game walking around with another boy.

Olli must've been growing uncomfortable too, or maybe he could sense Skye's skin tense being in the middle of a crowd. Everyone knew everyone here. If they hung around too long, they'd be the highlight of this week's gossip. *If they weren't already...*

"Can we go somewhere else, maybe somewhere a little quieter?" He leaned over some to make sure she could hear him.

If Skye wasn't uneasy, she was now. Not to mention feeling more nervous than ever. *Quieter? What did he expect at a football game?* Her brain was a mile a minute. They'd been alone before. Well sort of, Tiffany's brother was there.

Skye took Olli's arm, getting tired of trying to shout over all the loud instruments playing on the field. She guided him towards the concession stand's concrete building and then back behind it. They walked well past the tennis courts. At the chain-link fences they slipped between two bars. Skye got through easier than Olli's bulky form. Tiffany and Skye used to slip through this same fence to get into the football games free back when they were only in middle school.

On the other side of the fence, there was a yellow-painted building with another chain-link fence around the perimeter. She shakily pulled the clasp up on the cold creaking metal gate. As the night grew later and darker, she regretted leaving her gloves at home.

The two stepped inside. The sand was dusting around their shoes as they closed the metal gate with clank. Skye surveyed the field. There were the home team and visitor's dugouts, *quiet, but maybe not open enough.*

It took Skye a moment to realize Olli was following her every move. He seemed completely perplexed by where they were at or what they were doing.

"Don't tell me you don't have baseball in Italy?" Skye shook her head. *Maybe she should've stayed with Nick?*

Olli wasn't really sure if they did or not so instead of

responding he shrugged his shoulders, "There was a game I used to play when I was little. We didn't call it baseball. But we never had places like this to play. I think it was old baker's bags we used for bases?"

She tried not to, but her eyebrow physically moved halfway up her forehead out of curiosity, and her eyes widened. "Flour bags? When I was younger, we used egg cartons once, but usually we just took something from the garage."

"There, you've done it again. How do you do that?" Olli seemed to be dropping a heavy weight.

"Do what?" By this point, Skye was walking to the center of the Black Pine Panthers baseball field.

"As soon as I feel I messed up or that I'm out of place, you, you say something completely absent of judgment." Olli ruffled his hair with his left hand, dragging his fingers over his skull clear to the back of his neck.

Skye wasn't entirely sure what he was talking about, but she was tired from walking around the track or maybe it was the candies hitting her with a sugar crash, so she plopped down in the sand around the pitcher's mound, exhausted.

He looked down for a moment and then joined her in the dirt. "And you," she said, "how is it that you... have not only convinced me to watch a football game, but you get me to come all the way over to this empty baseball field? I hardly know you."

"You mean you don't like football?" Olli was sitting a lot closer to her than she would've liked, but she didn't move. The rubber mound wasn't ideal, but it was better than explaining to her mother why she had sand all over her clothes. "From what I saw I wasn't too impressed either. A lot of nonsense back and forth and back and forth. I couldn't make heads nor tails of it."

"I've been watching it for years, and I can't tell you anything about the first half of the game." Skye pulled her feet up towards her chest and wrapped her arms loosely around her knees. The temperature was dropping quickly tonight. The moon was creeping through the misty clouds.

"Then we can at least cross that off our list of activities," Olli replied nonchalantly.

Our list? Who was this guy? Was it time to send Tiffany a text to get her out of here? The large, towering lights illuminated not too far off. By the sounds of it, the football game had started back up again. Tiffany would be too busy cheering to get the text message. *Sink or swim, Skye, sink or swim?*

Skye looked at her hands gripping her knees a little more tightly now. They were turning a fair shade of purple. Without saying anything, Olli took his letterman's jacket back off. "Put this on, you're freezing."

There wasn't much she could argue. She *had* been freezing. The light jacket she was wearing wasn't enough to keep her warm out in the open baseball field. The warmth of the other bodies and towering bleachers weren't blocking the wind anymore.

"Won't you be cold?" Skye asked.

He laughed a little, "Cold... no, cold is standing out in this weather with no shirt on. Remember ten minutes ago? Besides in Gre—*Italy*," Olli corrected himself, "In *Italy* it can get pretty cold."

The bulky jacket felt strange on her shoulders, but it was much warmer, "Thanks."

Buzzz, buzzzz, buzzzzz... Buzzzz... Buzzzz. Buzzzz.
Skye sat up. Her nose and fingers were freezing. The rest of her body was warm. She smiled and then jumped. There was the panic of forgetting where she was. Her numb fingers swiped to unlock the phone screen.

"Hello."

It was Tiffany calling, "Where are you? The football game is over, and I'm in the locker rooms."

Skye's senses seemed to be de-thawing as she looked around. There was a little relief to realize she wasn't lying in her barn covered in egg yolk. It might as well be another illusion. She realized she was still sitting in the middle of the baseball field feeling the numb area on her side where the rubber pitcher's mound was beneath her body. Then there was Olli. His head was resting on her leg and his arms were pulled up around her knee.

Had they really fallen asleep talking? Perhaps she was more tired than she thought. The past few nights, she had spent either catching up on homework or filling out endless scholarship applications. Hopefully, the conversation wasn't all that boring. At least it wasn't another hallucination. As more memories came about, Skye knew things didn't go so bad.

"I'm heading back up to the school now, just give me a minute. I'll meet you at the car?" Skye was still tired, but the jolt of excitement got her heart going again, eager to keep her senses sharp in the crisp night.

Tiffany wasn't paying too much attention on the other end of the phone, but she definitely sounded upset and ready to go home.

Skye ran her fingers across the top of Olli's curls careful not to wake him up just yet. Before Tiffany could hang up the phone, she asked her, "Hey, if you're not too busy, can you go shopping with me tomorrow?"

The lack of details was killing Tiffany, but she didn't ask what for or why. "I'll meet you at the car in five," she said and ended the phone conversation.

Olli lifted his head and sat up as if he was armed to fight a large bear. Skye put her hand up to his chest, still showing patches of smeared black paint through the white shirt. He relaxed and then brushed off the grains of sand sticking to the dried sweat on his shirt.

"How long was I asleep?" Olli patted his face to wake himself up.

"I don't know, maybe an hour?" Skye glanced at the time on her phone screen, "I'm sorry, I may have fallen asleep first."

"No, no, no, don't apologize," begged Olli, still coming around, "If anything, I should be thanking you. I think that's the best I've slept in years."

"Years?" *How bad was his life in Italy?*

The two got up and started walking back through the gate and the gap between the fences. The football field was mostly empty now. Skye peered up at the scoreboard. The Panthers ended up just barely winning 18–14. There were a few junior varsity football players cleaning up the trash in the bleachers and the concession stand's gate was down, closed by now. Luckily the players hadn't come out of the boy's locker room just yet.

Skye took off the letterman's jacket and gave it back to Olli. He was grateful to have it back as he groggily rubbed at his green eyes. Inside he was beating himself up; he was losing focus. There was another part of him willingly accepting the looseness. Back home he couldn't even dream of doing any of these things.

Just then the back door to the school building burst open. There were several football players cheering and guffawing singing some chant together. Behind them strolled Tiffany and Davidson. They were bickering loudly back and forth to one another. Tiffany hollered something snippy. Davidson walked away from her towards his truck.

Suddenly Skye and Olli felt different with an audience around—not nearly as relaxed. Skye caught herself sliding the numb part of the tip of her tongue to the roof of her mouth. *How did you say goodbye on a night like this?* Olli lifted his hand and brushed Skye's cheek. He smiled, "I'll see you tomorrow night, then?"

"Yes, I'll see you then," Skye chewed the side of her cheek nervously.

Olli was sliding into the back of Davidson's pickup truck as Tiffany pulled at Skye's arm, almost yanking her body closer to her. "What were you two doing?"

Skye ignored Tiffany's question, "What happened to you?" Skye gasped looking at Tiffany's skin. She had a scrape along her face like rug burn and a bruise forming down her neck.

Tiffany reached up wincing. She didn't find Skye's sarcasm funny. "You know what happened. Everyone knows what happened. The entire town saw what happened. Even the people from Hawthorne Heights know what happened—wherever they're from!"

Tiffany was livid and obviously in a lot of physical pain. *What happened in the second half of the game?*

"It wasn't Davidson, was it?" Skye immediately tried to link their bickering departure to why Tiffany looked beaten up.

"What? No. I told you, you're not funny. Stop acting like you didn't see it."

As the two slid into the car Tiffany cranked up the heat that was sputtering along in the Oldsmobile. The car's fan struggled to clear the frost of the front dash. Tiffany seemed eager to get home. She was driving with just a small circle visible in the front window. Skye turned her head to the stop sign at the corner of the school building. Davidson had sped up did a doughnut in the parking lot and then peeled out into the road. *Idiot.*

"You really didn't see it?" Tiffany was completely perplexed as she squinted, hunched down and focused on the road. "What were you two doing? Were you making out and just missed everything?"

"See what?" Skye still ignored Tiffany's questioning, growing irritated without knowing how her friend had gotten hurt.

"Wow, you might be the only one in all of Alfaro that didn't. Well you and maybe Olli. Your date must've gone well. I don't think I saw either of you all night, now that I'm thinking of it. Tell me how your date went, and I'll tell you what happened to me. I'm sure you'll hear it from everyone else anyways. It might as well be from me first."

"Well," Skye blushed again. "He asked if I'd go to the Homecoming Dance with him."

Tiffany was trying to drive with one hand and scrape the inside of the window with the window scraper with the other. She took a break from scraping the window to stop the car in the middle of the back road they were driving down, "Boys in Italy apparently can be just as irritating as Americans. The Homecoming Dance. Does he realize that's tomorrow?!"

Chapter 10
A Thrifted Homecoming

Gresham, Second World

Fifty miles outside of Gresham, Cliffton closed his wings within his two green prickly pods. He landed safely onto the three-foot stone pillar marking the line of territory between Gresham and Preadence. It had been almost twenty years since he'd traveled this far outside of the Château de Beaucoup, and it'd been centuries since he'd dare travel this far alone.

The small black, yellow, and white striped caterpillar unrolled from the inside of his jacket pocket. His dainty antennas swirled up and brushed Cliffton's side as the small worm wiggled close by. "Gordan, you are the most impatient little being I've ever come to know."

Securing his direction on the horizon he pulled the rolled chunks of milkweed leaves he collected a few miles back. They were meant to last for the remainder of the trip. Gordan was eating them quicker than Cliffton could unroll the bundle, leaving small poop pellets behind. Cliffton had to fly upside down and do a shaky loop de loop to let them fall out of his tiny pockets.

He shouldn't have been scouting ahead this early, but after talking privately with Adam they both agreed it was wise not to waste more time. Alone, he would never make it to Lighthouse Point, but if he could get as far the edge of the desert on the opposite side of Preadence maybe they could get some idea of what they were dealing with.

Cliffton was small enough to hide from any of Fideleroi's soldiers he may encounter. He could never make the flight through the patch of desert, not at his age nor this time of year. The heat, winds, and sporadic storms were too unpredictable. The trip through the cemetery and valley were proving to be a great enough challenge. Cliffton found himself resting often and he was at least a half-day behind schedule. As much of an annoyance Gordan was, he was grateful for the company.

There was a rustling in the bushes up ahead. *Who else would be out this far?* He quickly placed Gordan back into his pocket and jumped down off the stone pillar. He crouched down along the side with a few dead white oak leaves and acorns for cover. Cliffton peeked around, as Gordan was nosily trying to glance out of the jacket pocket as well. The sound was growing louder. Whoever it was out here was getting closer.

He kept them both covered as he strained his eyes to see who it was. They were coming from the same direction he just flew. It was a girl wearing a familiar coat. Her tight pants were trudging along with her matching knee-high boots. At her waistband he saw the wand dangling without concealment.

Ike's girlfriend, Victoria?

Alfaro, First World

"How about this one?" Tiffany held up her tenth unappealing dress find in the shop this Saturday afternoon.

Skye rolled her eyes. Now Tiffany was just trying to be funny. The dress was a bright orange with feathers off to one side and almost no fabric covering the back.

"Well, you never know. Italians might have a thing for half-dressed birds." Tiffany sneered, shoving the dress clanking as it hung back onto the wire rack.

Skye would've laughed if they didn't have only a few hours left before the Homecoming Dance. "Maybe I just shouldn't go?"

There was a row of old tables with only two or three chairs and set of flannel recliners. Skye flopped into one of the recliner chairs with an orange sticker marked down from $25 to $15. She closed her eyes. *What was I thinking?* Skye's parents agreed she could go to the dance on two conditions... one if she paid for everything and two if they got to meet the boy at their house for pictures before the dance. It wouldn't have been bad conditions if Skye had more than $40.22 to her name or a rich boyfriend like Davidson who would buy anything she wanted.

Tiffany lent her a pair of old high heels that were a half size too small but were silver, free, and had a reasonable chance of matching just about anything. The shoes had only been worn once by Tiffany to junior prom last year with Davidson. As tight as they fit, they were still better than any pair of shoes she had in her closet at home or the ones she glanced at the store. Rain boots, tennis shoes, and steel-toed hiking boots were about all she owned.

The only school dances Skye had been to were back in middle school, when literally everyone went to dances and practically everyone wore jeans and hoodies. This dressing-up stuff was new to Skye.

"Don't sit down, we have to find something quick. My hair appointment is in less than an hour!" Tiffany sat in an old swivel desk chair across from Skye feverishly looking down at her phone. She was trying to touch up her heavy makeup over the scrape and bruises mishap at the halftime performance the night before.

"Tiffany, there's literally nothing here. Anything good was picked over weeks ago. If there ever *was* anything worth wearing," Skye was on edge, completely at a loss.

"Well, don't get mad at me," Tiffany had her fill of shopping today, this wasn't really what she had in mind when Skye asked her to go out, "It's your date's fault he's a procrastinator. If he would've asked you earlier, we wouldn't be at Save-a-Buck trying to find you a decent dress. Right now, we'd both be heading to get our hair done."

It bothered Skye how right Tiffany was, but it really wasn't helping.

"You're smart and resourceful, can't you like make something?" Tiffany looked back down at her phone again, clearly giving up shopping for a dress, and spun around in the swivel chair.

Tiffany had made her point. There wasn't a lot of time, but there had to be something in this mothball-smelling store Skye could wear. Skye got up out of the recliner chair with a new sense of determined energy. She pulled a peach dress she liked earlier that was too big off a mannequin, leaving the one-armed and stained body looking sadder than ever and completely bare.

There was another dress two aisles down. Skye had tried on the dress forty minutes ago. This dress was a nice seafoam green with beautiful beadwork and sewn sequins. When she tried it on the top fit, but the bottom was brown, frayed, and torn. Before heading to the checkout, Skye grabbed a half-used wrap of white elastic, a spool of floral wire, and a bouquet with some of the flowers missing.

Tiffany was checking the time on her phone religiously. She was used to Skye acting strange and didn't ask questions about the odd assortment of things Skye was flinging crazily into the shopping cart she shoved around with one wheel not quite working. The two pushed the wobbling shopping cart with a faint squeak up to the one working register with a flickering light up above.

The red bell at the front counter dinged three times without any worker in sight. If they took any longer Skye would be walking home. It took Tiffany hitting the bell with a hefty whop before a cashier in a green vest shuffled from the back up to the front end. The lady with short hair greeted them without looking up. In the rush Skye didn't even add up the prices of her items. The cashier wore a name tag that seemed to be missing a letter. Skye watched the register's blurry blue numbers adding them in her head with each beep trying to calculate the sales tax.

The last item the cashier was ringing up was the large

peach dress from the mannequin. With luck Skye released the air she'd been holding in. The dress was marked down fifty percent because of the wear and tear. Her total was just shy of $40 at $36.59. She had just enough money to buy a coffee at the gas station before getting home. She was going to need all the caffeine she could get if she was going to pull this off.

Preadence, Second World

There wasn't time for rational thought. As much as he wanted to go back and tell Adam what he'd discovered there seemed to be more to Victoria's escapades than a long walk. Cliffton shoved the milkweed leaves he still had clenched in his small fist into the same pocket as Gordan, and quickly and quietly began secretly trailing after Victoria.

As far as he could see she seemed to be alone heading away from the Château de Beaucoup. *Why was she leaving Gresham's territory and why did she have a wand? Wands had been banned from Gresham along with orb blasts years ago.* Cliffton reminded himself, but as much as he was aware Victoria couldn't be a magical being, or was she?

Cliffton was following Victoria too closely to fly so he dodged behind bushes, trees, and rocks trying to keep as near as possible without being revealed.

Alfaro, First World

Back in Alfaro, Tiffany dropped Skye off at her house. Skye took her stuffed plastic thrift store bags and pair of silver heels, jogged up to her room, and slammed the door. She didn't have a lot of time. Her closet was a mess and was getting worse as she threw clothes out to get to an old sewing machine, scissors, and hot glue gun.

She feverishly laid everything out on her unmade bed. A part of her flinched as she cut both dresses in half as neatly as she could. Skye flung the puffy green bottom on the other side of her bed. The top of the peach dress ended up on her nightstand at the side of a lamp. Carefully she stitched a new band of elastic on the peach tulle, holding it up to her waist three times before making the stitch permanent.

The next two hours were a wave of movement. Three times she pricked her hand and twice she had to change the needle on the sewing machine for trying to go through too many layers of fabric at once. The hot glue gun wasn't as harsh, but she did burn a small mark on her right arm trying to rush.

Her phone buzzed. Tiffany texted her to let her know her hair was taking a little longer than expected but was almost done. They would be over in the limousine with the boys in about half an hour. Skye was finishing up stitching and looked at her creation. It wasn't the best work, but it would have to do. *Sink or swim, Skye. Sink or swim.*

Skye looked up into the mirror. Her hair, she hadn't even had time to think about what to do with her hair? Her reflection jumped as the wooden door made noise. Her mom was knocking, "Honey let me know when you're done getting dressed. I have a surprise for you."

A surprise from her mom? What could that mean? Horrified Skye did all she could to hope the 'surprise' wasn't 'the talk.'

She undressed, putting the bottom of the gown on first and then the top—not being able to wear a bra under the dainty top made Skye feel exposed. In all the rush, Skye never considered how her farmer's tan would look in the skimpy dress. Making her best attempt, she brushed her hair and put it up, hoping it looked a little better than when Olli first met Skye.

As soon as she hit the stairs, she regretted putting the shoes on so early. They made her feet feel like she had only four toes. When she was brave enough to show herself outside of her room, she found her mom and dad were in the living room sitting together on the couch. Her dad turned the TV off; it was good to see he was awake and not wearing his scrubs. Skye's mom stood up, grabbing an old wooden box from the coffee table.

She gave Skye a hug, "You look beautiful," Diane took Skye's hand and led her into her downstairs bathroom. Vince stayed on the couch. This was their moment, not his.

In front of Diane's antique vanity and towering mirror, Skye looked back at herself. With her heels on she was almost as tall as her mother. Inside, she doubted herself. She'd gotten the top of the dress a little shorter than she intended, and her very white uncovered midriff was making her feel uncomfortable. Aside from obviously not being tanned in the right places, Skye considered if she had a skinny-enough waist to pull the dress off. Her mother didn't say anything even though Skye was certain she wouldn't approve of her going out in public with her belly button showing.

Diane pulled out some pink blush and powder foundation from the middle drawer. She delicately dusted her daughter's face, as Skye closed her eyes. Skye was asked to smile while her mom put just a little pink blush on her cheeks. With a few bobby pins her mom seemed to work magic on her hair. *Who knew she could do hair?* She kept it pulled back in a bun but pinned a few loose pieces by twisting the long strands. The last few bobby pins were used to hold the small crown of peach, green, and cream flowers into place. Skye would have never thought of doing that.

The box Skye kept staring at was on the edge of the vanity. Diane held it out in front of Skye and opened the lid. Inside there was a diamond necklace—too glittering and too large to possibly be real. The flower-styled diamond earrings matched the silver and flower insets on the necklace perfectly.

Diane lifted the necklace out of the box and placed it around Skye's neck. There was a strange clasp you had to twist to fasten the necklace in place. The earrings were just delicate clips. Their size made them appear heavy, but as soon as they were on her ears, they were almost weightless and hardly tugged on her ears, unpierced, as her mother well knew.

Skye almost cried; it was unlike her mother to give her anything or show much interest in any non-academic pursuit. But these were perfect.

Before she could ask, Diane responded, "These were my mother's. She wore them on her wedding day. I couldn't do so on my own. I thought you might like to wear them tonight."

Her eyes welled with tears and so did Skye's. She embraced her mom. Skye did all she could to whisper a simple, "Thank you."

Outside the farmhouse there was a high pitch honking

noise. Skye couldn't help, but think it was almost as annoying as the bus. *They didn't let Davidson drive the limousine, did they?*

Skye wiped her eyes carefully as she tried not to mess up the little makeup she did have on. She'd been so busy trying to get ready for the dance she forgot what she was actually getting prepared for. Quickly she was filled with nerves.

Her dad was already outside the house with his phone ready to take pictures or more so ready to size-up her date.

Olli appeared very nervous too. He seemed to keep it together enough to play it smart. The first thing he made sure to do when he got out of the limousine was shake her dad's hand like a gentleman. Skye stood at the door too afraid to get any closer and too worried she might embarrass herself. Vince didn't have long to harass Olli with questions. In Olli's mind he was fighting with too much. Today was a lot more to take in than he imagined.

He was fortunate to have Davidson to help him get ready for the dance. *Fortunate* may not have been the right word. As Olli was getting out of the car Davidson was leaning through the driver's space honking the horn repeatedly. *What was wrong with him?*

It was not too different than preparing for a ball at the Château de Beaucoup. Yet, there were a lot of bizarre traditions and customs to follow in the First World. He traded a fair amount of currency with Mr. Laux to afford renting a suit and shoes, not entirely sure why he couldn't just use a set from home. Davidson said you had to get something called a *corsage* for your date. It proved to be a rather expensive bundle of flowers on such short notice. If he told Adam how much he spent, he could start a business just selling flowers illegally to the First World and never work again.

Then there was the limo? What a strange carriage. Eight large wheels and enough space to fit a dozen people. Why it had to be purple he didn't understand. It wasn't very efficient or attractive. Nor did it often carry royalty, especially in these rural parts of Alfaro.

He knew Skye's father without question. The man they called Vince shared the same color hair and cheekbones as his daughter. *Was it him though?* This was Olli's chance to get a closer look at the man who could be the infamous Clint Teagardin. He shook his hand. He had a firm grip and many deep scars along his palms. His demeanor seemed to soften. *Was it possible this man, who he watched fumbling to take a picture without dropping the phone, really be responsible for killing thousands?* Skye did say he worked in the hospital. He introduced himself as Mr. Hope.

The only images he'd seen of Clint were old paintings. One of them was somewhat of a resemblance it was from an aged book. He still couldn't be sure. *Was it the graying hair that was fooling him?* All the paintings had a large muscular man with a trimmed beard or goatee. This man was clean-shaven and skinny besides a little bulge around his midsection. As Olli contemplated the image from the old book, he looked over Vince's shoulder. In the doorway stood Skye alongside her mother, whom she also looked like. Their shoulders rested at the same angle.

As much as he'd imagined finding the child of Clint Teagardin and Trinity Amadori, he'd always pictured a well-trained buffed-up fighting machine. Someone easy to kill or recruit. And always... always he'd envisioned the child to surely be a boy. Not the sight he saw staring back at him. Skye was breathtaking.

Any images of Clint Teagardin shaven or clean-faced were erased from his mind. All he saw was Skye. On her head she wore a simple crown of flowers, her hair was loosely pulled up with a few strands hanging at the sides. Her dress was reflecting the light from the limousine's headlamps with the beads and sequins forming shimmering flowers around her bodice. Her midsection was bare, and the bottom was a light peach flowing skirt to her ankles. A beauty full of radiant sorcery.

Tonight, was going to be more difficult than he imagined. Davidson must've also spotted Skye because he had stopped hitting the driver's horn and had crawled back to the center of the vehicle to pop his head out of the top of the limousine and resorted to a loud whistling placing two fingers in his parched mouth.

Vince did not approve of Tiffany's boyfriend on a good day and gave him a death glare before Davidson could start catcalling. Vince took his phone over towards Diane. Olli followed, still entranced. He and Skye didn't have time to chat before they were shuffled in front of any somewhat appealing backdrop the Hope farm had to offer. They stood and posed in front of the fruit trees and a white-washed fence. For the last few pictures Diane ushered the other couples out of the car including Tiffany and Davidson to get a group picture.

During the last hundred pictures or so, Tiffany leaned over to Skye. "I hate you," she said.

Skye didn't take the comment into offense as she forced her stiffening cheeks to smile just a little longer. She noticed Tiffany had even more layers of foundation on than earlier today still desperately trying to mask the scrapes on her face and arms from the fall at the football game. Tiffany dramatically shared everything that happened during the football's half-time show the night before while they were shopping earlier in the day.

As the cheerleaders were forming a pyramid, Becca Bergins sneezed, sending half the squad tumbling onto the track. Tiffany described it as horrible and embarrassing, but Skye's mental image was rather comical, and she was sorry she missed it. Not that she would have traded her time with Olli on the baseball field to see it. Skye noticed Becca was no longer riding with them in the limo today.

Tiffany went on, as Skye reimagined the fall to help her keep her smile through the neverending pictures, "I hate you," Tiffany repeated through pinched lips, "My dress was almost $200 and you go into Save-A-Buck and make *that* out of it. I hate you." Tiffany was fuming as she whispered.

Skye smiled, sidetracked as Olli slid his palm around her cold waist. From Tiffany, an 'I hate you,' was a compliment.

Preadence, Second World

Cliffton was on edge now, it was getting dark and he was well outside of their territory into Preadence. Victoria hadn't taken time to rest, so Cliffton was beyond exhausted without using his wings. *Perhaps it was dark enough now to chance flying without being seen?* Cliffton climbed the thinning branches of a lilac bush to the top, giving Victoria enough time to get ahead a couple paces. At the top of the lilac bush, Cliffton looked before him.

There seemed to be a gathering of sorts not far outside his line of vision.

The tips of tents stood up over the crest of a hill and there was torchlight and possibly a bonfire. He looked back and forth. *Where'd Victoria disappear to?* Cautiously Cliffton dove forward into flight trying to get closer to the flames. There was shouting and chanting. Someone seemed to be giving a speech.

A makeshift stage was up ahead with a crowd of maybe a few hundred. It was too far to tell who was talking. Cliffton strained forward and stopped behind a few shrubs. Those gathering on the other side seemed to be celebrating. He scanned the crowd trying to catch sight of Victoria. Instead of in the crowd, he spotted her at the front of the stage next to the man who was speaking.

Every piece of him was screaming to turn back. The white hairs on his ears were curling, his ancient instincts were never wrong. But he had to know what all of this was about.

"By the next full moon," boomed the voice, "we will receive our last shipments in the cove." The voice sounded like an older gentleman as his words echoed in the open space.

The crowd erupted holding out their torches and sending celebratory burst from their wand tips. *Shipment?* Cliffton was on his tippy toes leaning out over a dead leaf. He was almost certain it was Charles Teagardin speaking, but that couldn't be right! The man at the front of the stage began talking again, but this time all he heard were the words, "with the help from..." *WHAM!*

Cliffton smacked the ground five feet down, landing on the side of his face. For just a moment, Cliffton assumed the dead leaf he was standing on popped away from the branch, but as he turned his head to look up a small shoe the size of coin started crushing his face. Unable to comprehend he'd been attacked, Cliffton kept his eyes tilted above his head. Gordan had crawled out of his pocket and was hanging a few feet above him on the underside of a leaf in the shape of a J.

Alfaro, First World

Even Skye had to admit the limousine was rather impressive. However, the whole way to the dance Skye couldn't help but think how she would've surely enjoyed it a lot more if there was different company. Davidson and Tiffany must've gotten over their argument from the night before because they were now making out on one side of the limo's leather seats. Luke Stevens was sitting very close to another cheerleader Jesse Spallinger. Luke had his palms on each knee not saying a word while Jesse was taking selfies.

Skye was grateful to not be riding in the back of Tiffany's mother's Oldsmobile, but she had the strange feeling like they were riding the bus all over again, just everyone smelled and looked nicer. Skye was sitting on the edge of the leather seat at an angle trying not to let a belly roll show in her midriff and avoiding the stares of a football player sitting across from her. She was trying to concentrate on remembering the boy's name.

Olli hadn't said a word to her since he picked her up. She did like that his hand was still wrapped around her backside, as the limo bopped up and down through the dirt road and potholes.

"Would you mind finding a different place to stare?" Skye jumped, not sure what was going on. The limo slowed down as it made its way over a set of train tracks.

Olli sounded bolder than she had heard him talk to anyone before. His accent was a lot clearer now too. She thought he was talking to her but then realized he spotted the football player sitting across from them without a date, staring her up and down like a piece of meat.

"What are you going to do about it, you little grass fairy?" said the football player mockingly as he stared directly at Skye's cleavage.

Skye wasn't sure what was happening as she crossed her arms over her top half. Olli moved his hand away from Skye's back as he shot forward abruptly in the seat and firmly grabbed a hold of the boy's suit jacket. His force was propelled even further as the limo sped up on the other side of the train tracks and down a straight road. Davidson stopped kissing Tiffany long enough to hastily place himself in between the player's fist and Olli's face.

"Now, Jason," reasoned Davidson in a calm voice, "We don't want to ruin this good night by doing anything stupid. Now do we? We have the game at Kings Pointe next Friday we're going to be needing you for."

As Davidson called his name, Skye recognized the player. He was the kicker on the football team and well known for his own short temper. If her memory served her correctly, he was one of the ones left at the cemetery with his arm around Tiffany after Davidson dipped out on them just a few weeks ago. Jason was one of the players who didn't care about the team's curfew.

Obviously, Jason hit a nerve with Olli. Skye was scared; she hadn't seen him get defensive or aggressive at anything in the past few short weeks she'd known him. Davidson pulled a small flask out of his jacket pocket and offered it to Jason, "Here why don't you have a little drink. We'll find you a date when we get to the dance; there will be plenty of girls you can scare off. You're not going to want Valpot. Don't let her clothes fool you, she's all farm girl."

Olli hadn't sat back down yet or let go of Jason's jacket. All eyes in the limo were on him, Olli didn't seem to care what Davidson had to say.

Davidson slowly pulled Olli's arm away from Jason's jacket, "And you, you don't want to do anything that would get you kicked out of the country, now would you?"

Resentfully, Olli sat back down glaring at Jason's smug look as he finished off what was left in the metal flask. Skye didn't do as well with the attention as Olli. She was just glad they only had five minutes left until they arrived at the front of Black Pine High School. It felt more like an eternity. Skye didn't take Davidson's comments to heart, she was just glad that Olli didn't punch Jason in the face.

When they arrived at the front of the high school, the other couples and Jason poured, slightly wobbling, out of the limousine towards the school's cafeteria where the Homecoming Dance was taking place. They were a few minutes late. No one worth mentioning was ever on time. The streetlights were flickering to life and other students were straggling into the school doors to join the dance. Olli kept Skye back for a moment. Skye was uncertain about what was going on. She looked at him, and he seemed terrified sitting beside her.

"I'm sorry I got so defensive. Ever since I got here, I've had a bad feeling about Jason." Olli was still trying to de-escalate. His ears were even a little red.

"It's fine, really, stop apologizing for everything." Skye was still uncomfortable sitting in the back of the limo but could relax some now that everyone else was gone. It was nice to see Olli in something else other than his white shirt, letterman's jacket, and brown shoes, but it made him seem like even more of a stranger to her.

Davidson must've helped him pick out his suit, because it was almost identical to the other football player's. Olli's hair was even styled differently tonight, and he was sweating. Her brain was still trying to convince herself last night really happened. The sweaty black paint and stained white shirt came to mind.

Olli took her left hand that he'd placed the corsage on almost an hour ago. "Can I do something?"

Now Skye was the one who was nervous and sweating. Then he asked almost too quickly, "Can I kiss you?"

She couldn't breathe, but somehow managed a faint, "Yes." Without hesitating, he pulled her just a little closer beside him and a little more gently he kissed her, long and soft.

It was too much to take in. She'd kissed other boys, but not like this. There wasn't any other boy she *wanted* to kiss. Her nose was pressed beside his and his lips tasted like the woods smelled in springtime.

There was a *wheeeeeeeeeeeeeeeeerpping* sound. Skye pretended not to hear anything as he still kissed her.

Wherp, then she heard the driver clear his voice, "Sorry to interrupt, but my hour is over, and I've got a few other places to go tonight. You can stay, but I'm going to have to charge overtime."

Olli ignored the driver for just another second. He

didn't even look to the front where the driver was looking back at them through the lowered tinted window. He looked into Skye's eyes and then to her neck, where her mother's necklace shined back at him.

Chapter 11
Free World

It was her. The night was lost. He'd found the child—young woman, Olli corrected—of story and legend. Clint Teagardin and Trinity Amadori wed and escaped to the First World to have a child. It was all true. The mission was complete, yet somehow Olli couldn't find himself to move forward. They weren't really expecting to find her. The true heir to the sorcerers *and* wood fairies, possibly even future ruler of even more regions. All along he was preparing to kill the person they were looking for to ensure the peace. If nothing less, to destroy the entrance from the First World's side for good... but never this. There was no concrete plan of what to do next. The effort of searching took so much of their energy there was no direct step to follow if they found the true heir. Kill her? Seal the entrance to get rid of her for good? Impossible.

Instead of taking action, Olli chose to live out the moment. It was hard to ignore the necklace. He had recognized it without question. Clearly it was crafted in Yodére Forest centuries ago along with the pair of earrings he now stared at. It was royal jewelry pairs alike could be found on each royal portrait he'd ever seen of the fairy colonies. Adalina Amadori was wearing a near-identical set in all her portraits and renditions.

Now what?

Tonight, Skye was more mesmerizing than anything. He couldn't tell her the identity she held. For starters she would never believe him. Her parents had robbed her of her own right to succession.

As wrong as it was Olli couldn't resist the thought of *how lucky.* It felt peculiar to feel jealousy. For years he struggled with wanting to rule or not rule. He never had the choice. His parents would have never let him escape ruling the Kingdom of Gresham. Even worse, her parents were still around to help her. They were still protecting her from the evil within the Second World.

Why couldn't she have been a boy? Or a terrible, rotten person he could've offed and never thought twice about it? Not sweet, smart, and beautiful.

"Is everything okay?" Skye was looking up into his eyes again.

Jealousy dissipated with the sound of her voice and feel of her skin against his hands. They were 'slow dancing,' as they called it here. Her hands hung loosely around his neck, the flowers on her corsage brushing against his collar.

Olli had been acting weird ever since they got out of

the limo. Skye couldn't help but think she might be a terrible kisser and never realized it. The song had ended and there was a lot of hooting and hollering at the next song that came up. This was a lot more upbeat and not at all Olli's pace. Tiffany bopped over into them. Skye released her arms from Olli's neck, and he pulled his away from her waist.

"Hey, you two love birds," Tiffany giggled, while Skye rolled her eyes.

"Come to the bathroom with me I need help with my dress," Tiffany didn't wait for a response, instead she grabbed Skye's hand and started pulling her towards the cafeteria restrooms. Olli was a little dumbfounded but eager to get away. He mouthed the word *punch* and pointed to a table full of drinks. Skye reluctantly trailed away behind Tiffany.

It was nice to have a moment alone. His thoughts were frazzled for so many reasons. *Maybe it was best if he stayed in the First World to protect her. To make sure she stayed in the First World and never left. Destroy the entrance for good as his deal with Cliffton already entailed. It seemed like a feasible solution. His business was done.*

At the punch table, Olli scanned the contents of plastic ware and the gaudiest star-shaped table scatter. As he grabbed a paper cup and the ladle hanging in the orange punch, he dropped it splattering orange punch in every direction. He narrowly missed getting it on his rented suit. Olli couldn't believe his own eyes. He couldn't just pretend he didn't see him. Through the rounded punch bowl and dusting of glitter just behind the ladle were unmistakably the curled shoes of Cliffton Burroughs.

"Cliffton what are you doing here?" Olli hesitated

more concerned now as he came to his senses, "how did you get through?" *Could milkweed pixies sense what you were thinking?*

Olli tried to position his body in front of the table to cover Cliffton as best he could. He was hoping the splattered punch didn't draw too much attention. Luckily, the upbeat music continued for the next song and most of the students were in a large group across the large cafeteria jumping crazily up and down and not paying any attention to Olli at the punch table.

He turned his head so it didn't look like he was talking to himself. Cliffton slowly crept out from behind the bowl. His left leg would barely bend, and he had to use a makeshift stick crutch to be able to move forward.

"You look terrible," Olli was full of questions, but he refrained from asking them. He needed to find a way to get Cliffton to a better location. If he was spotted here, there were hundreds of cameras to easily snap a picture or take a video of him. Not to mention, Tiffany and Skye would be back from the bathrooms at any moment.

He put out his arm and without saying a word Cliffton ducked away into his damaged pod as best he could. Olli scooped Cliffton along with the small crutch up off the table. Slowly he lowered the pod and stuck it into his pocket.

When Olli turned around, he jumped. Skye was standing right in front of him. "Did you forget?" A long silence followed. "The drinks?" Skye specified, patiently waiting for an answer.

Olli didn't respond. "Here, I'll get them," Skye reached around Olli and grabbed two plastic cups scooping out the chunky orange punch for both herself and Olli.

"You said you were getting drinks, didn't you?" Skye asked taking a generous mouthful of her own, "Maybe I misheard, it is pretty loud in here."

Slowly Olli accepted the cup from Skye and took a sip. He could feel a tugging at his pocket as Cliffton popped out of his shell and peeked over the top of the creased side. Olli tried to unnoticeably push his head back down in the pocket of his suit. He needed to figure a way out of here and quickly.

"It is quite loud in here isn't it? I think that's why I'm not feeling very well." Olli dramatically put his hand to his head. Acting was never one of his strong talents. He'd give that one more to Ike.

"Do you want to go outside?" Skye was talking louder and slower.

If that was an out, Olli was going to try and take it, "Yes, I do. I think I'll go outside for a minute to see if it helps."

Skye made motions to go with him. She started to dodge around Ms. Cromsky trying to dance.

"No," said Olli a little too fast and too loud. "No. You should stay here. I don't want you to miss any of the dance."

Skye was concerned. She really didn't want to stay in the cafeteria on her own, but if he was going to get sick then she really didn't want to be around.

"Okay."

She refilled her punch and watched as Olli rushed toward the exit doors to the outside. Not sure how long he was going to be, Skye found an open chair and flopped down so the poof on her dress ruffled up.

Outside, Olli was sweating and truly not feeling well.

His head pounded with endless possibilities, and his empty stomach was tight.

He sat on the ledge of the sidewalk at the front of the school building and pulled Cliffton back out of his pocket. Olli unfolded the little creature in his right hand and shielded him from view with his left.

"What are you doing here?" Olli repeated, "*How* are you here? What happened to you?" Olli looked back and forth to make sure they were alone.

"Well, it's a long story," Cliffton began. It seemed painful for him to even speak without collapsing.

"Do try to fill me in," Olli was forgetting his own news.

"Adam and I thought," Cliffton breathed in a hoarse breath, "we thought it was best with how busy you were to try to scout ahead into Preadence."

"Preadence?" Olli copied, "You made it into Preadence *alone*?"

"As I was trying to tell you, before I was so rudely interrupted," Cliffton's body ached with every word, and he didn't come all this way to be lectured. "I went forward and was trailing Victoria..."

Again, Olli interrupted; he couldn't refrain, "Victoria as in Ike's obnoxious girlfriend... what on earth was Victoria doing in Preadence?"

"Carrying a wand nonetheless..." Cliffton wheezed.

"I'm still not understanding how you wound up like this?" Olli loosened his tie and undid two of his top buttons on his shirt. He was suddenly very hot.

"There was a gathering, I didn't get much information other than there's a shipment of something coming into the cove within the next couple of weeks," wheeze, puff, wheeze. Cliffton took a big breath in to try and finish, "I was spying on the sorcerers when my fellow milkweed pixie Replogle attacked me. It's a miracle I was able to escape. He took me completely off guard. The rotten traitor!"

"I guess I'm still not following you. How did you get through the entrance without the key?" Olli's adrenaline was surging. He really could get sick.

"It was already open, si-rrr?" Cliffton's lips hung onto the word *sir* a bit longer. A sign of exasperation and was that sarcasm as well?

Was it possible he'd forgotten to lock the entrance when he came through? Between the Second World duties and trying to understand the First World it was too much to keep track of. Something as small as locking a door behind him was hard to keep in check. The dance alone was making him forget a lot of things.

Instead of admitting his blame Olli came forward with his own news. He had to tell someone "It's her."

"What do you mean 'it's her'? You're sure?" Squeaked Cliffton, "You're *sure* you've found the daughter of Clint Teagardin and Trinity Amadori?"

"Yes, I'm certain." Olli had no doubt in this subject.

"Well then, I think it's time that we leave. If she is here she should be safe for now, but we have to get that entrance locked back up."

Olli reached into his suit pocket. It wasn't there. The key, the one thing he could not lose, he had lost. He thought through over and over again of where it might be. A lightbulb lit up in his head. It was still in his letterman's jacket.

"I don't have it." Olli's stomach did a backflip.

Cliffton seemed to stand a little straighter, "You

what?! I better have misheard you."

There was a pang of guilt inside him. He took his jacket back with him after exchanging the currency with Mr. Laux. He must've left the mausoleum unlocked as he left and never brought the key back when he entered for the dance wearing his rented suit.

A touch of calm came over him, when the place where he left the letterman's jacket lying in his mind came into focus. It was in the library where surely if anyone picked it up, was Henry. Henry would've known just what to do with it.

"We need to get to the jacket," Cliffton was determined to get to the key as soon as possible.

Cliffton had watched over it for years without losing it. Olli had it a few weeks and managed to leave the only surviving active entrance unlocked for an entire day. Because of what? A distraction?

Olli thought of the distraction. *What would Skye think if he left now without saying anything?* There wasn't time for explanation or excuses—they had to go. She wouldn't be a safe if the entrance was left unlocked much longer.

"Hey, grass fairy," came an obnoxious taunt.

Olli was irritated and on high alert as it was. He slid Cliffton back into his pocket.

"What are you doing out here? Did your date finally come to her senses and dump you or you just thought this was the bathroom or something?" Olli knew who it was before he even turned his head.

Jason was standing outside the exit doors discreetly taking a drink from a small glass bottle. He finished off the last few drops and threw the small glass bottle against the brick school building. It made a popping noise as the glass shattered on impact. Jason's arms were swinging as he headed towards Olli.

On the other side of the entrance Olli shook his hand. His knuckles had cracked where he punched Jason once and knocked the sense right out of him. As much of a poor condition as Cliffton's health was in, he refused to leave the unlocked entrance. He was convinced this was particularly his fault for letting Olli use the key in the first place.

Olli walked swiftly through Carpenter Hills and completed taking off his tie. It was almost eight o'clock, so it was unlikely there would be many scouts or townspeople out, but he needed to get the First World clothes off in case he was seen. He wanted to stop at Adam's to share the news, but he needed to get back up to the Château de Beaucoup to find the jacket. The other part of him wanted to go back to the school and have just one more slow dance before he left. He would feel a lot better if he could have the key back in his hands. Everything else would have to wait.

Chapter 12
Double Take

Alfaro, First World

It'd been three weeks. Three terribly long dreadful weeks, almost longer than the time she knew him. Skye hadn't heard from or seen Olli since the night of the Homecoming Dance. Jason had told everyone how Olli confronted him outside of the cafeteria.

There was talk at school about him getting sent back to Italy, but Skye just couldn't fathom it. She'd barely known Olli. Not once did she even ask what his last name was and no one else had seemed to either. There wasn't even a phone number left behind to contact him. He was strange and impulsive. There were even times when he was just naïve. But to just disappear without a word? It just didn't make sense.

As for Jason, Skye didn't doubt he got what he deserved, and Olli attacking Jason for no reason didn't add up. Skye tried to imagine him attending a different school or stuck at home on suspension, not halfway around the world. They had shared some sort of connection or so Skye kept trying to tell herself. Mr. Laux wouldn't tell any of the kids what was going on with the foreign exchange student, making French class even more miserable than ever. It was physically and literally eating away at her inside.

Skye pressed her head up against the bus window. It was going to be another gloomy day. The autumn weather had brought nothing but endless chilly rainy dark days. As she breathed, the condensation kept gathering up against the cold window. On the other side of the emergency exit doors there was a light drizzle falling from the sky.

As the bus was passing houses the pumpkins were still sitting outside of many houses half-rotten. The carved faces were drooping. Some you couldn't even imagine had a once more cheerful image. It was staying darker longer in the mornings. Outside it was nearly pitch black. The trees were barren, the last few beautiful leaves being knocked to the ground collecting along the other piles of brown soggy clumps. Tiffany had her feet up and head resting against the seat in front of them sound asleep.

This morning Tiffany saved the emergency exit seat as usual but gave Skye the inside spot today because the window was too cold and wet for her to lean up against. Tiffany had been out late the night before and was too mad at Davidson about something to want to text him back anytime soon.

The cold window wasn't so bad, and Skye didn't mind.

Her hair was already damp from the morning chores and she didn't have any makeup on like Tiffany to mess up. It was too early to argue seating arrangements and not much mattered to Skye lately. To pass the time Skye drew a little doodle smiley face on the window.

The bus was slowing down as it approached the first set of train tracks on their way to school. There was a small car in front of them the red brake lights shined through the front of the bus windows. In the distance, Skye could hear the horn on the train rickety-rack, rickety-tack, approaching slowly along the track. Skye was still peering outside, somewhat out of the smudged curve of the smiley face she'd drawn, as she neared drifting off into sleep. Her phone was connected by her headphones, and the music was switching to a new song.

Skye gazed at the train tracks in the distance. In the lull between songs, it revealed to no surprise the bus was quiet. Most of the students on board had headphones in just like Skye or were sleeping like Tiffany. Squinting through the dripping twinkling rain Skye saw something move on the double set of train tracks. It had to be a large animal. Maybe a deer, it piqued her interest.

More awake now, Skye sat up. The animal was getting closer. *Would it make its way off the tracks in time before the train came through?* The train's whistle sounded again and again. She found her heart pounding in her chest. Something terrible came to Skye. She peered over the bus's brown seats. As far as she could tell, the thing moving on the train tracks in the distance wasn't a deer or any other kind of animal.

Alarmed, Skye noticed over the seats no one else was looking out the window. The bus driver several rows up had pulled out her magazine from the side pocket of her seat and was flipping lazily through the pages, chomping her gum in the side of her cheek. A red glow of light reflected off her face.

Internally Skye was screaming. She looked back out the window. *Impossible.* The bright letterman's jacket was more visible now as the figure bobbed up and down walking away from the railroad crossing guards towards the approaching train in the distance. Skye couldn't be sure, but it had to be him—it just had to.

It was pure impulse. Her heart was racing so rapidly now she felt it would burst. The adrenaline was too much or maybe it was the cup of coffee she had this morning. The whistle on the train sounded again, but this time louder and much closer. Three times. A few more heads started to pop up on the bus, irritated, but it wasn't anything out of the usual. Some train engineers got a little happy with the train whistles.

She couldn't stand it any longer. Skye had to know, she had to warn whoever it was on the tracks, but she was so sure now. It had to be him.

Her headphones fell out of her ears, she grabbed the red lever to her side, cranked it hard to the left, and pulled up. Immediately a red siren flashed in several places on the ceiling of the bus. The alarm was ear-piercing. Every single student sat up and the bus driver flung her magazine up in the air in a panic. Skye didn't look back in the red glow, she couldn't. She pushed forward and out on the Emergency Exit door and leapt from the side of the bus.

It was slippery out and in the bustle of the urgency, she fell halfway down into the ditch along the side of the road. The man in the car in front of the bus flung open his car door. He shouted something, but it was too late.

Skye got up with muddy scuffed hands running towards the train tracks. Mud, rain, and grass splashed off of her body as she ran. The train didn't seem to be slowing down. *What was he doing?*

"Olli, Olli! Get off the tracks. Olli!" She was waving her hands frantically, like a crazy lady.

There wasn't a rational thought left in her brain as she got closer. He continued to walk along the tracks in the direction of the oncoming train. She was *sure* it was him. The rain was coming down just as hard as ever. Her hair was falling in her face and her legs burned from sprinting. He never stopped walking no matter how loud she screamed. He never looked back. It was his hair, his shoulders, his bare letterman's jacket.

The train was almost here now. Skye was on the tracks, racing towards Olli faster than ever. She was gaining ground between them, but as much as she pushed, her legs wouldn't go any faster. Her rain boots felt heavier than ever before on her feet. She wasn't going to make it in time. Her lungs were sore, her throat was getting raspy. Water flung from her arms pumping back and forth. Mud flipped up from her heels to her back. It was as loud as she could scream, but the whistle of the train was growing even louder. Skye fought hard against her best instincts screaming at her to stop. *Turn around, turn around, why won't you turn?*

Olli stopped walking and stood in the middle of the tracks facing the train just yards away. Skye had almost made it to where he stood. He turned his head to peer over his shoulder. Skye saw his eyes staring back at her, so deeply sinister as rain fell over his cheeks. His eyes didn't blink as the rain dripped through his wet hair and eyebrows. The train's light was glowing through the darkness and rain. Its whistle kept blasting over and over at this point. There were two young people facing their deaths on the train tracks.

Between the whistle and the sirens edging closer, Skye finally had the feeling of fear for her own life. Then he was gone, vanished, and she was tumbling. She hit the gravel and mud along the tracks and was rolling with someone whose hair was flickering against her face.

At the last minute before the train barreled into her, Tiffany yanked at Skye's coat, pulling her to the side. Skye could still smell the hot metal and feel the burst of wind whizzing by. Tiffany's hair was caked with mud and her mascara was running down her cheeks as she lay gasping for air.

"Skye, what's wrong with you?" Tiffany gasped for more air. Her fingertips flinging mud in all directions. "What," gasp, "were you," gasp, "*thinking*? You could've died!"

Completely out of breath and sore, Tiffany could hardly keep up with Skye and thought for certain she'd never reach her. Tiffany resolved to try a little harder in Ms. Crommmmsky's class the rest of the semester.

Skye was too stunned to feel the pain of the rocks in her hands. Too dumbstruck to worry about the people rushing towards them. She bolted upright. The train was slowing down but was quite far from where they were in the ditch. Beyond it there was nothing. He wasn't anywhere. Lightheaded and sick to her stomach Skye let her body slip away into the fatigue flooding her system it came just as fast as the adrenaline had overcome her. Red and blue lights flashed omnisciently in the distance. The mud felt good against her skin. Her whole body was stinging as large raindrops blasted her face.

* *

Grounded... suspended... emotionally unstable... fined... charges... These were all words Skye had to repeat in her mind. They were new to her vocabulary but were gradually becoming a part of her everyday life. It was now the week of fall break. The seven-day suspension a week prior was unbearable but was a fog in comparison to the amount of work she had to put in to catch up on in her honors classes.

The school board was thrown by her case, but it wasn't the craziest thing they'd seen. In the end they were lenient based on her having no history of criminal activity. Her parents agreed to pay the $500 fine to the fire department for being called to the scene. Diane and Vince also agreed to school counseling services for their daughter, blaming her spontaneous jump on too much stress.

Following the permanent ban from school transportation, Skye now had to ride to and from school with her dad Vince. Vince wouldn't admit it, but he was terribly disturbed by his daughter's behavior. He'd requested to be taken off call from the hospital and was now only working three twelve-hour shifts each week.

Their morning and afternoon rides were quiet, and Skye wasn't sure whether she was grateful for the silence or terrified. She was all the talk at school for a couple days. After the football team lost at regionals everything seemed to die down. Davidson had a field day with jokes, but it was old news after a while. Tiffany didn't know what to do or think. The attention for saving Skye's life was nice, but Tiffany strangely felt like she still lost her best friend that day.

Skye had to take mandatory counseling during her only elective gym class, the one time she ever got to see Tiffany besides when they passed at their locker. Her counselor told her she could make up the credits next semester. Tiffany tried texting Skye, but she kept forgetting her parents took her phone. *She could've at least found a way to say thank you.*

Being grounded wasn't so bad, Skye thought. She spent more time with the animals than ever before, and they never talked back or poked fun. The barn was still hard to go into, so most of the time Skye took Buckwheat out.

The barn still reminded Skye of him, even if she was never technically with Olli in the barn. It took all she could not to be back along the ocean beside him. Why she longed to be with him completely drove her crazy. Ever since he came into her life, she had done nothing but get hurt and feel insane. No one else saw a boy walking on the tracks that morning. Not the train conductor, not Tiffany, not the car in front of the bus, and no other student. *Was it another illusion?*

The counselor at school wanted her to talk about things. Skye couldn't bring herself to tell the counselor Elita Hurschbach the truth. Even when Skye tried to explain things to herself, she thought she sounded crazy. *What was real and what was imagination?* It was too hard to tell, and Skye wasn't interested in more counseling, especially after Mrs. Hurschbach told her there was nothing she could share about Olli's whereabouts.

Instead, Skye talked about her grand future plans to attend college. There weren't official charges filed by the school or train company, so her permanent record was still clear, and her grades were better than ever.

Her studies helped keep her mind off other things and her parents made her retake her college entrance exams last week. To Skye's surprise, she had scored much higher on them than the year prior and was eligible for several more scholarships now. Unfortunately, this just meant more applications and essays. It was neverending. *Would her parents even consider letting her leave home for school now after all this mess?*

Mrs. Hurschbach seemed content with their meetings, but Skye knew better. Inside she was struggling more than she thought humanly possible. As well as she was doing in school, none of it mattered anymore. There was a growing emptiness welling up inside her. The extra time alone was making her live more and more inside her head.

Diane hid Buckwheat's saddle somewhere in the house or garage during her 'grounded time,' but she should've known it wouldn't make much difference. It didn't stop Skye from riding. *What else was there to do?*

On this particular November day, the sun was shining. It was growing colder, so Skye wore two light jackets and a stocking cap. The trees were completely bare. Before long snow would cover everything in sight. The animals would be tougher to visit in the coming months. The news channels were calling for a bitterly cold winter with lots of snow. There was always a chance they'd lose a few chickens if the temperature fell low enough.

Skye was riding Buckwheat bareback along the perimeter of the fence. It was cold enough you could see the air winding in moving swirls from Buckwheat's large flaring nostrils. Dad was up at the house making dinner while Mom was probably making her way home from work. It was so peaceful out here. The dairy cows on the other side of the fence were grazing quietly on what was left of the frostbitten grass. The fields adjacent were bare from a good fall harvest. Twilight was approaching as the glowing pinks and oranges crested to the edge of the empty horizon.

Buckwheat came to a stop. Skye rubbed his tightly styled mane. He enjoyed the extra company but only tolerated the additional grooming Skye found ample time for during being grounded. She managed to learn a few new braids for horses from an old library book.

There was the sound of leaves crunching through the woods. Skye squinted through the trees. Whatever the sound was coming from wasn't approaching very quickly. It seemed to be hovering close by. Buckwheat was hesitant. Skye thought of a raccoon, possum, or skunk. Maybe it was her cat Maiji? He'd been missing since the night Olli disappeared.

Hopeful Skye dismounted Buckwheat's bareback. She could use a break after riding without a saddle for so long. Buckwheat was cautiously walking with Skye as a guide. The wind blew a few green and black walnuts from the surrounding trees with a racketing thump. A squirrel jumped from branch to branch above her head.

Then, there it was. A faint, "Meow," and Skye jogged forward into the trees a little way. Sure enough, flopping around in a pile of leaves scratching his backside was a healthier than ever Maiji.

Excited and feeling happy for the first time in weeks, Skye rushed to his side and scooped up the black and white cat.

She held him up to her face, "Oh, where have you been?" it came out in annoying baby voice, but Skye couldn't help it; she was almost giddy. Skye assumed Maiji was hit by a car or caught by one of the Grabers' dogs. Maiji felt heavy and full from having been well fed while he was away. *Maybe he'd been hanging out at the Grabers' all this time enjoying field mice and milk left in the barn?* Maiji never stirred, but by the time Buckwheat let out a loud neigh it was too late. Standing in front of Skye were two figures.

Immediately she recognized Olli but had no clue who the other one was. The girl had to have been around Skye's age. Skye still held Maiji, too confused to fight or run. The girl standing beside Olli snickered. "This is her?"

She grabbed a stick from her waistband and said something in a different language. Then Olli was lifting her up onto Buckwheat's back and the stranger was holding Maiji.

Chapter 13

Gaining Strength

Preadence, Second World

What a crazy messed up dream. *Strange* wasn't the right word, nor was *terrible*. It was somewhere in between bizarre and uncomfortable. Skye pulled off her covers. She didn't hear her alarm, but it felt like she had slept for a long time. She was worried she'd overslept but then she remembered it was fall break. It was fine. As she rolled onto her belly there was some relief in the pain she was feeling in her back. Maybe it would be best if she went back to sleep.

Her head was throbbing, but it was likely because she didn't have any dinner. There was a knot in her stomach and Skye felt like she was starving. Dinner? Wasn't her dad making dinner last she checked? Skye couldn't recall eating the tuna casserole and green beans her dad was making on the stove before she went out to the barn.

Why did she smell burning leaves? Skye's senses were fuzzy as she turned over again and then sat upright. Did she sleep on her floor? There was a stabbing pain continuing to shoot through her back and something covering her head. Skye's palms brushed the dirt floor. Alarmed, she discovered her hands shackled together and she was laying on the damp solid earth.

Skye managed to raise the shackles high enough to pull the burlap sack from over her face. What she thought were covers turned out to be nothing more than her second jacket. All Skye could remember was grabbing it last minute before going for a ride with Buckwheat. *Was that yesterday already?*

Outside, Skye could hear a horse bellowing through the thin tent. *Was it Buckwheat? Were they hurting Buckwheat?* Skye thrashed her arms about trying to loosen the chains. The end of the linked metal was somehow attached to the tent pole.

Her heart was racing. *Where was 'here'? Was it even worth calling for help?*

Gresham, Second World

Meanwhile Adam was pacing inside of his small house. Cliffton had his bum leg propped up on an old box of matches, and Olli sat on the wooden chair in the corner. Julianna was holding down the watch post at the mausoleum. The three had been doing shifts ever since Olli came back through the Second World and confessed he could not find the jacket or the key. Adam was left out of the lookout rotation but not because of his eyesight. Of the three, he by far had the best self-defense combative skills.

Adam was physically unable to pass back through the entrance into the First World. He lost his eyesight through the enchantments placed on the entrances by Leonardo da Vinci hundreds of years ago when Adam was forced into the Second World at a young age. If he tried to pass back through the mausoleum to the First World, he would be killed by the same enchantments. Because he had no magic blood in him and he was born in the First World, he would never be able to go back home.

Henry and Olli trashed half the Château de Beaucoup searching for the jacket, leaving the rest of the Château's staff in the dark and frustrating most, like Ms. Hockenberry who was left to clean up the mess. When one of the housemaids asked what they were looking for, Henry snapped and made up a story about losing a silver button for the coronation robe. All this lie accomplished were random attendants turning in buttons at all hours of the day. Apparently, a lot of buttons had been lost over the years, or workers were taking them off their own clothes to stop the mad clutter and extra work.

There was nothing. Almost more furious than Cliffton, Henry was tempted to confess to the council how irresponsible Olli was just to have him dethroned. Right now, he knew it was best for as few people as possible to know about the entrance being unlocked. Still, the thought of Olli not being king in a few months made him feel better about his current bout of youthful negligence.

Henry reminded himself Olli had found Clint

Teagardin. He was also successful at finding the known heir to the sorcerers and the wood fairies. Clint Teagardin and Trinity Amadori were alive and for certain had a daughter named Skye. That was something.

Julianna sat along a stump-shaped gravestone. She was only an hour into what must've been her twentieth four-hour shift and was absolutely bored out of her mind. It was only about six o'clock, but it was already getting dark. *What was she supposed to do out here all alone?* Julianna watched a few large sycamore leaves float down to the ground while she shuffled an old, faded set of tarot cards in her smooth palms.

After doing a few of her own readings, she had to force herself to stop. Convinced she was messing up her dealing skills or shuffling the cards all backwards. Misfortune, loss, nothing good. *Where was her love, where was the good luck?* The mausoleum seemed to rumble as the ground beneath her feet shook. She really could use all the good luck she could get right about now. There hadn't been a great deal of time to respond.

Instead of standing to defend herself, Julianna dove to the backside of the tomb. *Was that a horse?* The entrance was clearly opening. *How long had they been on the other side? Had they crossed through during someone's watch?* It sounded like stone grinding on stone.

These were undoubtedly the sounds of horseshoes trotting the solid earth and stone. Julianna tried to be patient while she waited. It wasn't until she heard the door close that Julianna decided to move. By then, several minutes had passed before the audible clink came together. There weren't any screams or signs of a struggle. Whoever was coming through the other side was originally from the Second World.

When it felt safe, Julianna looked around the side of the mausoleum. It had been almost three weeks of watching. Finally, Adam and Olli were letting her in on all their secrets. Dodging the lies and snooping was getting old. Aside from being included, she really *was* grateful to do it to allow Cliffton to get some rest, and now of course something exciting would happen while Julianna was here alone.

As she watched the first arrival emerge, it proved to be a large black horse with white splotches. There was someone on top, but they were more just a body slung over the back, tied forward around the horse's neck like they were sleeping. Then, unmistakably, there was Victoria's backside, her streaky long straight hair swooshing behind her. It did not come to Julianna's surprise that Ike was following closely behind on foot.

Victoria tried to mount the large horse along with the limp body—Julianna thought it was likely a Clydesdale. If Theodore were here he would know. Ike was trying to help her up, but Victoria seemed irritated.

There was a faint *tink tink* noise jangling at her midsection. Julianna winced; she'd forgotten about the three orb blasts in her pocket. As she leaned forward to get a better look at the couple, one slipped out the side of her jacket and rolled forward about ten feet. Neither Ike nor Victoria turned to look, but there was enough force created from the fall that when the orb stopped rolling, it ignited into a powerful blast.

All she could do was brace for impact as she held her

breath. Her fingertips clawed into the crevices on the side of the mausoleum. She instinctively went to cover her ears next, but there was only a blast—no echoing boom. The only sound came from the pieces of ground debris and flying dirt.

Julianna was both elated and alarmed by the accident. She and Leona Harlow had tried for several months to get the blast to silence. It must've been the extra fragments of mermaid scale. Those were expensive and hard to come by. They never would've imagined the scales would work. Julianna purchased a few from the man in the moat. They could've been fake for all she knew.

Now wasn't the greatest time to celebrate. Ike and Victoria were caught off guard, not sure what had caused the sudden explosion. Julianna was grateful they didn't seem interested in sticking around. Ike was kissing Victoria goodbye, fumbling as she raced off on the reluctant horse while Ike sprinted on foot alone towards the stables.

The dust and dirt were settling by the time Julianna was able to stand straight. Julianna wasn't sure what she just witnessed. She checked the mausoleum door: it was locked tight. Either Ike or Victoria had the key. Was the person tied on horseback the mysterious girl Olli had been talking so much about?

There wasn't a lot of time to waste. The horse was swiftly disappearing off towards Preadence and Ike was nearly to the stables. Clutching an orb blast in her fist, Julianna sprinted the whole way to her old home.

Preadence, Second World

Outside of the tent, there were voices. It was hard to make out what they were saying. Skye recognized there was some English, a bit of French, and something else. The few French words she could make out were vulgar terms. Itching to get the shackles off her wrists, Skye scavenged around for anything to try and work the metal chains from her hands.

There was an old cooking pot, some metal utensils, and a cup. Skye scooted across the damp earth. Her arms would only separate about eight inches, enough to grab a fork and the cup. She couldn't get the chain to reach the edge of the tent so she could peek out the flap. Quickly she slid back to the pole in the middle of the tent. The post was anchored deep into the cold earth. She took the blunt end of the fork and started stabbing at the ground.

After half an hour or so of digging, there was a rustling outside of the tent. Skye was sweating, and her hands were covered with blisters. The chains had created raw red bands of rug burn marks along her wrists. As the tent flap folded in, Skye threw her jacket over the hole by the post and turned around with her back to the post. She did all she could not to seem too startled. The half-bent fork was tucked hastily under her bottom.

A new face entered. There was a gleam of morning light shining in along with a cool breeze. It wasn't the girl she'd seen in the woods or Olli. Who was this man? He didn't seem terribly old, except for his eyes. They were a stone gray with specks of green. There were wrinkles framing his eye sockets and the broken creases went as far as his graying hairline. The muscles in his forearms and broad shoulders seemed strong. The light reflected from his side making him appear taller than he really was.

His nose was like her father's. It was pointed but it had a flat edge off to the left side. It was difficult to know what to do because he didn't say anything. He simply looked at her up and down. It wasn't like a hunter seeking prey, to Skye it seemed strangely like admiration.

Skye felt simply pathetic. She brushed her sweaty hair to the side with her blistered fingers, so she didn't look as intimidated as she really was by his presence. What other choice did she have except for to stare back at his stony eyes? The silence was not appeasing to her conscience, so Skye broke it. *What else was there to lose?*

"Where am I?" Skye's voice was frail and cracked. Her mouth was desperately dry.

The man seemed uncertain of how or what to respond. He was trying to read her. There was an aura of her blood so much like his, but so many other parts completely baron of all the Second World's offerings. *Ike was certain this was her?*

The features seemed true, but as he read her body language and searched what he could of her mind, there wasn't anything he could find. He hadn't seen Trinity in years, but the hair was the same and she was beautiful. As beautiful as wood fairy could be.

He didn't answer her question. "It's a shame you've been robbed of your identity," he said instead.

The man really seemed pained to look at her now. *What did he mean? Robbed of identity? Were these guys trying to take her identity for credit card fraud? Was that even possible?* Skye's thoughts were straying with the nerves as she tried to recite her social security number in her mind. *Bad news, I don't have any money.*

He was too curious not to stare. He edged closer to her. The man focused his eyes on her back. He wasn't disappointed not to see anything.

She followed his moves. *Could he see where she was digging? Did he notice her palms? Why was he checking out her back and shoulder blades?* Skye tried another question wanting him to leave or at least back away, "Who are you?"

This man with old eyes and middle-aged build was letting out a combination of a sigh and a menacing laugh together. "Who am I? Oh, young Skye, I believe I am what your kind call *grandfather.*"

Then, as if he regretted his own words, the man left the tent. Skye couldn't process anything. It was all lies, it *had* to be all lies. Who Olli was, who this man was. The lies were making her feel stupid and sick.

Glad the man left so soon, she didn't give it much time before she pulled the fork from under her bottom and brushed the jacket to the side. With more energy she fought through the stinging and the blood and dug into the dirt around the tent post deeper and faster than before.

It was hard to judge what time it was, but outside it seemed to be getting brighter. The tent wasn't getting much warmer, but the constant digging was making her hot. If the guy was her grandfather, the least he could've done was bring her some food and water. She placed her hands down in the shallow hole around the tent's post. It had to be the bottom ridge of the pole.

Absently Skye had been listening to the conversation outside by the two men in the strange language. The constant banter had seemed to stop. This may be the only chance she was going to get. With both hands she clasped them around the pole and lifted slightly. The material was heavier than she imagined it to be, but Skye didn't have to lift very high or hold it for very long. It was just enough to shimmy her bonds down the pole and underneath the ridge. Carefully, she nested the pole back into the hard earth, stabilizing the post.

As she celebrated her freedom from the tent, the ground around her reverberated, shaking the tent fabric over top of her. She held the fork boldly in her hand. There was loud shouting and a bustling of horses outside. *What was going on? Did they know she was trying to escape?*

A shadow approached through the tent's entrance. The flap to the tent flipped back open. Skye recoiled as far back into the small space as she could. It was difficult not to reveal she wasn't attached to the tent pole anymore.

The shoulders, the eyes, his hair. It was all she could do not to leap forward and stab him with the fork.

Through the entrance of the tent stooped Olli.

She wasn't shy anymore. She was angry. "You make me sick, and you think you can just do this to people. What's wrong with you?" she said. Skye wasn't paying attention to the racket outside. She'd been wanting to scream at him since the Homecoming Dance for abandoning her. When he appeared on the train tracks, she later wished the train would've just hit him, erasing Olli from her life. But she knew that was a lie.

Yet, why didn't she strike him? He placed out his left hand, holding it with his palm upright, "Skye, we need to go."

She didn't grab his hand. Mostly because she was still

trying to act like she was tethered to the tent. *Didn't he know her hands were bound?* There was something different about Olli. *Was it his clothes throwing her off?* He was wearing a thick brown leather coat and tan trousers. Those were his same brown shoes though. It wasn't what he would typically wear to school, and it wasn't what he was wearing last night in the woods.

"You don't understand," Olli gritted his teeth, like he wanted to be saying something else, "we need to get out of here. We aren't going to be able to hold them off very long."

"Hold who off? What's going on?" Skye was livid and didn't care to go anywhere with Olli. Then she saw it, along his waistband somewhat covered by his long coat was a ridiculous-looking sword.

Growing impatient, Olli said, "You aren't safe with these people." Skye laughed inside: *safe* was the wrong description, "We have to go."

"These people. You mean *you*?" Skye was disgusted. Lies, lies, and more lies. *A sword, really? What a weirdo. Was this some strange medieval reenactment they were caught in?*

"What, no!" Olli crinkled his face. He reached out his hand again more forcefully, "Why are you acting like this? I'm trying to rescue you."

"Rescue, that's hilarious, it really is," this was getting old and there was only so much bitter sarcasm Skye could dish out. Whether this was fake or real it no longer mattered. It was time to leave.

While Olli had been talking, Skye had been waiting for the right moment. When he had gotten far enough into the tent, she thrust the cup and pot into his direction. She saw him raise his arms to block his face as she darted outside the tent. As she exited, she flung the fork back at him just for good measure.

It was as far as she went. Outside, things were burning. People were fighting with swords, bursts of blue fire, and strange geometric glass bottles were whizzing about. *What in the hell was going on?* Skye tried to turn back and duck for cover in the tent. She ran right into his chest. Olli wrapped his arms around her body, but not to restrain her. It was more of a protective hug. Skye held her bound arms to her chest, helpless. It felt too good to resist.

A tall lean girl with light brown braids spotted Olli and came closer, "You both need to get out of here. I only have about half a dozen or so blasts left. Adam is doing all he can to keep what's left of the watchmen back. We're going to have to retreat soon."

The new girl threw Olli a brown leather bag. "Would you be careful with that?" Olli caught the side bag and slung it carefully over his head. The girl's braids flung left and right as she ran back towards the fighting.

Skye looked out and found who she was talking about holding out a sword. What was his name again? Adam? Whoever this Adam was, he seemed very skilled. He stabbed one man effortlessly and was holding his ground well. The sword wasn't very funny anymore. It was real, and they were really killing people. There were at least three other dead bodies scattered around the small camp.

The girl was helping Adam fend off the other man. What was his weapon? Was the other guy holding a stick? A magic stick? Skye couldn't bring herself to call it a *wand*. All she could picture was a black rod with a white tip. There was no bunny appearing from the end of this wand, only death.

It was hard not to buy into the lies or was this a light show... special effects? Her eyes strayed from the fighting as she scanned around the charred grass and bare shrubs. Skye didn't see the old man claiming to be her grandfather anywhere, dead or alive. *Where had he gone?* There wasn't much choice but to follow Olli. She could be mad at him later. If he was going to get her out of here alive there wasn't anything she could do to protest. There was a stone pillar with Buckwheat tied off with a long rope. It was good to see he wasn't harmed. She brushed his mane with her shackled arms, pulling away the leaves and burs. Buckwheat seemed to relax his tense muscles at her touch.

Skye jumped when she saw the rope tied around Buckwheat's neck start to move. It seemed to be untying itself. Then the small fantastical figure appeared. He had a little hat and green foliage on his backside. His coat looked like it would fit a doll and the shoes reminded her of an elf. Dream.

He stood looking back at her, realizing she was staring. "Aye, your father is going to kill me."

There wasn't room for questions. Olli was talking to the small creature or was it a very small person with odd wings? Did she hear him correctly? This little man knew her father?

Olli helped her get onto the horse's back, and Buckwheat knew to kneel gently. Buckwheat wore a strange saddle and a rather intricate harness. He seemed just as eager to get away from this place as Skye. Skye held onto Buckwheat's mane with her blistered hands. If she wanted to get away this was her chance. It wouldn't be difficult to command Buckwheat to kick back and leave this craziness. But where would she go? Just off the landscape she could survey by normal eyesight nothing appeared to look familiar. There was no telling where they were. It seemed a long way away from town nowhere near the farm or even the Grabers' place, and daylight was fading away.

There weren't a lot of places Skye knew outside of Alfaro. Still, there had to be a gas station or motel somewhere nearby. Right? Skye stopped imagining a diner as hot ash fell on her shoulders and rested on Buckwheat's backside.

The soldier-looking man was still battling the girl and the boy named Adam. There were blue sparks flying from the stick as bursts of light contacted the blade of Adam's sword. Another missed his head by an inch, striking the tree behind to the ground like a bolt of lightning. A third flash of blue ran into the girl's chest, knocking her down.

Skye was startled suddenly as she heard Olli shout, "Julianna!" Olli bolted away from the horse and ran to help Adam and Julianna. Instead of his sword, Olli drew out a dagger. The tip was not metal. It looked as if it were made of stone or slate. Though Skye didn't know it, it was heavier than any metal made on earth. A piece of rare meteor had been sculpted to fit the blade of the dagger for King Benevolence in the 1500s. It had been passed down for generations to now be in Olli's procession.

Cliffton shook his head sadly. They were never getting out of here alive.

It was something Skye would've never pictured Olli doing at home. He seemed so awkward and un-athletic. This boy in front of her—more like a young man—was leaping into the air naturally. Olli passed the girl, Julianna, who lay motionless. He then tackled the man with the wand to the ground. The stick rolled out of the man's grasp. They wrestled as he pulled back his arms, then rolled several feet on the ground. Their intertwined legs and arms were thrashing about. Then, as fast as he'd ran off, Olli was atop the man forcing the short dagger into his chest. The man stopped moving and then a wisp of gold light seemed to escape from his chest. He was dead. All Skye could think of was how lucky Jason was to walk away from a fight with Olli the night of the dance, if in fact Olli really did attack him. He'd have been toast.

The opportunity came and went if she was going to leave. Skye was too focused on what she was witnessing. Did Olli just kill someone with his bare hands and a dagger? Would self-defense be enough to keep him away from prison?

Adam was shaking Julianna on the ground and then he laid her in his lap. She wasn't opening her eyes. Skye wanted to know if the girl was alive but couldn't bring herself to get down from Buckwheat's back. It seemed a great deal safer this high off the ground. Olli knelt beside Julianna and shoulder to shoulder with Adam. Julianna didn't seem to be breathing her body was lying still and the glass she had in her hand was sitting beside her limp arm.

Adam and Olli both startled as Julianna suddenly sat upright. At first, she seemed disoriented and then rapidly pulled herself together. She grabbed hold of the glass bomb and pushed Adam and Olli away who were crowding her trying to help her up off the ground. With one hand she brushed off her thighs. Julianna looked at the dead man nearby.

"How did you know he was carrying extra life?" Julianna was facing Olli as she asked.

"I didn't," Olli was being honest, "It was a lucky shot, besides Adam wasn't able to kill him."

"How much time do you think he had?" Julianna asked again, not looking away from the dead body.

"Maybe another, thirty or forty years, tops," Adam responded. Skye was straining to hear what was going on. There wasn't much proof, but she was pretty sure the Adam guy who was talking was blind. *What were they talking about?*

With a slow head shake Olli tried to make sense of it. "My guess is there wasn't any recent activity of Agenesis, but it's going to be a lot harder to tell. It may be best if we start tracking down some more of the Ureilite meteor. With any luck we may be able to harvest a piece of black diamond large enough for another blade. We will need more weapons that can kill these monsters with extra life."

The little fairy man was talking. "It'll be a wild goose chase if they think they're going to find any more black diamond. People cleaned the boundaries dry of the Ureilite stuff long ago."

Skye was listening but wasn't sure if he was talking to her or not, "Well I guess finding you was sort of a grasshopper in a bush. And look, here you are."

She wanted to ask the little man more questions. Like how he knew her father and how it was even possible for him to exist.

Not hearing the rest of their conversation Skye watched Olli heading back towards her. He hugged the girl

Julianna farewell and with Adam he did a slow knuckle fist bump where their fingers seemed to intertwine. It was a sign of goodbye with Adam. It seemed more formal than a handshake, but not as intimate as a hug. *Who were all these girls Olli was hanging around?*

Olli helped himself on top of Buckwheat's back behind Skye. He was hoisting a side bag over his shoulder. The sword, Skye noticed was hanging to the opposite side.

"You'll have to take her with you, I'm afraid there's no good place she'll be safe while you're away," the little creature was well-spoken.

"Shouldn't we just take her home?" Olli asked even though he already knew the answer.

"I'm afraid not," there could be others who follow you through. There's not time to take her home and get to the lighthouse. You're wasting time as it is."

"What about back up?" Olli asked, uncertain.

"Egh, the council will never approve troops. They'd probably detain the girl or worse..." Cliffton hesitated but chose to continue, "If your brother is involved it's not clear if there are others who aren't—how you would say—on our side."

Olli couldn't help the nagging tarot reading and dice. The tarot cards were usually accurate even coming from Julianna. She said he would not journey alone to the lighthouse. Originally, he thought Cliffton, Adam, or Julianna, possibly even Henry would join him on his trip. Olli just never imagined Skye would be the one to tag along.

"Cliffton," he pulled the heavy key out of his breast pocket, "I believe this should go back to you, then, at least until we know more."

"You're damn short of luck you got that back. It seems you and your brother might have that much in common," Cliffton reached out for the key.

"Never say that again," Olli flung up the hood of his leather jacket.

The little figure chortled then tucked the key to his side.

"Rest easy if you're hibernating before we make our return. Be sure to tell Adam at least of the key's location in case we need it?" Olli was pressing trying to get out of the campsite. The blast seemed to have stopped shaking the earth beneath their feet. It was time to go.

"Ride safe, you have precious cargo. If she doesn't make it back alive, you have my word, he will kill you." Olli eased up on the reins, thinking it was probably true. If they made it back alive, Clint would likely *still* hunt him down for putting his only daughter's life at risk.

Skye didn't ask questions. Soon she'd wake up. Her hands would stop hurting. Maybe she'd even be in her own warm bed. *Should she say goodbye to the little creature? What was his name again? Cliffton? Hibernating?*

Instead of a goodbye she forced a faint smile. Olli took the reins and wrapped an arm around Skye's waist. She still had her wrists shackled. Warm, now his touch felt real and her horse beneath her seemed alive enough. *Lighthouse? Skye had never seen a lighthouse in person before. Where was the closest lake or ocean to Alfaro? Why were they heading there on horseback?* Dream.

The air was cold and the light rain beginning to fall hurt her face too much to keep her head upright. The only cover her exposed hands had were the dark hairs on Buckwheat's mane. Her other jacket was still inside the tent. Olli seemed to read her mind as he draped his own body over her just a little more closely. As they sped away, the smoke billowed up in the sky and the last rays of sunlight faded into the darkening rain clouds.

Chapter 14
An Evening with Mr. Laux

Alfaro, First World

There were green shutters against an Irish Crème paint and old planters with brown flower stems along the white porch. There was a small eight-sided window at the center peak of the top story. The house was at least fifty years old like the house on the Hope farm. Some of the wooden floorboards on the porch were warped. The door had intricate wood along the door frame and a braided metal rail along the stairs.

It was a quaint two-story home just inside of the town limits of Alfaro. Leaves gathered in the corner of the deck along with a few stray pieces of trash. They wiped their feet on the faded welcome mat. Diane knocked first, and she pulled her long coat up to her cheeks and ears to block the bitter cold wind. When no one answered, she tried the stylized doorbell to the right of the forest green door. A faint *ding* echoed on the other side.

A day without seeing their daughter didn't worry them so much. She was a teenager and a grounded one. It would only make sense that she took her horse to a friend's house to get away, to retaliate. They called several parents without any of them saying they had seen Skye. Tiffany's mom was confused about the situation but glad she wasn't with her daughter. She'd heard about the crazy girl who ran off the bus almost killing herself.

On the second night, however, full panic swept through the Hope family's household. They searched the Grabers' property and the entire two acres of woods. Their little girl had grown out of sleeping in the barn years ago, but it didn't stop them from checking the hayloft both nights. Diane and Vince didn't even bother with the local police. In this world, it wasn't common for a girl and horse to just vanish without a trace... Deep down they knew this was worse—far worse—than what local deputies Dan Shepard and Gary Harding could fix.

They decided to dig deeper into the boy who they met only once. The young man named Olli seemed to enter their daughter's life as quickly as he left it. Maybe they should've caught the signs sooner? They could've moved farther away, packed their bags and changed jobs. Then, as soon as Diane got the old necklace out, against Vince's wishes, their daughter started doing crazy things. "Foreign exchange student" seemed like a terrible cover-up, and so obvious.

The entrance had been closed for a long time. It

should've been destroyed by Cliffton over seventeen years ago. Then again, *he* was supposed to destroy the mausoleum in the First World as well and yet never was able to bring himself to do it. A person from the Second World wouldn't know how to act. Maybe if he wasn't working so much, maybe if Diane could connect with Skye... a million maybes crushed Vince.

There was some movement on the other side of the curtain in the window next to the front door. Vince tried knocking again, shaking off an all-too-familiar guilt. No one would open the door.

"That's it, I'm not going to stand here all day," his hands twitched at his waistline.

"Wait," Diane held up her arm before Vince could knock down the door, "Wait, we're not out in the country anymore. Look around; there's cars and houses all over the place. They have neighbors; they might see."

"Fine," Vince wasn't wasting any more time standing in place. He briskly stomped down the porch steps along the side of the house, until he reached the side door along the back of the garage. "Better?" was all he said to his wife who was trying to keep up with his pace. Then Vince busted through the door at the side of the house within a few tries thrusting his whole body forward.

Diane couldn't help but roll her eyes at her husband's show of masculinity but was glad to not have to wait around much longer. She didn't like being out in the open in a strange part of town. Diane felt exposed standing outside the Laux's house.

They let themselves inside, stepping through the broken door hinges. The garage was dark and had two cars parked. The lights flickered on the front of a black BMW, almost blinding Diane and Vince who stood directly in front of it through the broken door. The door now lay at an angle in front of the car. Inside appeared a terrified middle-aged woman and two children in the back. The garage door whirred open. Diane and Vince let them leave in the black car, down the sloped driveway, bottoming out the car at the edge of the road. The car peeled off down the street. They hit a button to close the garage, already worried about the unwanted attention they had already called to the house. As the garage door met the concrete, Vince wasted no time pushing through a second door to enter in a narrow kitchen.

"What is the meaning of this? I told him everything he wanted to know. I don't have anything else to give. I swear I didn't know it would come to *this*. I wasn't aware of what I was dealing with, or truly *who*, my mistake."

A disheveled Mr. Laux stood in his bathrobe with flannel pajama bottoms and slippers. There was still half-eaten breakfast on the stove and dishes started in the soapy sink. He held a long gun in his reaching hands. *Would a normal bullet be able to kill the intruders?*

"Sit down, we're not here to harm you or your family. We— we just want to talk." Vince paused, trying to read Mr. Laux's mannerisms. "And for god's sake, put that away."

Vince was enraged but curious as to what Mr. Laux was talking about. He might be their only link to finding their daughter. Mr. Laux lowered the hunting rifle he had in his hands.

Diane sat beside Vince on one side of the family's kitchen table, and Mr. Laux sat colorless on the opposite side, twiddling his thumbs nervously. He laid the gun on the stained table beside his cold morning tea not far from his trembling fingers.

As best he could, Vince suppressed his aggression because it was the right thing to do. Give Mr. Laux a chance to plead his case.

On second thought, he couldn't wait, and he pressed Mr. Laux to talk, "Where is she?"

"I don't know," Mr. Laux stammered, "All I know is I left the Second World twenty years ago and sought asylum in the First World. I wanted nothing to do with them. There are papers to prove I'm a citizen along with my family. My family knows nothing about that terrible, loathsome place."

Vince believed most of what Mr. Laux was telling him, "What about the boy? The exchange student?" his hands were twitching.

Diane added, "He wasn't from here, was he? He was like us, yes?"

"I didn't know who he was. He claimed he was trying to permanently close the entrance in Webb Cemetery. He seemed like a good kid, he knew a lot about Gresham and Yodére Forest."

"How did he know who you were?" Vince asked.

"An old friend—or who I thought was a friend—gave him my contact information. He used to visit before the entrance was locked."

"It was more than locked," Vince tried to cut him off, but he knew it wasn't blown to pieces like it was supposed to have been.

"The fool I was, I believed him." Mr. Laux was almost talking to himself, "I didn't realize who his family was... what his real intentions were..."

"Who was he? I don't think we ever got a last name, just Olli..." Diane pictured the boy: polite, handsome, and a liar.

Mr. Laux seemed to second guess telling them, still torn with his own interactions. The first few months with the boy he seemed like an ordinary teenager. He was just full of hormones and always borrowing money. Then just this week he came storming into his house threatening to kill his whole family if he didn't give him directions to the Hope family farm. *The boy should've already known that, he'd been there several times.*

"Loucentious, Olli Loucentious, the next living heir to the throne of Gresham and proprietor of the Château de Beaucoup."

Diane wasn't sure whether she should be alarmed or not. When they left the Second World, the wood fairies weren't necessarily enemies of Kalli and Helge Loucentious. *Had they lost their lives the night they themselves fled the Second World? Who had won the deadly final battles of the war? The Château de Beaucoup survived, perhaps the humans had won... and the milkweed pixie Cliffton was surely alive? Still... what was a human doing with the key to the First World? What business did he have with their daughter?*

"I know who you are, I know *what* you are." Mr. Laux tried not to shake, "Four years ago, I saw you at freshman orientation with your daughter. Is she why you left?"

He was getting too personal. Vince didn't know this man outside of him being a teacher at the high school. Aside from his connection with this boy he hadn't known he was from the Second World until today.

Mr. Laux was speaking again. This time it was a

combination of French and Latin, "Le Monstre." Mr. Laux spat at Vince's face.

It was going to be difficult to convince Mr. Laux to look past his old life. The man Mr. Laux was imagining didn't exist anymore.

The teacher turned to Diane, "And *you*," he flicked his nose in a sign of disgust, "how could you abandon your kind for this?" Mr. Laux gestured a disapproving head nod, eyeing Vince up and down with repugnance.

She was already ashamed for not recognizing him earlier. He would have lived within the colony. Did he lose family? Were there others who left their home living among humans here and she was too blind with her own problems to see?

"You left too," she couldn't hold back; his judgments weren't fair. Tears threatened to fall down her pale cheeks.

"I was a gatherer, not a *queen*. Not someone who could stop what was happening, not someone with beings' lives in my hands," Mr. Laux's hands were making a fist against his kitchen table. He'd repressed a lot of anger the last few years.

"Your wings, though?" Diane wasn't thinking. She hadn't been in contact with her own kind in so long. As rude and unwelcoming as Mr. Laux was, he was a part of home.

"I sold them at a reasonable price for safe passage, *not* to his kind," Mr. Laux gave an off-putting look towards Vince. "I sold them to a human woman who braved the boundaries of the Château de Beaucoup. I'd imagine it was just a few months before you two lost hope. I have no regrets."

"Yours? Did he take them?" Mr. Laux was lavishing the

unrest. He'd waited almost four years to confront them for their lies and betrayal.

Vince interjected, "Now you've gone too far. I think it's time you tell us where our daughter is, and we'll be going."

"I think you already know the answer, Mr. *Teagardin*. The question is: what are you going to do about it? If it's not already too late."

Chapter 15
Sink or Swim

Preadence, Second World

Skye moved over to her side. Dirt was underneath her palms. Her arms were still shackled. Not a dream. She had been afraid of that. The smoke was going out of the fire, just a few black and white coals remained in the small fire pit. They were glowing ghostly orange against the morning light. Unlike the last time she woke up in a strange place, there was no tent protecting her from the foreign elements.

Olli and Skye hadn't talked. She was exhausted and collapsed on the earth almost as fast as the two dismounted her horse Buckwheat the night before. Skye wasn't ready to talk. There was too much to try to wrap her brain around. If this wasn't all a dream, what *was* it?

The pain in the empty pit of her stomach was making her want to eat everything nearby. Now, even grass looked good enough to eat. Her mouth was so dry she could barely stand it. Water.

A few yards away, she found Olli sitting with his back turned towards her on a large downed tree log. His brown coat was encapsulating her. She went to move but it was bitterly cold away from the hot coals. Her body was shaking, not just because she was chilly, but because she needed to eat and drink.

It was tempting to roll back over and sleep. Light-headed she forced herself to sit up. There was a small stream on the opposite side of where Olli sat. She noticed Buckwheat was getting a drink from the cold running water, and a rope tied him off to a tree. Holding the jacket around her shoulders she went to the right side of Buckwheat and leaned down carefully over the slanted edge, steadying one arm on Buckwheat's towering legs. Buckwheat's body was radiating a glow of warmth.

Why didn't Olli have any bottled water or something? After about a dozen handfuls of water later, Skye's hands were pruning and turning purple. Her heart lurched when Olli walked over to her side. He reached out touching the shackles. "We need to figure out how to get those off you."

Skye didn't look up, refusing to make eye contact with Olli. The water had given her some strength and with the strength came anger.

"What in the hell is going on?" Skye was as blunt and to the point as she could possibly be.

The burst of excitement was tiring. It was all she could do to not tumble back into the shallow water behind her.

Olli caught her before she could somersault down the sloped earth into the freezing stream and be whisked away. She brushed him off. "I don't need your help," Buckwheat neighed defensively but kept drinking, "I need something to eat. Those friends of yours didn't really have the greatest manners with their guests."

"Not exactly friends," Olli was still reserved, but a part of him was holding back a laugh.

"Nothing's funny right now, I could keel over any minute," Skye was exaggerating, but she really wasn't doing so well. Maybe she needed to rest?

He couldn't hold it in anymore he let a laugh roll off his cheek. Skye shoved him in the chest, and felt dizzy all over again, "I'm serious; get these things off of me so we can go get some french fries or something."

Olli reached into the bag he had slung over his shoulder and pulled out a small wooden bowl with a carved spoon. "I need a little more time to figure the chains out, but for now I do have some food. Here, take this."

Skye reached out for the bowl and spoon, "Oh, thank god. You don't happen to have any chocolate cereal in that bag, do you?"

Another laugh nervously escaped his body, "You are kind of cute when you're mad."

More irritated. *Who was this new version of Olli and what made him so confident?*

"Here," Olli reached out his hands taking back the bowl. He turned it on its side and started to swirl the small wooden spoon around the bottom of the bowl clockwise three times. Something brown and mushy started to appear out of thin air inside of the bowl.

She blinked again just to make sure her brain wasn't

making things up. The air wafted cinnamon. Olli watched her closely. He handed the bowl back to her and lifted the spoon up to her mouth. "Try this, it's banana bread pudding," he kind of seemed sorrowful, "too bad it's the only thing the reckoning bowl can conjure. Julianna is still learning the basics."

Who cared how it got there? She'd ask Olli more about this Julianna girl later. Right now, there was food—real food—in her hands. Anything would've tasted good, but as Skye opened her mouth the glop of the banana bread pudding slid off the spoon in Olli's hand and onto her tongue. The sensation was wonderful. It was warm too, like it had just come out of an oven. The pudding was sweet, wholesome, and rich. She begrudgingly accepted the spoon and slowly ate the rest of the pudding without Olli's help. When it was all gone, she turned the spoon three times in the bottom of the bowl as she had seen Olli do and more pudding appeared.

He stared as Skye scarfed down a second helping of banana bread pudding from the reckoning bowl. She was so stubborn sometimes. "I don't think I can break through these chains with just my sword. I would've tried, but I didn't want to wake you. Besides, I can't deny it has been a lot easier to keep tabs on you this way."

"What does that even mean?" Skye asked as she sat down the bowl on the fallen log and leaned up against the tree. She might've eaten too much too fast. Her stomach gurgled. She swallowed hard, refusing to get sick in front of Olli.

He was still edging entirely too close. Her stomach was starting to settle, "It means, I missed you."

The more self-assured Olli didn't ask like he did in the

limousine the night of the Homecoming Dance. This time the more confident Olli just leaned in, pulled her waist closer to him, and kissed her. Skye didn't push him away. She pulled her shackled arms up and over his head, resting her forearms on his broad shoulders and kissing him back. As mad and confused as she was, she'd also missed him terribly.

Alfaro, First World

Diane and Vince stood at the gate to Webb Cemetery. Neither of them had been back here since the night they left almost eighteen years ago. There were several new rows of grave plots, but the cemetery itself must've been almost all filled. A few sections were added in the back where the new gravel was laid on the paved path. Diane and Vince left the car parked and running at the side of the road.

Each stone they passed was the grave marker of a person who died decades before their lives in the First World. Vince looked at the names he didn't stop but took note of the grave they saw the night they left. The last name Hope was written across the mossy top. There were no new flowers in the cracked cement planters on each side. This grave gave them their chosen last name here. *Was hope all they were left with yet again? Hope for their daughter's safety. Hope the entrance would be open. The hope that Mr. Laux was lying?*

Vince stood facing the mausoleum like an opponent. Behind him, Diane held his arm anxiously. Her touch was filled with a gentle ease.

The entrance should've been destroyed. He trusted

Cliffton with his life, his family's life. *Why hadn't he demolished it as they had the other four? Did he betray him? Was his dear little friend even still alive? Had he run into trouble the night they fled?* Vince was never able to destroy the entrance. With a full investigation of the two dead children found near the mausoleum and a missing child, he had no choice but to stay as far away from Webb Cemetery to avoid suspicion.

His years had been so full raising a child, beginning a new life, and trying to save the sick and the dying in this world. The thoughts never had time to seem possible. Now they were all flooding his consciousness. It was his fault she was taken. Vince shook the memory of the two lifeless bodies they left resting almost exactly where they now stood.

Vince braced himself as he reached forward to open the door to the mausoleum.

Preadence, Second World

Too much was still confusing. Incredible. The landscape was nothing like Skye had ever seen. There were hills behind them, large trees, and was it her or was it getting warmer? They were traveling through a country Olli referred to as Preadence. Skye had never heard of it. *Was this all just more of Olli's lies?*

Just like she had never heard of reckoning bowls or winged people small enough her cat could ingest with one bite. What did Olli call the little man, a milkweed pixie? *Where was Maiji?*

They had packed up and were both on Buckwheat's back again. "Olli, if you weren't the one who took me from my house, who were those people?"

It was a lot for Olli to be so forward with Skye. He'd been lying and hiding his identity for months. Now, the time still didn't feel right to share everything, "Unfortunately, I have a twin brother named Ike, and I believe the girl you are describing is his girlfriend Victoria. They've made quite a mess around here."

Skye thought back to the night she sat on the swings next to Olli. He told her he had a brother but never mentioned he was a twin, "Was it your brother who was on the train tracks too?"

Olli pulled the reins back on Buckwheat so he would come to an abrupt stop. "When was this?"

"A little over a week ago," Skye left out the muddy details. He didn't need to know she about died trying to save someone she thought was him or how she had to endure hours of counseling because everyone thought she was crazy. Skye was beginning to think she was crazy too. Maybe when she got her hands on her phone again she could look up signs of schizophrenia.

He guided Buckwheat forward trying to piece things together in his head. *Just how long were Ike and Victoria in the First World?* The days were adding up in his head. *Three weeks—what could they have possibly been doing for three weeks in the First World? Why did Ike lie to Olli and say he was vacationing in the mountainside?*

"How can I be sure you are you and not your brother Ike?" Skye was so convinced Ike was Olli both times she hadn't thought to find something different about them.

Skye was pretty sure this was Olli. The way he kissed her was the same. He was still different than the last time she'd seen him. Here he was cockier, but she'd seen the rage in him and the power to kill like she'd seen in the limo.

The question bothered Olli. Many people struggled to tell the difference between his twin brother and himself. It was a characteristic that in his younger years he enjoyed. It often got him out of things he didn't want to do, and it was helpful if he needed to pawn some mischief off on his brother. Some of the council members could tell them apart, but not everyone. Henry had always possessed the knack since birth, but he *had* changed both their diapers. Adam always knew, not leaving many others who could. Olli was hoping Skye would be one of those few. Maybe he was being unfair; after all, she hadn't known he had an identical twin.

"As for looks we are too comparable. Ike has a scar on the bottom of his left foot and small birthmark under his right underarm." Olli rambled the dissimilarities he'd pointed out to hundreds.

Now it was Skye who observed Olli. She cut Olli off, "And you, you like to take your left hand through your hair when you get nervous. You were also throwing the football around with your left hand. Is Ike right-handed?" Ike had used his right hand when she saw him in the wood beside her house.

Olli thought about this because he'd just done it a few moments ago. *Did he really brush his hand through his hair every time he was nervous?* He resisted the urge to do it again as she finished. She leaned closer to him.

"Yes," was all Olli could say. He was left-handed and Ike was right. Ike used to mock him because he said he would always be 'right.'

He smiled. Maybe she did have her own way of

knowing.

"Can I ask you one more question," Skye was hesitant kind of playing with her right band.

"Anything," and Olli truly meant it. He owed her at least that much.

"When I was back at that camp," Skye pictured the inside of the tent awakening alone and cold, trapped. *Camp* didn't seem right, maybe more a jail, but she stuck with it, "at the camp there was a man who came and visited me."

Olli followed along trying to speed up Buckwheat enough but not too much so they couldn't carry a conversation. Adam had worked out a shortcut through the eastern Tromperie Desert. They were crossing territories Olli had been forbidden to enter as a child. His father King Helge Loucentious never took him or his brother through these parts. The enemies here were too unpredictable. There was no secret truce as they shared with the wood fairies in Yodére Forest.

He pursed his lips, prepared to tell her who this man was or who he thought it was. The trouble was he'd believed it was a man named Fideleroi, but now Cliffton thought it was Charles Teagardin. Olli could only describe this man as pure evil and long dead.

"He said he was my grandfather. Is that possible?"

Alfaro, First World

"Two to three weeks!" Vince blasted, slamming the keys on his desktop computer.

Izzy, the intern from the hospital, was at the Hope farm trying to help Vince and Diane get their things around to get a passport online. The small outburst didn't bother her in the slightest. Her own father was a heavy drinker and it wasn't out of the usual for her to witness Vince Hope have a fit of anger at work every now and again. It was especially common after the loss of a patient or when he confirmed a misdiagnosis. As an intern, you just learned to look past some things.

Diane and Vince weren't too much older than her own parents. Izzy would've expected them to handle the technology without much help, but without their own daughter to work with them, maybe it was harder for the couple. They had explained they were trying to book a graduation present for their daughter overseas. *Must be nice to have that kind of money*, thought Izzy. Her parents got her a stuffed animal and a black marker for her graduation present just over two years ago.

She was quick to answer, squinting at some of the fine print, "Here it says if you pay extra you can try to get it expedited if the other paperwork goes through. Anywhere from twenty-four hours to ten days."

As they finished their paperwork and got their official identification downloaded for Diane, Vince, and Skye Hope, Diane sent Izzy home with a few dollars and a couple dozen eggs for her troubles.

The plan was for Diane to stay in Alfaro and keep monitoring the mausoleum entrance in Webb Cemetery for any activity. Vince had used his wand for the first time in years to create a small security device at the mausoleum using a couple of green emeralds Diane managed to carry through with the rest of her few belongings from the Second World. They would use the charms to send an alarm back to the corresponding emerald in Diane's pocket.

If and when their passports were approved, Vince would head to the other four entrances to see if by some miracle one was opened. If they weren't then at least he would know he succeeded at closing them properly and would have just the one entrance to watch. Neither he nor his wife could sit around and just wait for something to happen. They would have to try and get back through to the Second World somehow.

The other reason they wanted Izzy's help today was so he could break the news to her he had to assign her another RN at the hospital with whom she could finish her internship. At first Izzy was upset; she was worried she wouldn't be able to complete the semester. Vince made sure he got someone good to replace him. Nurse Arnold was a seasoned veteran at the hospital and although she was boring and some of her practices were outdated, she would do Izzy justice and possibly give her an even better chance at passing her boards than Vince could.

As much of the First World practices he'd picked up on, there was still a great deal of healing he did with his magic other than from actual treatment. The hospital approved the six-week paid sabbatical, and Diane would remain working at the daycare. It would be safest for her and the best place to keep an eye on the young children, in case anyone who had the key to the entrance was going to try Agenesis. If she kept working, it would raise less alarm with how strange they'd been acting. As for Skye, Vince forged a doctor's slip for a diagnosis of Mononucleosis.

As they waited for the passports to arrive, they packed everything Vince might need for his international trip. They practiced old enchantments, found ways to disclose his wand in his carry-on luggage, and prepared themselves for the worst. He desperately wished he had kept his sword. If the entrances were sealed, it didn't mean those who were caught on the other sides weren't angry they were closed off all these years. They could be living nearby and watching closely for activity like he and his wife were doing with the Webb Cemetery entrance.

He worked endlessly, researching the locations for any sign of activity. They needed a place to start. Where was there most likely to be a breach in entry? Together he and Diane drew out where odd happenings took place in articles, tabloids, and entrances he was certain were destroyed. There wasn't much to go by, which was good news. Most sightings of Second World creatures were prior to the internet.

It seemed their greatest chance was between two entrances. There was the entrance in the Ruins of Benevolence, not likely leading to where Skye was. From the information they gathered from Mr. Laux was they were humans from the Château de Beaucoup who had access to the key, that'd put him hundreds of miles from where he'd need to be. Not to mention he'd have to explain why he was suddenly traveling to the Middle East. The second possible entrance was in Scotland. There wasn't any exciting news to support the entrance being opened, but it was one of the only entrances he knew wasn't properly sealed.

Preadence, Second World

"I'm not saying I don't believe you," Olli stopped to take off another layer of clothing. He assisted Skye gingerly off the backside of the towering horse. The weather was starting to get hot as they neared the outskirts of Tromperie, "I'm having trouble believing it myself."

Charles Teagardin was believed to have died twenty-five years ago. Olli was processing again. The last two days were a lot. He continued to be astounded by how much Skye so willingly took in. She was so accepting of the mysteries the Second World had to offer.

"I have no doubt he is who he says, but you have to understand your grandfather is not a good person. He was the leader of the sorcerers for centuries. They almost wiped out entire populations of beings under his reign." Olli did not live during the reign of Charles Teagardin, but he knew the stories well.

Sorcerers? It didn't matter to Skye if this man was telling stories, she wanted to know who her grandfather was. It was a topic she always fantasized about. Skye didn't have family. Her father said he grew up within the foster system and was never adopted. Her mother claimed to have lost both her parents as a young adult. The only family Diane would admit to having nearby was her own husband. End of story.

Skye wanted to take off her thin jacket but couldn't figure out how to get it off with her arms bound together. She hoped it would get cold again. She tore off what she could of the sleeves and used a piece of the fabric to stuff under her metal cuffs to give her wrists some relief.

"So where has he been all this time? Even my parents said he died long before I was born."

"I don't know," said Olli, and he really didn't. As legend had it, Charles Teagardin was killed in battle and his oldest son was sworn in as the successor almost immediately following his death. *Why would Charles Teagardin fake his own death? Was Charles Teagardin the alias of Fideleroi? It would make sense.*

What of his new appointed heir? *Wouldn't Skye still be next in line for the throne? Was that why he didn't kill her? Did he think she would be on his side?*

If Charles Teagardin was meeting the shipment at the lighthouse, this little mission could be far more dangerous than he originally imagined, especially with his new traveling companion. He needed to get those chains off her if she wanted any sort of a fighting chance. The shortcut through Tromperie Desert up ahead may be their only chance to get to Lighthouse Point before the others.

"I can't explain everything to you now, but I promise in time, I will." Olli was pulled something else out of his side bag. This time it was a small round glass jar. Inside there was a blue and pink mist. She doubted this mysterious item would be food and was curious how something so small would help her get out of the restraints. Skye was mesmerized by the tiny sparkling galaxy dancing inside. The two moved away from Buckwheat and placed the chains across a rock. He gave her his coat to shield her face. Skye had nothing to lose. She desperately wanted the chains off her.

Slowly Olli uncorked the bottle and placed two drops on each end of the shackles and jumped out of the way.

There was no sound, but the blast was enough to send Skye on her back. When she sat up most of the shackles were gone and some of the metal pieces were fizzing from the heat as well as parts of her skin. The right shackle popped off entirely and the left just had two links left dangling like a bracelet. She rubbed her right wrist. It burned but it felt liberating.

"You couldn't have tried that sooner?" Skye was only in a little pain and was happy to peel her jacket off to get some relief.

Olli let the smart-alecky response go, he was just glad it didn't hurt her too much. The little explosion could've gone terribly wrong.

"What was that?" Skye asked.

"The powder is a combination of a few enchantments we use in our orb blasts. It's similar to gun powder in the First World. However, this is very potent and very temperamental."

Skye nodded like she understood. What she was really hearing was she could've been blown to pieces.

Olli pulled out the map from his pocket and laid it out on the stone pillar next to the large rock he blasted the chains on. Skye watched Olli put the stopper back in the small jar and carefully stick it back in the sack. She looked at the old paper he spread out on the stone pillar.

There was fancy cursive writing next to what must've been Olli's chicken scratch handwriting. She could make out the words *Gresham*, *Yodére Forest*, and found the familiar word *Preadence* right of the center in the map. *Why didn't Olli just use his cellphone? Was there no reception out this far?* Olli pointed to the place Preadence just as she found it.

"We are about here," he slid his finger up above the word to the path freshly drawn. "We're trying to get just north to here," Skye read the place he'd stopped at. There looked like small waves scribbled and a small picture of a lighthouse was drawn in sepia ink.

"The quickest way to get to Lighthouse Point is

through the farthest Western Region of the Tromperie Desert. It's likely whoever is meeting the shipment there has been taking the easier terrain and keeping inside the boundaries of Preadence."

Skye said, "So, what makes you think we can make it through a desert?"

This dream-like state made it easier to be honest. She thought of all the things she knew about deserts. It really wasn't a place she wanted to be. Skye tried to leave all reason out of her questioning and to just exist. Her body felt like it was traveling through a time machine.

"Well, I've ridden your horse before," Olli admitted. "He's the descendant of a very prized breed in Gresham. I think he can make the journey. Thanks to Julianna's reckoning charms we should have enough food and water to make it through without stopping as long as Buckwheat is up to it the journey."

"It was you who took Buckwheat out of the barn? Why would you do that? I was terrified to do chores for weeks," Skye was busy looking at the rest of the map. It didn't seem like it covered anything she knew. Where was the United States, Russia, or even Australia? There didn't seem to be any countries, cities, or states she recognized. Nowhere did she see Alfaro.

"He was one of the reasons I knew you were who I was looking for. Him and your mother's necklace," Olli said.

"What does my mother's necklace have to do with anything?"

"I told you, I'll share everything when the time is right." Skye rolled her eyes. *Just when would that be?*

She'd had enough. She grabbed the rope along Buckwheat's reins and started walking back the way they came from.

He quickly stuffed the map back in his pocket and started walking after Skye, "Come on what do you think you're doing? You don't know where you're going."

"I think it's time for me to go home. I don't want to go to your stupid lighthouse. If you're not going to tell me anything, I'd rather be with my parents who also don't think I should know anything." Skye's feelings and brain were playing a game of ping pong.

Whatever fog she'd been under after she'd been knocked out in the woods was lifting. If she wasn't going to wake up, she needed to get out of wherever this was and go home, get back to school, and maybe actually participate in counseling. With any luck, she could still graduate at the top of her class, go to college forget everything she knew about this boy who called himself Olli.

He was glad she had her backside turned as he slid his hand through his hair, before shouting. "I am Olli, first son of Helge and Kalli Loucentious, future King of Gresham. And you..." Skye had stopped walking, "You are Skye, daughter of Clint Teagardin, King of the Sorcerers, and Trinity Amadori, Queen of the Wood Fairies, future Queen of the very land we walk on and possibly even more, I can't be sure."

It was her turn to laugh, "Why would you say something like that?" Skye couldn't believe anything he said anymore. She still didn't turn around; she was looking ahead to the towering hills and vast landscape.

"Because it's the truth," Olli was trying so hard not to tell her his lineage—not that she knew any of their people's history.

"What difference does it make if I stay or return home? I want my life back. My simple, boring life." *Did she really mean that?* Skye took a few more steps, trying to breathe deep just when the air seemed to be getting thinner.

"You can't go home, not yet." Olli was shouting to her backside. Her hair flicking behind. Inside he knew he couldn't force her to want to stay. He himself questioned leaving the Second World, abandoning Gresham several times these past few months.

"What do you mean, I can't go home?" This time, Skye stopped walking away. She really had no idea which way the direction was to lead to home. Skye wasn't even sure which way the camp would be from where they were now.

"I don't mean you can't, not in the way Adam can't go home. He would die if he tried to go back through the mausoleum. I mean the entrance is locked. We thought it'd be safer this way. Leona Harlow said you have to come to the lighthouse with me or we could both die."

Skye didn't know what Olli meant by Adam not being able to go home. She didn't care about him, "Die? Open your eyes, I could've already been killed several times." Skye tried to straighten the lumps in her hair tightening her ponytail, "Who's this Leona Harlow?"

"She's an advisor for the Château de Beaucoup," Olli stretched the truth, really anyone who knew he was a regular with her would make fun of him. "Her life is dedicated to fortune-telling. It's rare for her to be wrong. You need to come for our safety. I can't let you go home yet."

Skye thought about this a moment. She didn't like not having a choice, "What if I told you, I've already been to the lighthouse with you?" Skye turned back, still trying to sort reality from lies. Somehow traveling alone with Olli didn't feel so out of place. She'd felt it and even seen some pieces.

"What do you mean?" Olli was completely thrown off by the statement. He hadn't been to any lighthouse with Skye before. They'd only been in the same places traveling together a handful of times and always in the First World.

The vision she had in her barn when she woke up covered in egg yolk was itching her memory. Maybe all these crazy things made sense in some strange way?

"I saw us, I felt us there, but I don't remember seeing any shipment. Just you, me and the sun setting over blue waves." Skye felt dumb after she heard herself say it, like trying to share a fond dream. Words couldn't quite explain what she'd seen and felt.

"You saw us together, in a vision?" Olli furrowed his brow. *What else had she seen?*

"I think so; it all started when I got hit with that football. I smelled the salt of the sea and then after you were in my barn, I fell from my hayloft."

Olli was genuinely concerned. Now he was more certain about Leona Harlow's prediction. They had to keep going. He felt safer and slightly more confident with Adam's route through the desert. There was a greater chance they would make it through alive if Skye's visions were accurate.

Skye signaled for Buckwheat to kneel as she climbed on top. Her mind was all mixed up. Olli was speechless; if she took off on Buckwheat, he would never be able to keep up with his speed. They'd never make it to Lighthouse Point, and he'd be stuck trying to retreat on foot. She didn't ride off. No, instead she turned Buckwheat around and put her hand out, helping Olli pull himself up onto Buckwheat's back. Skye knew she had to go now; she needed answers; she needed proof she wasn't crazy.

The truth was she liked Olli's company and she had no idea how to get back home. There was no way to tell if Buckwheat knew where to go either.

"Lead the way, prince," Skye said jokingly, as she rolled the word *prince* off the tip of her tongue.

"As you wish," mocked Olli, "my princess."

Chapter 16
Guardians

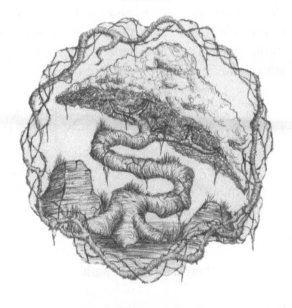

Gresham, First World

On the eighth day, their passports cleared, and Diane and Vince quickly spent a fair chunk of their life savings to pay for a one-way ticket to Scotland. He took three credit cards just in case he would have to take any additional flights and one single carry-on bag. Diane hadn't even pulled out of the airport's parking lot yet and was already feeling more vulnerable than ever.

Vince sat awkwardly on the plane next to a large woman wearing too much perfume and a man in a cheap suit who kept his legs in Vince's seat space. Vince had never flown before except for the few times he'd gone with Diane when she still had her wings. Heights didn't bother him, but he lacked trust in the First World's technologies. Being completely surrounded purely by humans was an adjustment Clint made years ago, but he still struggled with it sometimes. It wasn't unless they were incapacitated like they were at his work in the hospital that he felt comfortable. Looking around, his chances of getting away with sedating all the humans on the plane was not likely.

The man in the gray suit started talking about baseball. Wasn't it still technically football season in the United States? Vince neither wanted to hear about it nor did he care. This was going to a long nine hours. Vince placed his hand on the man's arm, releasing a silent enchantment through the man's body until he noticed his head fall into a deep sleep.

Preadence, Second World

Their last night outside of the desert, Skye and Olli settled in for dinner early. The landscape had drastically started changing from the green grass and colorful trees to the dry tall grass and ground full of cracked dirt. The plant life was curious. Some of the plants looked ordinary, while others couldn't possibly be real. The cacti and succulents were the most familiar. As they traveled onward, it was like experiencing many seasons in just a few days.

Insisting he was tired of Julianna's banana bread pudding Olli disappeared for about an hour. He left Skye at a quiet secluded area they made for camp. She was given the small dagger for protection. She thought it was funny because she had no idea if she would be able to use it even if the occasion called for it. He returned to the bare patch of land with a few berries that reminded Skye of large prunes and handful of strange glossy purple leaves.

She watched as he cooked the berries over the small fire until they puffed out into a shape and size of a kiwi with spikes. The outsides of the food were a crispy brown and inside they were soft pink. The fruit tasted like roasted almonds. Olli was wrapping the leaves around his and eating them together like a wrap. Skye did this only after eating two of the spongy nuts plain. As she got past the texture, she decided both were good.

"I haven't had these since I was a little kid," Olli said briefly reminiscing his youth, "We don't do any trading with Preadence anymore and few beings travel through the Tromperie Desert. They'd probably fetch a fair price in the market. I was lucky to find them," Olli talked about his find like he was just a Boy Scout trying to earn a badge on a camping trip.

"Just what exactly are they?" Skye was enjoying her fifth helping, unable to control her endless hunger.

Olli finished his wrap-like creation, "It's called amande rose, a tree that only grows in these warmer parts of Preadence. The leaves are purple when they're in full bloom. Look at this, when you crack open the pit," Olli took the small black dagger from Skye's side and popped open the hard center of the amande rose. He revealed a seed in the shape of a heart. He went on, "They used to be popular around our holidays. Very high protein, it'll be a good snack for the next couple of days in case we don't find anything else to eat. They're much better roasted than they are raw. I packed a few handfuls to take with us."

"Just how long will it take us to get through the desert?" Skye found her words out of place again. The only time she thought of a desert was when she was trying to spell *dessert*. Right now, she didn't want any more desert.

"It's about sixty miles of straight sand," Olli pointed using his dagger in his outstretched hand and popped a couple of the amande rose in his mouth as he continued to talk, "Some of the areas are flat and will make for quick riding. The rest have dips and crests of deeper, looser sand. It'll take at least two days of straight horseback riding."

Two more days? Skye was adding up the days in her head trying to figure out how long she'd been away from home. It was difficult to count without knowing how long she'd been unconscious. *Maybe a week? How were her parents handling her absence?* Skye wondered distractedly playing with a rip in the thigh of her pants.

For a moment she felt guilty only now thinking of her parents and worst of all with her parents came the thought of school. She looked back at her horse. "And you think Buckwheat will be able to make it that far without resting? He's never ridden through any sand before. Let alone for sixteen hours or more at a time."

"We're going to have to try. Any less and we might as well have taken the longer path around. That's about a hundred miles. Some of it is all rock. If you don't think Buckwheat will make it, then I trust your judgment." Olli seemed disappointed but sincere.

"I didn't say it because I don't think he can make the trip; I'm just not interested in risking his life or mine for that matter for whatever this is. He is my horse." Skye wanted to feel helpful. There were a lot of things out of her control right now.

"I would never," Olli stressed, "intentionally put either

of you in harm's way."

Skye thought his words were ironic. She remembered the football on the track in gym class and then about how he was really the only reason why she was stuck here in the first place.

"And what will we do for water?" Skye continued to probe, "I didn't see any oases on that map of yours."

"You have a quick eye, I'll give your stubbornness credit," Olli was reaching into his bag. He grabbed out a metal disk, "I've got something else to show you."

He sat the metal disk flat on the ground and then pulled up the sides. It was folded together like a collapsible telescope. When it was to full size it was about as big as a five-gallon bucket but looked more like a vase to Skye. He turned the rings on the large chalice until they became one solid vessel. It seemed made of brass.

"Here, look inside," he said. Skye obliged, curiously peering into the chalice.

"Now," he instructed, "take your hand," Olli continued as he raised her hand up to the rounded side of the chalice. He made her fold all her fingers into a fist and then he took her pointer finger to the rim of the old vessel. "Connect the circle one time around, clockwise."

So, she did, and he guided her hand the whole way around the top ring. There was a strange slurping noise and then just like the food in the reckoning boil, water appeared to rise from out of nowhere on the bottom of the empty brass container. *Was this somehow still a dream?* Was she supposed to add magician to the list of names she had for Olli?

"Did your friend Julianna make this for you like the bowl?" Skye still wasn't sure who Julianna was to Olli.

"No, no, no... water is a lot harder to conjure than food for some reason. This vessel is old, and the enchantment for it seems to be lost. I think it's been in the Château de Beaucoup since the time you would know from the First World as the Middle Ages. A man named Francisco Melzi was famous for his ability to make water appear. These water vessels are very hard to come by. A lot of them were destroyed or damaged in battles. A great deal of soldiers used to carry them. Others were forgotten and are probably used as regular cups or displayed in museums in the First World."

"First World?" Skye still couldn't talk to Olli as clearly as she could before. It was his normal English with the odd accent, but it was like a whole new dialect. "Why do you keep saying that?"

He sighed again forgetting she had no knowledge of anything, "The First World is where you live, but it's not where your parents are from, where we are now, the Second, is a space between the First and Third. There used to be a time when all beings could travel safely between worlds, but now not everyone can travel safely through. Some people lose their eyesight when they enter if they don't have enough blood of a Second World being. I'm not entirely sure how it knows. Old enchantments, I suppose. It's very bad if you try to return to the First World after entering the Second. You lose your soul and die."

"So where is the Second World exactly? Is it like a different dimension?" Skye was fishing for a reference she could relate to her knowledge of geography.

Olli couldn't really explain but thought he'd better try. To him the Second World was his home and the First was the strange foreign place. "It's more of a realm or extension of the world you live in. We coexist. A disclosed... layer almost... of reality."

Skye thought about this, trying to use a combination of 90s movies she'd seen to find a reasonable answer. She tried to settle for *alternate reality*. Yet, she was more concerned whenever she left here, the Second World, if the First World she knew would be back to normal?

"And the Third World?" Skye asked.

"The Third is even more complicated," Olli enlightened. He had never been to the Third World and didn't want to go there anytime soon, "The Third is a world which only souls can cross through to."

"So, death or an afterlife like a heaven?" Skye concluded.

"Yes," was all Olli could come up with.

She still didn't get it. How any of this was possible was baffling all logic she built inside school. The image of the blind man striking the soldiers at the camp were flashing through her memory. Is that what he meant by the man Adam not being able to return home. Was he from the First World too?

"Here drink up, we'll want to get ahead of the dehydration. Buckwheat should drink his fill when we're done too."

Jackson Field Airport, First World

The tarmac was slick this morning. A light freezing rain had rolled in at about four o'clock that same evening. On top of the delayed flight, the plane had yet to take off because of plane flaps freezing over. Vince looked down at his phone and switched the button from airplane mode since they weren't moving. He was desperate for any distraction and slightly regretted putting the hairy man beside him to sleep. He could use some senseless baseball banter to listen to if it meant keeping his mind off the delay. His phone suddenly vibrated vigorously in his hand. His wife was calling him along with missed text messages.

"Hello," Vince was glad to hear her voice even if the woman beside him was giving him an evil glare.

"The alarm, the alarm went off!" Diane was driving, as fast as she could toward Alfaro. The closest airport was in a town forty-five miles away. The emerald they used to detect the movement at the entrance was warm to the touch.

"What!" Vince tried not to sound too startled. He cupped his hand around the phone. He wanted to bolt up out of his seat and scream. Instead, Vince settled for, "Are you sure?"

"Come back and get me," he said, "you can't go alone. We don't know who's gotten through the entrance or how long they'll be here."

Diane slammed on her breaks, swerving left and right on the thin ice and pulled over on the side of the highway. Shaking, she flipped on her hazard lights. She had no idea his plane hadn't taken off yet. He had already missed several messages and the last two calls went straight to voicemail.

"What do you want me to do? I'm at least twenty minutes from the airport." Diane was at a standstill; several vehicles were whizzing past her small car, not paying attention to the patches of ice.

Vince didn't know what she should do either. An extra twenty minutes both ways could mean they'd lost their chance. There was no telling how long the entrance would be open for this time. The man beside him kicked the tray latched into the back of the seat in front of him. It was sent flopping down, almost knocking the phone out of his hand. Vince had had enough of this. Anything more than twenty minutes would be too long on this plane.

Preadence, Second World

They talked for hours into the night like they did on the baseball field. Except as many questions Skye asked, she felt like she had ten more for every answer. The sky was so much clearer here. The pair had stopped traveling on horseback towards the lighthouse to set up a new place for camp on the bare earth. She laid in a small patch of damp grass on her back looking up. There were stars and constellations she had never seen before on the clearest nights back in Alfaro. They seemed to all be backwards too, *was that even possible? Was Preadence in a different hemisphere?*

There was a homey feel to sleeping outside. She had always liked it out in the open. It reminded her of when she would sleep out in the barn with Buckwheat as a young girl. A shower would be nice, but she didn't think Olli had one of those in his bag.

As warm as it had gotten in the day, the night seemed to be making up for it with a brisk chill. She had her jacket around her neck, and Olli must've been cold too, because he didn't offer up his own jacket as usual. Instead he did something new. As Skye was running out of steam, her head bobbing from staring up above. "You look tired," Olli said.

"Me," Skye was somewhat surprised he had noticed. She *knew* she was tired. Skye didn't need to have Olli tell her that. Her body was tired. She'd been sleeping on the ground for days and her stomach was feeling bunched up in a knot from all the exotic food she'd eaten. All the horseback riding wasn't helping either. "Have you seen yourself lately?" Skye asked Olli back, just being honest.

He had dark rings under his eyes and had lost at least ten pounds since she'd last seen him. It must've been the truth because of instead of another smart-alecky remark, he simply propped his bag up under his head, rested his sword upon his left side and spread open his other arm.

Skye ogled in how silly he looked. Olli rubbed his eyes, not laughing, "What do you have to lose?" Skye was on the opposite side of the fire trying to adjust her back on the hard earth. He was right. What else was there to risk? At least she'd be warmer.

She brushed some of the dirt off the back of her bottom and walked the few steps over to his side. The warmth was familiar and when he took his hand up to her face to pull her loose strand of hair behind her ear she knew the only thing she'd lost was the wall she'd put up between them. Within minutes Skye fell asleep, peacefully blinking away the strange bright stars.

When Skye woke up alone, she thought for sure it would be in her own bed this time. No more Second World mumbo jumbo. It was warmer outside; the sun was just rising above the rocky hills on the horizon. Was it rising in the west? Her arms woke up last the stinging tingly feeling moving out of them as she adjusted her body on the uncomfortable earth. She pulled her hair back up into a tighter bun, trying to seem like she hadn't been roughing it for days.

Olli was tucking the map he'd shown her from the day before back into his pocket.

"We need to get moving, the heat will be unbearable by noon. If we leave early enough, we'll enter Tromperie Desert within a couple of hours."

He didn't say anything about the night before or even as much as a good morning. Olli must've gotten some sleep. Skye was out cold, exhausted. She liked him better tired. He seemed more serious now and focused on the travels up ahead. Buckwheat was drinking from the brass vessel. She ate breakfast on horseback. Skye still felt hungry after she ate but kept the feeling to herself.

In less than three hours of riding, they hit sand. Most of it was compressed and the once abundant scenery of dry plants was now less dense. Their pace started to slow, but Buckwheat seemed to be holding up okay even with two riders.

When the sun was directly overhead, Skye could feel her pale skin start to burn. As hot as she was getting, Skye kept her jacket on. She used it to cover the top of her head making sure to conceal her ears. It was hotter than she could ever remember it getting in Alfaro, not even in late July. The sand seemed to just amplify the heat. Underneath her she could feel Buckwheat begin to dip in his usual steady stride.

"Can we stop for water?" Skye didn't wait for Olli to respond. She knew her horse very well; they needed to stop. Olli had hoped to get a little farther, but he couldn't deny he was getting thirsty too. Red rings were starting to appear on his darker cheeks just under his eyes. On the horizon he could still see towering rocks, but they were getting shorter and fewer as they rode along.

Skye let Buckwheat drink two helpings of the full chalice before cleaning it with her jacket, which dried all too quickly. Then she moved on to making a fresh bucket for her and Olli to drink. Olli pulled the map from his jacket. He checked the position of the sun. At most, they were maybe twenty miles into the desert. It was hard to calculate their position, the sands were often changing direction and where the desert started on the aging map could be several miles off in either direction.

"I think it's best to keep going; we can eat more of the amande rose and pudding as we go. We'll have to hope Buckwheat grazed enough before we left to keep his energy the rest the way. This will be the toughest part of the trip. If we get through the hottest portion of the day, the remainder of the journey will be through the cooler night."

As the hours slowly passed it was like driving through Alfaro except instead of cornfields it was just neverending mounds of sand. The plant life and color seemed to wash away with every hour they rode. Sand was building up in Skye's mouth around her gums and teeth. They had to stop twice more for water before it started to get dark.

The cooler weather didn't seem to come with the looming darkness. Their skin was sunburnt, even after trying to soak their clothes in the water of the chalice to block the sun. It wasn't enough. Skye tried to cool Buckwheat's coat after the sun disappeared. The sand was hot to the touch.

"Are you sure we can't stop and rest for just a little

while?" Skye was concerned for Buckwheat, and she thought about admitting to Olli that her legs were tender from riding. This was by far the most riding she'd done in her lifetime, but Olli wasn't complaining about being sore, so she kept her discomfort to herself. She tried scooping chunks of sand away from Buckwheat's nostrils and took the time to try to fix her hair again. The grit of sand in between her teeth was like taking a nail file across her mouth.

"How do you know we're going the right way and not in circles?" It seemed like they had been traveling longer than just a day's worth and everything looked the same to Skye.

Olli was looking up at the sky again, but there was no sun. The stars weren't as clear as the night before, but still behind the dark clouds and moon there was a guidance system, "We use the most reliable navigation system in existence. Unlike in your schools, we still highly value the study of our stars, moon phases, and position of the sun. It's as basic as your alphabet."

Skye looked up at the glimmering balls of fire, somewhat annoyed, *like she could control her quality of education.* She knew many constellations and names for stars but did not know how to orient herself from there.

In her head she tried to recall the names of the constellations she saw above her. Cassiopeia, Draco, Ursa Major, Ursa Minor, and Orion... but those were all she could think of at the moment.

There was no way she could remember all forty-eight constellations named by Ptolemy over thousands of years ago, but she did know a decent amount of astronomy. Stars were a phase she was fascinated by when she was younger. Back when she was about eight years old, she wanted to be an astronaut. A virtue that seemed to terrify and intrigue both her parents. They knew a lot about the stars too and most of what she knew about them came from what her dad talked to her about. It was a long time ago when he didn't work all day and night. The days when he would still spend hours around the farm. *Why hadn't her parents taught her to navigate with the stars?*

After a few more hours the evening ride was finally starting to give some relief. Skye's clothing was almost dry from soaking them earlier and the temperature was comfortable as they rode horseback. It was much easier to talk now. Without the sun beating down or having to cover her face she could hear Olli more clearly. She was also getting used to the sand being in her eyes, eyelids, and nostrils. It was difficult to sleep sitting upright and all around them the earth was coming back to life.

"There's Polaris," Skye was confident she had the right star, but the orientation was still off in some way, "Is it all reversed here?"

Olli shook his head, not prepared to deal out Second World practices.

He was somewhat impressed by her knowledge of the heavens. It wasn't like he was trying to sound like he knew everything earlier. In all honesty, he was only fair in comparison to his brother, at least regarding his sense of direction and navigating the stars. It was nice just knowing something Skye didn't for a change. The whole time he spent around other humans in the First World, he seemed clueless about most of their technologies. From what he had observed, most of the electronics appeared unnecessary or as distractions.

"I believe you also refer to it as the Northern Star in the First World?" Olli was checking Skye's understanding, "Here we call it the Southern Star, but it is just as useful to find our way in the night sky."

Olli took Skye's arm and held it out in front pointing it up at the star Skye was referring to as Polaris. "You see these two bright stars around Polaris?" He connected the parts of Ursa Minor and Skye winked one of her eyes closed to truly see which stars he was pointing her to.

"Kochab is about here," he continued to guide her arm making a swirl with her hand, "and Pherkad is here, they're the guardians of Polaris," Skye never knew the star had 'guardians,' but she liked that there was something about the sky here and at home she could see. She brought her arm back down with a yawn.

There was more: "They're helpful in telling time too, and right now the guardians are saying it's time you should get some sleep."

They had done a lot of riding and as much as she wanted to hop off and lay down and be off the saddle, as they rode, Skye had spotted at least a half a dozen snakes slithering through parted moonlight as the dark hours grew later, not to mention the other scurrying creatures she didn't have names for. She caught a glimpse of something too big to be a scorpion that kept flashing a shadow behind them. She never asked what they were called; it was an answer she didn't want to know. Buckwheat would have to serve not only as their form of transportation through the night but also their fortress of protection.

Carefully, she locked her feet into the stirrups and bunched her jacket around the saddle's horn. The leather strap wrapped around her arms she laid forward willing herself to sleep. Thoughts of guardians and bright lights swirled in her dreams.

Sharp rain pelted on the metal rooftops and waves were crashing through the breezy day. Olli had been in a very deep sleep. He thought she had left him, but there she was fast asleep, his arms tucked around Skye's waist, and her hair whipping about in the wind tickling his unshaven face. *Was that drool at the side of her lips?* He kissed the back of her neck, careful not to disrupt her sleep. His body bobbed ever so slightly up and down. Then Olli leaned softly back forward and rapidly fell asleep with his face buried in her hair shielding his own skin from the rain, not realizing it was sand pelting his burnt face.

Awakening again, Olli's body bounced. He did not awake this time in comfort. The world around him was slightly on its side. *When he'd awoken before, wasn't it raining? Did it rain in these parts of the desert? Now there was no sign of it.* About falling off Buckwheat's back, Olli sat as straight as he could manage. Buckwheat was moving—not very fast—through deep white sand. Frantic, Olli couldn't help but question where they were. *What time was it? What was that roaring noise? What he could see of the sun, it might have been ten or eleven in the morning?*

He forced his eyes to focus. Then he looked around. There were no more plants, no more rock forms on the horizon. There was just sand in every direction. Some of it was flying up and swirling around make the visibility in the distance difficult to see through.

What was the awful sound he kept hearing? It certainly was not a heavy rain or the sound of the Cardarrious Sea. Flicking the reins to spark some energy into Buckwheat, there was an urgency burning within him to get moving. They needed to ride away from the sound at all costs. Buckwheat could've been heading in the wrong direction for hours. *What if they traveled west? They'd never make it out of Tromperie now.*

The jolt shook Skye. She heard the rolling wind too. *What was going on?* Her soothing dreams popped like bubbles before her own eyes. *How long did she sleep? It was clearly too long. Were they already at the lighthouse?* Skye coughed, trying to clear her dry throat. Would it be too much to ask for the chalice? She rubbed Buckwheat's side; the horse's coat was caked with a layer of heavy sand. Buckwheat's colossal legs felt weak beneath them.

"How much farther?" Skye asked groggily. She waited, but Olli didn't respond. As she gazed up, she knew why. A few miles in front of them there was a high wall of angry smoky-like sand. The noise was echoing away from it like a train.

Without asking, Skye took charge as she pulled the reins out of Olli's hands and slid her feet back into the stirrups. She didn't know where they were headed, but she knew which direction she *wasn't* going to lead them. The adrenaline surged swiftly through her tired, thirsty veins. Buckwheat was startled from his restful state; he'd been walking too long. All Olli could do was hold on and trust that Skye knew what she was doing.

They were going as fast as they could away from the wall of screaming sand. Buckwheat fought uphill and back down. There was a stumble as Buckwheat landed his front leg wrong along his feathering. They were nearly all thrown forward. He caught his footing in time to save them from rolling down the sloping sand like they were caught in a dusty avalanche. Steadying himself, Buckwheat put every ounce he had left in him to pull them forward with each step. The ground started to level out and the sand didn't seem quite as deep as he kept going. Then that's when it happened.

As fast as they were going the sandstorm was coming at them too quickly. It covered them like a dense fog, along with the haze was a sense of being buried alive. Blinded, their lungs filled instantly with more sand. Their bodies felt heavier. Skye pulled her hood up over her head and her sweatshirt as far up to her eyes as she could pulling tightly on the metal zipper. If he wasn't still holding onto her waist, she wouldn't have even been able to see if Olli was on the horse or not. She would just have to trust the feeling.

The whirlwind of sand kept coming, it got louder, and everything seemed to be going slower. Her body kept getting heavier to the point where all her skin felt was numb and her mind dizzy. Buckwheat seemed to somehow miraculously keep bobbing up and down under their bodies. It was impossible to tell if they were moving forward or if it was the wind blowing him back and forth as easily as a flag in the air.

Alfaro, First World

Vince was behind the wheel. It was by luck that the plane had to de-board and the flight was delayed several hours because of the inclement weather. He was only moments away from pretending to have claustrophobia or shouting he had a bomb. Anything to get himself off the wretched aircraft. They got their flight miles, Vince's carry-on bag, and took off in the opposite direction. He drove as fast as it felt safe to drive on the icy roads.

Not caring for anyone who may be around, they drove the car through the pathway in Webb Cemetery. When they got out Vince kept his hand over his wand. Diane held the emerald out in her palm it was beginning to cool. In front of the closed door of the mausoleum they found themselves standing anxiously for the second time in less than a few weeks. The sensor was still in place, but when Vince checked his anticipation sank. The entrance had been locked.

"You're too late," the couple turned around, startled at who they found staring back at them.

"Davidson?" Diane's heart raced, but she relaxed when she recognized the familiar face, "What are you doing here? What do you mean we're too late?"

Lighthouse Point, Second World

As the storm settled, the air around them began to clear. It was like the desert didn't like them being there and spat them back out. Skye's nose realized where she was before her eyes could. Her hearing was muffled, but the same rhythmic splashing of water hummed low in her ears.

There was still a lot of sand everywhere, but unmistakably they had made it to the sea. What she thought was another sandstorm was actually the sound of real waves crashing. Making sure an unconscious Olli stayed on Buckwheat's back she flicked the reins and guided her horse toward the waves.

Buckwheat galloped, happily limping through the shallow tide. As Skye hopped off, she fell into the water. She let the water run into her dry mouth but was careful not to drink any of it. The salt tasted terrible as she spat the water back out trying to get the gritty paste out of every crevice. Skye continued to splash water up into her face and submerged her head. Sand was not only all around them, but the stuff seemed to be in everything. It cleaned smoothly from her hair, nose, and ears. She had to scrub her cheeks and arms to get the areas where sweat and sand built up for days. As most of the sand washed away Skye felt both cleaner and lighter than just moments before.

Seeing Olli still on Buckwheat's back, Skye flung water up from the steady waves with both hands. He stirred, but Olli was already waking up. He was able to dismount Buckwheat a little easier than Skye. *They were alive, they somehow made it through the Tromperie Desert.* Elated and feeling drunk, he wrapped his arms around Skye. Lifting her up, he spun around. They both collapsed into the water. Olli lifted his head, "Good boy, Buckwheat, good boy."

She was proud of her horse too. Skye may have been the one holding onto the reins, but there was no way she was taking credit for navigating them through the sandstorm. Maybe it was just good luck, or it could've been Buckwheat's natural instincts. Skye rang out the water and sand from her jacket and her hair before pulling it back up into a bun on her head.

The air was cool after getting out of the warm water.

The beach itself was quiet and seemed abandoned. Skye didn't see any litter from tourists. No plastic cups or straws in the tall grass, no bottle caps along the receding tide. There was just the white sand and lots of water. It was like the lighthouse had its own private beach.

The tall grass met up to the edge of the desert on one side and on the other there was some green foliage, but it was mostly sharp rocks along the cliff's side. There was a little whitewashed house missing parts of the red clay roof and there was no glass in most of the windows. Beside the small house there was the jutting land, a wooden crossing to the beach, and then there was the lighthouse.

The details of the lighthouse in her vision were foggy. The thin spiraled building stood several stories high. There was a metal railing around the top portion which seemed to be the same as what she'd seen when she blacked out in her barn before falling from the hayloft. The company in the vision was the same too. Skye imaged having to ride back through the desert and hoped there was an easier way to get back home. *It had to be all forward from here.*

Olli was having his own internal struggles. *Did they beat the others to the cove? They must have. It was calm and whoever these 'others' were seemed dangerous.* For now, Olli kept his concerns to himself. He and Skye were alive, not necessarily safe, but alive.

Thankful not to have lost anything in his bag, Olli cleared its contents and poured the desert sand out onto the beach. He pulled out the chalice filling it to the brim for all three of them to get a drink. Even unkempt and abandoned, this place was beautiful. They walked with Buckwheat until they cleared all the sand they could find away from their sun and windburnt bodies. *How long were they asleep?* The sun was already lowering behind them and dipping into the desert away from the sky.

"I think it's best we find somewhere to rest for the night. If they're not here yet, they should be soon." Finding shelter would be an easy task. Skye was already fantasizing about the possibility of a television, warm bath, and maybe even a bed.

Defensively, Olli drew his sword as Skye remained back far enough to mount Buckwheat if there was danger lurking inside the small home. After a few minutes of tension, considering someone could be hiding inside, Olli came out jumping and hollering. He scared Skye half to death. She clumsily tried to climb halfway up Buckwheat's backside who had also startled at the unnecessary shouts.

Inside the small lighthouse keeper's quarters, Olli started a fire in the old black wood-burning stove with some driftwood and dry grass. They laid most of their damp clothes out along the dusty furniture. He used a dry reed to light a few old lamps and candles. It was difficult to tell how long the lighthouse living quarters had been abandoned. There were still a lot of the supplies and furnishings. Apart from the layer of dust and grime there were piles of sand in the corners. The large blue floral print area rug and a fabric-torn armchair didn't seem completely ancient.

The paint and wood inside smelled a tad damp and musky and in some spots, there were clusters of green algae growing. Dozens of creepy pictures filled the space with assorted frames nailed to the wall in odd places. The images were blurry from the layer of dust but from what she could see some of the frames were filled with sketches or pen drawings, pictures of ships, and a few watercolor paintings of the seascape or portraits. *Was this Second World a form of time travel?*

For dinner, they had some dried vegetables that may have been potatoes, turnips, or carrots at some point. Olli broke the lock to the cellar. He found the vegetables along with a questionable-looking large jar. The vegetables were just fine for Skye. A little butter and pepper would've made them taste better, but after days of nothing to eat besides sweet bread and strange nuts, the salty food was more than she could've asked for. As for the jar Olli pulled up from the cellar, it had a brown translucent liquid with silver chunks floating in it. After Olli cooked the pieces on the stove they looked and smelled awful to Skye. It reminded her of the school cafeteria, when 'surf and turf' were listed on the menu. She never ate the surf.

"Eat, it's just pickled herring," Olli coaxed Skye to take a bite from a three-pronged metal fork they'd found under the kitchen cabinets.

Not sure of what that was or why someone would store it in a jar, Skye went ahead and tried it. She still couldn't get over how it looked in the jar, and the taste was too much like old sardines. The cellar hadn't just been storing stale vegetables and pickled herring. There were also a few bottles of well-dated wine and champagne. To her surprise Olli had popped open a bottle of red wine and was drinking it from a smoky glass. She wasn't sure why she was surprised. Olli did hang out with Davidson.

"It's perfectly legal to have a glass of wine here. We drink it with almost every meal. Young and old alike. It's very mild, not much alcohol. This looks homemade— possibly fairies. Would you care to try some?"

Skye contemplated the offer. Legal or not, did it matter? On occasion she'd had a drink at home or around the holidays, especially New Year's Eve. Her dad usually snuck her a glass every now and again. When she was out with Tiffany she never just drank for fun. However, Skye had survived a kidnapping and sandstorm this week. If anything, a taste of wine seemed normal.

Olli wiped out another grimy glass that wasn't broken and filled it half full of wine. Skye took a sip; it wasn't very cold. The wine also wasn't as sweet as she'd had at home, but it was nice having something to drink other than water.

They'd been at the lighthouse only a few hours and it was incredible how at home they had made themselves. Buckwheat was grazing calmly just outside the house tied to an old wooden railing. Olli had laid out a row of green stones along the perimeter of where the dry grass met the sandy beach, high enough to keep out of the tide. He said it was an alert system. They would alert any movement. *Where was the electricity?*

When it came to bedtime, they gawked at each other. There was one bed about the size of a full-size bed in the First World, not much bigger than the twin Skye slept in at home. It was odd that they hesitated. They both slept beside each other on the ground and on a horse. *Why did a bed suddenly feel more... serious?*

Being the gentleman as always, Olli didn't give Skye the option. He plopped down on the throw rug on the floor with his dried coat as a blanket and the pillow from the armchair. Skye didn't argue. She shook out the dust and sand before getting in. The springs weren't very comfortable, but it was nice to stretch out after being vertical on horseback for two days. The fire was down to the coals and the two lamps just ran empty.

Skye laid on her back staring up at the ceiling. She heard every crackle of the coals and rustling of grass outside. Olli must've been exhausted because within minutes she heard a dull snore coming from the ground. No phone, no radio, no television, and no... Skye stayed awake for at least another hour before she gave in. Hoping she didn't step on him, she wrapped the musty old blanket around her legs and stepped to the floor. She was trying not to wake him up, so she carefully placed the blanket over his body and laid on her side just behind him on the wooden floorboards.

Chapter 17
Catwalk

Enchanting, Olli thought. When he rolled over the next morning his side was sore, and his legs were raw from the days of riding horseback. The sunburn was starting to heal, and the back of his neck itched from where it had already started to peel off flakes of his skin. As he rolled to get a little relief by itching his neck, he nearly elbowed the sleeping Skye in the face.

Had she been here all night with him? Could they just stay here? He was handy enough, all he had to do was fix up the windows, replace some of the roofing? Olli had watched Adam do these things on many occasions. *If Cliffton was wrong about the shipment maybe no one would ever come this way to bother them. Faking their deaths would come easy. No one would question if they were consumed by the harsh desert and its tricks. He could escape his right to the throne—if only temporarily—and she wouldn't have to come to terms with her own destiny.*

When she suddenly opened her eyes, it was too late to pretend like he was asleep and too obvious he'd been staring at her, completely ensnared in the moment.

Cardarrious Sea, Second World

Charles Teagardin pulled the gray hairs together on his lengthening beard. He looked out at the land in the far distance. The crew was pulling the last of the barrels aboard. Most of the large heavy barrels were below the deck of the ship. If they were going to make the trade deadline, they would need to have the fifty barrels packaged and ready to transfer.

He watched as one of his soldiers put their bloody fillet knife back in its holster. It had felt good to do a bit of killing. However, the old man was cautious to stay away from any battles he couldn't win. No one ever knew how much time they had left in their life without a Fleur de Libellule, but somehow, he knew. There was a feeling that came with age. His bones were achy—even fighting today he felt tired. All he wanted to do now was rest. Charles checked his own reflection in a pool of water aboard the ship and then stomped his boot into it.

It'd been too long since he'd performed Agenesis.

Unable to lay around forever, their growling bellies finally coaxed them off the hard floor. Skye and Olli had a strange assortment of food for breakfast. There were a few leftovers from the night before and the bread pudding from the reckoning bowl. The late start to the day made anything taste good.

With nothing better to do after breakfast they took a walk along the shore to see if there were any other signs of a shipment or people carrying about business in these parts. Skye noticed Olli took his sword and dagger with him, but aside from being well-armed, the walk was relaxing. They left Buckwheat up at the house to graze. He needed the extra rest just as much as they did. Skye's legs were feeling much better getting to walk instead of ride. She left her rain boots and socks in the deeper sand while they walked through the shallow parts of the clear water.

The sun was warm and kept the waves reflecting enough light to walk for hours through the brisk winds. Skye found shells and a dead jellyfish and noticed radiant shining pieces reflecting in the cloudy blue water. Olli seemed tenser than when they arrived at the lighthouse. *Where were they?* He had wondered to himself.

One of those shining pieces popped out of the moist sand through each breaking wave. Skye thought it was a full shell, so she waded out into the cloudier water until it lapped up against her knees where her pants were rolled just above her ankles to avoid the chill. When she turned it over in her hand the clumps of sand rinsed away in the next wave. Then she held it delicately out in the sunlight.

Olli realized Skye had stopped and turned to see she was holding up the scale.

"You should hold onto to that," Olli said to her seriously.

Skye pulled her hand back she was just about to drop the piece into the moving water.

"What is it?" Skye was now admiring the beautiful little piece from the sea more curiously. It seemed more like a piece of light metal than a shell now that she had examined it more closely.

Olli walked back to where Skye stood looking at the scale, "It's a shed scale from a mermaid."

"Come on, a mermaid scale, really?"

She rolled her eyes, unable to see this one through. The food and the water were obviously some kind of illusion. Now he was going to try and convince her mermaids were a real thing. It'd go right along with the magic wands and milkweed pixies.

"Yes, they shed them kind of like a snake or how sharks lose their teeth. It doesn't hurt them. You should keep it. Julianna tells me they're still pricey these days. The scales are useful for all sorts of things. They're hard to come by in Gresham because we don't have many calm shores in our territories and the mermaids prefer the cove or the caves."

He really wasn't kidding. "What would you use something like this for?" Skye rubbed her finger along the shiny iridescent smooth surface. She thought of jewelry right away.

"Oh, there's all kinds of uses: medicines and weaponry. Many years ago, you would see them worn as good luck amulets or woven into clothing. Personally, I think it was more of a fashion statement than anything."

Skye tucked the scale in her pocket with the rest of their finds. It was getting chilly and they hadn't found anything unusual or out of place in the few hours they'd walked. At the end of the cove, Skye burst forward with excitement. Olli looked behind them at the opposite side of the cove. The lighthouse was starting to look small in the distance. He checked the emerald. It was a flat green and cool as ever to the touch.

He met up to where Skye was stooping down in a bunch of rocks some sharp and jutting out of the water, others smooth from years of waves crashing over them. The tide was low, and the cloudy blue water had left behind a series of active tide pools. Olli smiled at her child-like amazement. There wasn't anything he'd seen her get this excited about in the First World. The only thing he could compare it to was when he'd asked her to go to the dance that she showed any interest in what most the girls obsessed over.

Then here was Skye, inches away from the water, letting a starfish-like crab crawl up her arm. *How did she know the creature wasn't poisonous?*

He found himself lost in the memory of the dance and said, "I'm sorry about leaving you at the Homecoming Dance."

Skye was distracted watching what she was certain must be related to a sea crab or starfish climb back down the edge of her fingertip and back into the shallow tide pool. It clasped its white and blue claw and was now eating something gooey and white out of a brown shell.

She didn't look up from the tide pool. Homecoming seemed a long way away. Another time entirely, but she did hear him because she asked, "Why did you leave? Did you really attack Jason?"

Skye's own mind was drowning in the tides. She suddenly had Nick Burkley's arms around her neck as they danced away the rest of the evening. He took her home that same night too on his motorbike. Instead of the strong smell of salt the memory of the menthol cigarettes and body spray clouded her senses. Real.

Olli breathed deeply, poking away at the small pools with a stick he'd found. "I really didn't want to leave the night of the dance—but my friend, the milkweed pixie you saw me talking to a few days ago—he was badly injured. He had also overheard about where the sorcerers and a man named Fideleroi was going to be next."

"Who's Fideleroi?" Skye was following along, trying to fill in the gaps. She physically had to shake her head and blink her eyes to remember where she was. Olli was gone a long time while she was left to fill in the blanks. *Why didn't he come back for her sooner if he knew she needed to go with him to this place?*

"No one is sure who Fideleroi is," Olli answered, but Skye wasn't sure if she cared for the answer. She had other more important interests in mind. Olli continued, "We had speculation that he was working with the sorcerers, but we weren't certain until more recently. With your grandfather involved there could be a lot of trouble heading our way. It's likely we will have to cover our tracks better and maybe have our bags packed. We don't really want to involve ourselves if we're outnumbered."

"And your brother and his girlfriend they're somehow mixed up with this bunch?" Olli didn't talk anymore about the dance, and she wasn't ready to tell him about Nick.

Distracted, Olli kept fidgeting with the stick. He had poked it through a few little swimming creatures that looked like giant shrimp. "I was hoping it wasn't true, but it seems that's the case. Cliffton thinks Victoria may even have some sorcerer bloodline in her to boot." He kicked a mussel off the rock it was attached to.

"What do you think the shipment they were talking about was?" Her mind was thinking of mail or oil. *What did people of power here value? Gold or maybe the green emeralds?*

Again, he shrugged—tired of not having the answer and frustrated he had made it all this way without any more than he started. "It could be anything. My friends and I have been trying to get to the bottom of this for almost a year. It's what we've been working on these past few weeks and trying to figure out how to get ahead of them to the lighthouse before the full moon. Depending on what we find, I'll be able to get the council involved."

The council sounded so official. For being a prince, he didn't seem to have a whole lot of authority. "Won't that get your brother in some sort of trouble?"

"I hope so," Olli threw a rock out into the waves looking out across the choppy water, "maybe it'll knock some reality into him. People have died, they're at least three reigns coming of age this year and the contract is at a greater risk of corruption than ever before."

"All this over a contract?" It seemed this world's politics were just as messed up as her own country, just without the news channels and social media.

Olli turned, looking directly at Skye across a small tide pool. He leaned up against the stone wall. He was careful where he stepped to not tumble into the roaring waves or sharp rocks, "Not just a written document. A magically bound contract. It was written and sealed hundreds of years ago in blood. There's no way to break the ordinances and laws written within it, unless all the rightful heirs are present and use their blood to make revisions. It's why you are here. The five nations are wanting change. The sorcerers have always hated the contract, the humans tolerate it, and the fairies as usual are neither for nor against anything. Then there's..."

He paused. Skye was looking intently back at him trying to soak in everything he had to share. *If only the council and his people showed the same respect or interest as Skye demonstrated at this very moment.*

"There's the Rodinians and then the mermaids."

Was he at it again? Fairies, mermaids... and whoever the Rodinians were... It all sounded made up. "So, let me get this straight, your birthday is in a few months and you'll be the rightful ruler of the human beings of your home, Gresham? I'll be of age in June covering both the sorcerers and wood fairies. Who is the successor of the place called Rodinia and the mermaids?" Skye's brain immediately went to a pale, red-headed cartoon, but she had to keep some fun to herself. He probably had never heard of her anyways.

"We believe we have the bloodline of the mermaids to Jamison Atlas, but there's a few questions I may have for your parents about your father's lineage in that department. The Rodinians have been such a private region for so long that we can't be sure of the bloodline. They've lost a lot of their kind over the years. During the battle the night your parents fled into the First World, many lives were lost."

Wherever this was seemed like a dangerous place to live. "What happens if I don't want to be in charge here?"

He never thought about someone else not wanting to rule or Skye not wanting to stay. There were so many people he knew who sought power, it never came to him. "According to the contract you would have to. If you died...

well, we'd have quite a different story on our hands. Then the disclosed young ruler of the sorcerers will take your place. I suppose that would leave Marconi to the wood fairies. I believe he's technically your cousin."

"My cousin?" There was more family in this place? A lot of family. *Why didn't her mom and dad talk about them?*

"Yes, your mother has a sister in the wood fairy colony. Marconi is the reason we believed you existed and that your parents hadn't been killed. Marconi is just shy of a year older than you, I believe. The wood fairies tried to have him crowned, but the ceremony never worked."

"You know more about me than I do." There was a much darker thought that popped into her head. *Why was she still alive? Why did they think her parents were dead? Were they just waiting to kill her?* Skye knew things were bad when she woke up shackled in a tent, but it was a joke, a bad prank, not because some people or sorcerers wanted to kill her. Suddenly she didn't feel safe along the shore childishly frolicking along the tides as the water began to rise. For the first time in days, she wanted to go home.

And then she didn't. She was up against the tall rocks now beside Olli.

"There's still a lot I have to learn," she said. He couldn't help it. As he watched her innocently and so invested in the discovery of each new creature in the tide pools, he knew he was falling for her still. Resting the stick against the rock he pulled her towards him, both arms wrapped around her back. The waves were sprinkling a light spittle of salty mist along his pants and the bottom of where her feet and her pants were rolled to her knees. Olli hated the contract.

They spent hours just being, they tried to not think about the contract or why they were here. They just were.

It was going to be getting dark again soon, so they headed back up to the lighthouse. It was hard for Skye not to take an extra glance between the waves and at the rocks. *There was no such thing as mermaids.*

She got back before Olli, who insisted on getting a few more pieces of driftwood to cook dinner and for the fire to last a little longer through the cooler night. Skye was ready to look around the house some more. Everything seemed so old like antiques, but if it was as old as the items seemed, they would've certainly aged more.

Walking around, Skye found an area that must've been like a bathroom. There was a spout with running water when she pumped a large lever. The water smelled of the sea salt and sulphur that must've pulled up from an underground well. There was a large metal basin and something like a toilet and when she peeked in seemed to lead to a small tunnel that went on forever. *And to think she'd been going outside the whole time they'd been here, including once in the ocean.*

Another door was a closet, revealing old musty blankets and a broom which fell on her head. The third door she opened led to a smaller room with a black spiraling staircase. It seemed sturdy enough to hold weight even with some rust crusting around the edges. There was light shining in from windows high above. Skye put her hand on the cold railing and wanted to head up the stairwell.

She jumped, realizing Olli was standing behind her in the doorway, "It leads up to the lighthouse lens and catwalk."

Olli was holding one of the pans with the creatures he caught in the tide pools earlier in the day. She was curious about what it looked like at the top of the lighthouse but didn't want to be rude. Food was harder to reheat here. There wasn't any microwave.

She turned and closed the door. The rest of house was warm running the stove. The shrimp-like creatures Olli called *bogini* tasted a lot better than the pickled herring. He'd even found a jar of olive oil from the cellar to dip with. They finished the rest of the vegetables and bottle of wine from the night before.

She was taking the dishes to clean them off outside when Olli took them from her. He stopped looking her over. Her hair was matted from the wind and dry sand was still visible at her barefoot toes.

"Here, why don't you go take a bath," he said. Skye let him take the plate and one fork.

"What do you mean 'a bath'? Are you saying I stink?" It really wasn't a question. She knew she stunk. They both did. There didn't seem to be any deodorant or body spray in this so-called Second World along with the electronics.

"No, I just thought you'd want to, since we have one now." Olli sat the dirty dishes on the little wooden table. "I'll put some water on the stove."

"Where's this bath at?" After he put the water in the pot on the wood-burning stove they went into the small bathroom with the faucet. Skye realized the metal trough-like basin in the corner must've been what he was talking about.

"How do I work it?" Skye felt stupid but was interested.

Here, Olli hand pumped the faucet rinsing the barrel then filled it about halfway full of water. Olli had watched Henry do this for him at least a thousand times before. He brought in two of the lamps they'd been using to light the other rooms and put new fuel in them. He came back with a potful of boiling water and small glass vial. First, he emptied the boiling water and then added a few drops from the stopper. Skye about backed up into the wall, thinking it was the same thing they used the blast the metal chains from her wrists.

"My butler, Henry, sent these with me. They're supposed to have soothing healing properties. I guess we'll see if they work."

The drops smelled like lavender and peppermint. Skye didn't have to ask. Olli left with the pot and vial to go clean up from dinner. There was no lock on the door, but she trusted she was fine to remove her clothes. The sea had cleaned her skin and most of the desert sand from her clothes but had left a layer of grit behind.

The bath was lukewarm, and the light was enough to see to get washed off. She dunked her head underwater several times in the sudsy water to try and clear her head. The droplets Olli put in the bath left some bubbles behind. The water did seem to soothe and cleanse. As for the healing, the sunburn was fading before her eyes and her legs weren't as sore. The smell of the smoky fires seeped away from her soaked hair.

Feeling somewhat refreshed, Skye waited until the water was almost cold before hopping out. She had the moment when she realized there were no towels. Instead Skye grabbed one of the dusty blankets she'd found in the nearby closet to dry off. It would've been nice to have a clean set of clothes to change into.

She settled for her long sleeve shirt and shook what was left of sand from her pants. There was no drain for the bathtub so for now she left the water sit. Piles of sand were settling on the bottom of the metal basin. It was nice to feel clean.

Carrying her clothes and one of the lamps while putting out the other, Skye opened the bathroom door. It was quiet. Remembering what Olli said about needing to be ready to go at the drop of the hat she put all her things together. It looked like everything he'd brought on Buckwheat's back as well as his shoes were sitting together by the bed.

He was fast asleep buried under the puffy blanket. Olli must have given up being a gentleman. She carefully pulled back the covers and laid down. It was dark, but the one lamp left illuminating the room was keeping her awake. In less than an hour the rest of the oil burned down.

The darkness and the company didn't help her get to sleep any better than the night before. She tossed and turned, trying to fall asleep. Skye worried she'd wake up Olli. So instead of fighting her restlessness, she slowly stood. The creaky rusted springs made a lurid shrieking sound as her feet touched the floorboards beside the bed. Skye walked, tiptoeing towards the window. She peeked behind the sheet they'd placed over the broken window to keep the bugs and wind out. Buckwheat was still tied outside.

They were safe, but it must've been at least two o'clock in the morning. *Why couldn't she sleep?* Even if nothing was outside besides the sea, she didn't want to leave for a walk. Instead she grabbed her jacket from the pile of her things and headed back to the closed door beside the bathroom.

The spiral staircase had holes illuminating the ground around her bare feet. Her hand went to the staircase railing and then Skye began to walk upwards. She slowed down only to look out the little windows along the path. These windows still had most of their glass. They were enough to see through, but not crystal clear. She glanced out of one window about halfway up the stairwell. This window had a small corner at the bottom of it with no glass. She was able to see the water stretching out far across the horizon. It must've been a reflection because there seemed to be a bright light just below where the water met the cloudy night sky.

She kept taking steps upward until she came to a door at the very last creaking step. The door was cracked in parts because of the old wood. There was a little latch keeping it closed. She expected it to be locked, but unexpectedly the latch could easily be lifted. With a quarter-turn of the rusty clasp Skye pushed inward against the draft. The door pushed inward, revealing a tiny room. Her feet passed through the entrance with an echo.

As she looked around the small space, she realized she was much higher than she thought. There were many large windows looking out over the sea in all directions and her body swayed slightly with the tower as if standing out on a dock over water. She felt uncertain of her footing, and the water surrounding her made her seem like she was moving. There was a railing around the room in a circle and another ring of metal at the center of a room mostly enclosed. At the center of the room and slightly over her head there was something like a giant lamp surrounded by several mirrors.

Skye didn't know how lighthouses worked. She was a little preoccupied by how her body felt like it was swaying slightly side to side. The glass chandelier-like device in the center of the lighthouse tower was beautifully and masterfully crafted. It had to be very heavy. There were odds and ends around the lighthouse. There were glass bottles with bright colorful liquids. Something she recognized as a sextant and glass prisms. Then Skye noticed there was a green glowing emerald laying on the ground.

The door behind her swung back. Olli was standing with his bag slung over his arm, a lamp in one hand and his sword outstretched in the other, "What are you doing awake? The alarm was firing, but I didn't know where from. Then I noticed you weren't in the house."

"I couldn't sleep," Skye was looking out at the water still. She wasn't any more tired than when she'd laid down in bed. "I'm sorry I woke you."

"No, it's fine. I'm just glad you're safe." Olli lowered his sword and felt for Skye's cold hands.

Skye turned back around feeling guilty. She looked back out the window. The light she'd been watching bob up and down along the horizon while she walked up the stairs seemed to be getting bigger. She noticed Olli had been looking out at the sea as well, "Could it be a beacon or a buoy out in the sea?"

Olli let go of Skye's hands and put his sword and bag down on the wooden floorboards. Olli squinted looking out at the open water, "That's not a beacon."

Skye kept watching the light illuminated a pair of dark

sails in the moonlight. Olli didn't have to tell her what it was. "What's a ship doing so close to the shoreline?"

This was bad, he didn't even consider the shipment taking place miles out at sea. There appeared to be only one ship. It was moving too fast to be willfully making landfall. Ships of its size didn't port in this cove. It would risk running through the sharp rocks in low or high tide. They'd have to send a smaller boat. Only a few minutes went by as they watched the ship grow larger and larger on the horizon. *Why wasn't it slowing down? It should've dropped anchor miles ago.*

Without thinking twice, Olli lifted the lamp to examine the large glass lens and mirrors at the middle of the room. The fuel was still inside the center. He took the lid off a green liquid jar and poured it in the basin first. It was hard to see everything in the darkened space. Some of the concentrated green fluid dripped to the ground beside his bag.

Skye was near the thick glass looking out at the sails getting larger. *Did ships usually go that fast?* She'd only seen ships in movies. *Was Olli trying to save friend or foe? Maybe he recognized the maroon sails. Or was there a flag?* She couldn't make out a skull and crossbones, it seemed a good enough sign to help to Skye.

Olli threw the lit lamp up into the fuel pit at the center of the lighthouse tower. He honestly did not know where the lighting post was to ignite the rest of the fuel and be able to reflect off the mirrors to reach the cove. The fuel must've been more concentrated than he thought because it lit rapidly. The blue and yellow flames were also brighter and hotter than he would have guessed they'd be. It was almost too hot to stay up on the top of the lighthouse.

The lighthouse near Gresham used a more sustainable fuel. This fuel seemed sporadic and difficult to control. The sparks from the flame spat down at the wood floorboard making small burn holes in the baseboards as the hot glowing embers fell. Too busy looking out at the ship, neither Skye nor Olli saw it coming. The floor around them ignited. When he noticed, Olli grabbed his hot sword from the floor and went to get his bag.

He was too late. There was an implosion as one of the small orb blasts rolled down the spiral stairway. The stairwell, door, and lens room were filling with smoke and alit with blue sparkling flame. Olli covered his face and grabbed Skye's scared hand. He shoved at two metal hinges in the wall and pushed them forward. Smoke rolled outside; Olli stepped forward into the open-air of the lens room at the top of the lighthouse tower. Skye followed his lead, not sure what else she could do.

The catwalk seemed sturdy regardless of its age and wear. The light inside behind them illuminated the night. As it moved their silhouettes reflected bumpy in the water. They were trapped on the balcony outside and the ship still wasn't stopping or wasn't able to. Skye held onto the railing looking down. The sand and rocks were directly below them.

The water was too far out to make it if they fell or jumped. The flames filled the inside of the tower. "What do we do?"

He didn't have an answer. *What a terrible stupid idiotic thing to do. How long would the stone hold up? Would it be able to survive the flames?* The ship was almost to the rocky shores. Anyone aboard would surely drown or die from the impact once they hit the sharp rocks hiding in the high tide.

Skye held Olli's hand more tightly. There wasn't a chance to wait it out. There was a second and third explosion rocking their feet as the flames made their way to the rest of Olli's bag. The railing lurched forward just as the ship suddenly got caught in the waves and on the rocks. The massive ship started to fall on its side, a third blast threw Skye and Olli forward and over the catwalk railing. Something inside of Skye told her to jump, and she propelled herself as far away from the catwalk as her shaking legs would allow. Tightly her fingers kept hold of Olli's hand. He'd jumped too.

From his own ship, Charles Teagardin collapsed his enchanted telescope. He was watching the fishing vessel with maroon sails collide with the sharp rocks as he'd intended. The waves were quick to beat and batter it to pieces. The large sails were the only thing he could still see.

More amusing, he saw the old lighthouse completely engulfed in flames. The tampered fuel ignited just as he'd planned. *How could he be so lucky to get rid of two eyesores in one night?*

Chapter 18
Pulse

Skye rolled over on her side. Her whole body ached, and she felt like a semi was on top of her legs. She blinked her eyes over and over again to try to see more clearly. *Wake up!* Blink, *eyes please work.* Blink, *why can't I see anything?* Blink, blink, *why can't I feel my toes?* her mind screamed.

There was sand caked along the edge of her face. She tried to swat it out of her mouth, but it turned out her hands were covered in it as well. Her eyes burned. The whooshing and crashing of the waves almost put her back into a deep sleep. Blink, blink, *wake up, Skye!*

Large blobby birds were diving and swooping over her head. The white shadows twirled in circles. Skye felt dizzy. She tipped her head to the side and got sick right in the damp sand. Now with her head turned she blinked again. Water. She was so thirsty, but nothing was willing her to get up just yet. Her body parts wouldn't work together.

The water was beginning to take on a glow in and out of each breaking wave. The strands of clouds turned from their pale grays to purple and orange, as the sky behind them reflected a calm baby blue. For a moment Skye had completely forgotten where she was or how awful she felt. She didn't feel pain. She didn't move. She hardly breathed. Slowly she allowed the peace of the moment to surround her entire being. Gently the sun began to rise breaking over the horizon quickly filling the water with a warm kiss. Blink.

It was then that Skye truly was awake. How had she forgotten? She was not alone in this oddly home-like place. As she lifted her head, the tranquility she had been feeling vanished. Pain was real. It coursed through her body. There was an emptiness in the pit of her stomach. Her body was covered in debris and her skin was cut, scraped, or bruised everywhere she looked.

The feeling returned in her torn hand. At the end of her fingertips there was only sand. Panic was setting in. When Skye pulled her head up to see what was on her legs a seagull was glaring back at her from the top of a piece of stone.

There was strength coming from somewhere within as she pushed her cut palms into the sand, somehow, and she scrunched her hands up enough to get her body into a sitting position. One by one she flung pieces of stone from her legs. The seagull hopped off her but continued to peck at the sand nearby. Every few pieces she'd try to wiggle her toes to make sure she wasn't paralyzed. As much as everything hurt, she was feeling optimistic that nothing appeared to be broken during the explosion's impact.

It was morning and there was worry surrounding her clouded thoughts. If she was stuck in this mess, where was Olli? When her legs were finally free, Skye stood shakily in the sand and rubble. The massive ship was about five meters ahead, water splashing up against it in the low tide. It was slightly on its side among the sand and what was left of the destroyed lighthouse.

Her eyes scanned furiously back and forth, searching for any sign of Olli. She began flinging pieces of debris aside in desperation. In one pile she found the water chalice still warm to the touch from the flames continuing to burn all around. Then she unearthed the small dagger out of its case and half-buried in the sand. In the same heap was also Olli's sword. She used the heavy sword carelessly to leverage large rocks. The last thought on her mind was the possibility of slicing her hands even more.

When she found where his body was, only a brown torn shoe was visible. Frantically, Skye began throwing rocks again. As pieces of her own flesh broke on the palms of her hands, Skye kept hurling aside rocks powdered with white sand. Each piece she moved caused her heart to sink further.

Parts of her nails cracked and bled grappling with the damp and heavy pieces of wreckage. His legs were uncovered first. The one was off to the side; his waist was turned on top of more rubble. Then Olli's chest looked too still to be breathing. There was his face. He was hardly recognizable. The blood and the swelling distorted his features. It was painful to even to look at.

Delicately, Skye brought her shaking hands and rested

them on his pale cheeks. She brushed away strands of his hair on his forehead. Inside she felt a great loss, praying he was still alive but prepared for the worst.

With one hand she slid it down to his chest. His body was still warm. At first there was nothing. No rise and falling of his chest. Not even a low heartbeat. Then there it was a light hiccup beneath the fabric of his torn shirt.

Something strange was happening. A part of Skye seemed to be leaving her body. Each of her hands was still upon Olli's skin. One was placed firmly on his chest while the other cradled his face. His eyes were still closed, but Skye could almost feel a part of him who wanted to wake up. The light flicker in his chest was growing to a rapid pulse.

An emptiness was growing within Skye's own body. Her eyes were blinking hard. The sick feeling returned to her stomach. Floating black specks came into her vision. She was feeling faint and weightless. The marks on Olli's face began to close and heal around dried blood. Olli's chest rose steadily higher, pushing against Skye's limp hand. A sharp pain came to Skye's temple.

Olli's eyes shot open as he inhaled the salty air, and he took his first deep breath in hours. Skye looked out across the ocean one last time, the warm glow disappearing from the edge of the waves. The seagull lingering nearby leapt up into flight. She closed her eyes and collapsed backwards into the sand.

Alfaro, First World

Davidson stood leaning against his bag of golf clubs, all alone on this cold Sunday morning in December. He was just about to stop for the day; his hands were raw from trying to swing the club too hard and from the cold wind. He'd also run out of golf balls and wasn't in the mood to go fetch them today.

When he heard the clanking sound, he ducked behind a tree. If it was either of the town's officers, he wasn't going to risk getting kicked off the basketball team, even if he was just playing to stay in shape.

Less than an hour ago he'd watched Skye and the foreign exchange student step out of the mausoleum, and now Skye's parents were just out here probably trying to track her down. Davidson thought for sure she was sick, but what was Olli doing living in the old mausoleum? He hung around out of curiosity and there really wasn't anything better to do in Alfaro on a Sunday. Maybe he could ask the poor guy to live with him for a while—they had an extra bedroom.

When Skye's parents turned around, he didn't know what to say. They looked completely frantic, but he supposed her parents weren't as used to Skye sneaking around as his were. He didn't mention the foreign exchange student but really didn't want to be around other people today.

"If you're looking for your daughter, she left on a horse about an hour ago."

Diane and Vince Hope weren't in Webb Cemetery to make conversation and didn't wait around much longer. They wanted to question why Davidson was out here all alone, but with the entrance locked, the thought of their daughter being found alive was all they needed. *Were those golf clubs?*

"Thanks," was all Vince told Davidson before they got

back in their car and sped off out of Webb Cemetery.

Under his breath, Davidson rambled, "What a weird family."

Davidson picked up a stray golf ball by the side of the mausoleum. The thought of Skye and Olli made him kind of jealous. He and Tiffany had been going through a rough patch for weeks. Davidson had just turned eighteen and had chosen to enlist in basic training for the Navy right after graduating high school, a pursuit Tiffany didn't agree with. She was worried he wouldn't come back or would find someone else while he was away.

Tuning out the rest of the world, Davidson walked with the golf ball in his cold hand. He bent over and teed off one last time on his brother's grave. The snow finally broke from the dark clouds in the sky, the first of the winter season. The thick fluffy snow quickly made a thin white coat on everything it touched. All that was visible was the Dec... in *December* on his brother's headstone. It was a tough enough day as it was to be dealing with other family's problems. He shouted to the empty void, "Fore."

When Diane and Vince made it back to the farm, they found large horseshoe prints leading up the drive. Maiji greeted them as they opened the car door. Diane picked up the cat as they checked the barn. Sure enough, there was Buckwheat. He had a new saddle hanging on the post. *Was that sand on the seat?* He'd been fed and seemed content. Aside from their only horse being returned and cared for the other animals who had also been freshly fed. There was no sign anyone else was around.

At the house, they went upstairs, gently pushing the

door open to Skye's bedroom. There she lay in the same clothes they'd last seen her in. Diane sat on the edge of the bed and Vince pulled the covers up to her face.

"For god sake, let her sleep," Vince told Diane, who was about to shake Skye's side, "I have a feeling she's been through a lot these past few weeks."

Diane didn't protest. She was grateful to see her daughter alive and... was that a suntan? While she watched she made sure Skye was breathing like she did when she was a little baby. When Vince nudged her arm, Diane leaned down and kissed her head, "Sweet dreams, my princess."

To my husband Jordan for finally making it
to the last page.

For my son Dawson, who was with me through every
word, and my daughter Brixsyn, a true princess.

About Atmosphere Press

Atmosphere Press is an independent, full-service publisher for excellent books in all genres and for all audiences. Learn more about what we do at atmospherepress.com.

We encourage you to check out some of Atmosphere's latest releases, which are available at Amazon.com and via order from your local bookstore:

The Short Life of Raven Monroe, a novel by Shan Wee
Insight and Suitability, a novel by James Wollak
It Starts When You Stop, a novel by Johnny Abboud
Orange City, a novel by Lee Matthew Goldberg
Late Magnolias, a novel by Hannah Paige
No Way Out, a novel by Betty R. Wall
The Saint of Lost Causes, a novel by Carly Schorman
Monking Around, a novel by Keith Howchi Kilburn
The Cuckoo of Awareness, a novel by Andrew Brush
The House of Clocks, a novel by Fred Caron
The Tattered Black Book, a novel by Lexy Duck
All Things in Time, a novel by Sue Buyer
American Genes, a novel by Kirby Nielsen
Newer Testaments, a novel by Philip Brunetti
Hobson's Mischief, a novel by Caitlin Decatur
The Red Castle, a novel by Noah Verhoeff
The Farthing Quest, a novella by Casey Bruce

About the Author

Tabitha Sprunger is an art educator, illustrator, and writer. *Readers' Favorite* said of her debut novel, *"Hart Street and Main* is imaginative and creative," filled with, "vibrant characters." *Hart Street and Main* is the first book in a trilogy. Sprunger began writing the trilogy while still a student in high school. She has also written and illustrated children's picture books such as *Lefonso by Numbers* and *Lefonso and the Picture Day.*

She does her best writing in a coffee shop or out in nature. Sprunger enjoys traveling and spending time with her husband and two children. She resides in Northern Indiana with her family.